Dreaming Wakes the Fool

Book 1

Books in this Series

Dreaming Wakes the Fool

Book 1

Jan Bear

A World of Speculation Press

Woodburn, Oregon, USA

Cover Design by Leslie Ann Akin
Cover art by Lisa Bagherpour aka Fairiegoodmother and Abigail Larson

Acknowledgments

Thank you to my family for years of understanding as I lived in two worlds to write this book.

To my critique partners, Bev Cooke, Katherine Hyde, Lynnette Horner, and Gloria Smith (in alphabetical order) for their insightful comments.

To my friend, Leslie Ann Akin, for help and support that goes far beyond the beautiful covers she created.

To Marlene Howard and Oregon Writers Colony for teaching, support, and use of the magical Colonyhouse on the Oregon Coast.

Contents

CHAPTER 1

Summer Dreams

THE HOPEFUL FEELINGS ECHO HAD MANUFACTURED for this job interview collapsed when she saw the receptionist.

In the optimism of the 2019 spring term, Echo had thought it would be easy—get a job, rent an apartment, start making adult decisions for her life. Now her prospects dwindled with her stack of resumes. Assistant, trainee, intern, gofer, junior this or that—no, no, no, no, and no, with nothing to show for her efforts but miles and miles on her bus pass.

And now the young woman sitting before her—Madison, Mackenzie, something like that—gave her the pitying look she thought she had left behind in high school, along with the middle-school nickname, Broken Mirror, that continued to follow her through the halls until the last day of school. This girl—the receptionist—had not been the worst of the tormentors—Echo knew *their* names—but part of the crowd of girls who had everything Echo didn't—beauty, popularity, enough money—and who looked at Echo as at a pathetic creature, beneath their notice and beyond their help.

It's not high school anymore, Echo told herself and held her head high as she walked up to the desk where Mackenzie or Madison was talking on the phone. "My name is Echo Shearwater," she said when the receptionist finished. "I'm here for an interview for the sales assistant job. Sorry I'm late—the bus—" She let the sentence drop, because riding the bus ought to explain everything, but probably not for someone who never had to ride public transportation.

"Hi, Echo," Madison or Mackenzie said. "I'll let Pete know you're here."

Echo turned to sit in one of the cloth-and-plastic waiting room chairs, but Mackenzie or Madison stopped her with a question: "Haven't seen you since graduation last year. What have you been up to?"

Echo turned to her. "Mackenzie, right?"

"Madison." She smiled apologetically. "A lot of people make that mistake. Mackenzie was my best friend." She waited, smiling.

Oh, yeah, the question. "I've been going to Portland Community College. Now I'm looking for a summer job."

Madison nodded knowingly. "It can be hard. I was down at U of O, and my dad found me this job in April."

How nice for you, Echo didn't say. *Ten thousand a year tuition plus expenses—and a dad.* She turned to the waiting room chairs again.

"Do you still keep up with Gray?"

Echo faced her again, like staring down the lions in the Colosseum. "He's still my best friend."

Madison's eyebrows raised, and one corner of her mouth quirked upward. "Really!" Her eyes drifted away into a memory and returned. "Interesting guy. Not bad looking, but kind of weird."

Now Echo felt like the lion, ready to scratch this girl's eyes out. *But why? He* is *weird.* She asked anyway. "Weird?"

Madison squirmed almost imperceptibly. "Well, you know, the guy who knows everything he shouldn't know and nothing of what he should."

An uncomfortable truth, but Echo wasn't going to tell Madison that. "There's more to Gray than meets the eye," was all she said.

Then Pete emerged from his lair, and the all-too-familiar shock that crossed his face at the sight of her scars told her all she needed to know about her prospects here. "I—I'm sorry," he said, stumbling over the words. "The job has already been filled."

Echo might have protested, but what good would it do? At least she no longer had to deal with Madison—and hopefully Mackenzie—possibly ever.

Gray pushed open the door to the Ugly Mug Cafe wondering what he would find today. When he first walked in, it was the fantasy pub he usually saw—well-worn wood polished to a shine, pewter mugs on a shelf above the bar, and the owner a friendly dwarf with wild hair and an intricately braided beard. Gray ordered the usual, and the second cup set before him reminded him of his purpose today. By the time he turned to the table he usually shared with Echo, the scene had changed to a sidewalk cafe in a beautiful city.

It was a sunny day with a lacy net of shadow falling through the tree branches overhead. A bouquet of roses, red as dark blood, appeared beside him as he took the chair facing the entrance to the cafe. The roses surprised him, but they were *right* for the moment, even though they represented a feeling he was not ready to reveal to Echo.

His heart pounded like a drum at the prospect of sharing his reality with her. The Srelevart—"Travelers" in Oge speak, a group of people who met to explore Ytilaer, the world beyond the mirrors—said that it was better to allow Ytilaer to remain a secret. You can't just tell other people, they said. During his years in the foster care system, Gray had learned what happens when you try—they don't believe you, and even if they believe *you* believe, the consequences are dire. Gray had been labeled deficient, delusional, and histrionic from the time he was seven, and if Douglas Burroughs of the Srelevart hadn't saved him by adopting him out of the system, he couldn't imagine where he might be now.

But Echo was different. At least that's what Gray had been telling the Srelevart pretty much since he met her in middle school. Recently, that august body had reluctantly agreed that she might be that one in a million who could be shown. They had agreed in principle, but not for this day, this conversation.

But, he argued, the Paris cafe disappearing and leaving him standing before dark-robed Inquisitors, *her aunt is moving, and I need to show her before it's too late.*

With a parting glance at their stern, familiar faces, he dashed into his esuoh—the "house" of his psyche—and closed the curtain on the outside world. Alone in this small space—big enough for him—he pulled up a thimble-chair next to a thread spool he used as a table and tried to recapture his former mood. His heart was still pounding, and he kept picturing the way the Srelevart would react when he told them he had helped Echo cross over. One way to get rid of this feeling would be to let them set the time. He shook his head. He wasn't a kid anymore—he looked around at his Borrowers-inspired esuoh, furnished with odds and ends of Big People's lives, and felt his face flush red. Well, he wasn't a kid anymore, despite that.

He got up and lifted the curtain again for a peek. The Inquisitors were still there.

He pulled down a graphic novel from his shelf of memories. Older than most of the books on the shelf, the paperback book occupied a place of prominence and safety, a buffer against the trauma in a box of pictures that sat next to it. He never opened that box.

Sitting on the thimble again, he set the graphic novel on the spool table and allowed it to fall open to a page from seventh grade—a dark prison full of cruel, mocking faces—an overall impression of teeth and the shadows of prison bars. Then in his peripheral vision, light dawned like the coming of the sun. It was a girl—Echo, though he didn't know her yet—who walked in a bubble of light, lifting his darkness. He turned the pages, again experiencing the day he met the girl who changed his life.

He wasn't ready—neither he nor Echo was ready—for lifelong commitment to each other. But the invitation for her to join him in a secret world of magic and meaning—a commitment both bigger and smaller than the personal—well, he had decided today was the day, and when Echo arrived, he would tell her. His heart pounded with the excitement of an amateur gambler putting everything on the line.

He went back into the world, to the beautiful cafe. The Inquisitors were gone, consigned to oblivion, and the roses were on the table again, waiting.

He pulled a coin-sized mirror—a rorrim—from his pocket and examined his reflection. It showed only one of his eyes, but the image rippled, and he hovered a finger over its surface. Would it be easier to talk to her if he crossed back into her world? If he looked into her eyes?

A shadow crossed his vision, and he slid the rorrim back into his pocket.

A man wearing an expensive blue suit and a gray fedora leaned against a tree shading the sidewalk, talking on a cellphone. He looked at Gray, and their eyes met—which gave Gray a shock, because it meant the man was in Ytilaer as well. The man was generating his appearance—there were signs Gray recognized but couldn't explain—a traveler in Ytilaer but not of the Srelevart. It was troubling, but the strange man was not the monster Gray had been dreading most of his life.

And then Echo appeared, her smile cool and weary, but nevertheless lighting up the already bright day like sunshine breaking through clouds. The man put away his phone and opened a door for her. She waved to the cafe owner behind the counter and came to sit across from Gray.

CHAPTER 2

Missed Connections

ECHO THREADED HER WAY ALONG A SIDEWALK full of people who strolled among the shops and restaurants of Portland's bustling Sellwood neighborhood. She looked forward to meeting Gray at their favorite coffee shop. After today's interview, she felt even more hopeless than usual and had begun thinking *I need to treasure this opportunity to be with Gray because I'm about to lose it,* instead of just enjoying it for itself.

The glass door of the Ugly Mug Cafe reflected Echo's face—a hash of scars that had earned her the middle-school nickname Broken Mirror. Through the glass, she could see her friend Gray at their usual table with two mugs in front of him, his eyes closed as always, his shoulders slumped like someone afraid to be seen.

She pulled open the door, nodded to the coffee shop owner behind the counter, and sat opposite Gray. "Sorry I'm late. The bus."

"I don't mind waiting." He pushed one of the two mugs toward her. "But your coffee might be cold." He leaned forward on his elbows and studied her face. Yes, with closed eyes he looked at her. It was a fact most people didn't get about him—she hadn't understood either, right away, but having been best friends with Gray since seventh grade, she'd gotten used to most of his oddities.

Echo took a sip. The coffee was just the way she liked it, except cold, and that wasn't his fault. "It's good. Thanks."

"Your light seems dimmer today."

"Wrung out," she said. "It was hot on the bus, and we got stuck in traffic for what seemed like *hours*." She leaned back in her chair and glanced at her phone before dropping it into her shoulder bag again. "But I'm a half hour late, so maybe it wasn't really hours."

Gray was still watching her with an expression of intense concentration despite his closed eyes. "How did the interview go?"

She sighed, pushing her bag under her chair with her foot. "There was a girl from school there—do you remember Madison?"

Gray shrugged.

Echo matched his shrug. "Anyway, the interview didn't happen. The manager said the job had been filled, but I could see the real reason in his eyes."

Gray waited, his mouth closed tightly, his eyes moving back and forth under his eyelids.

"I didn't want that job anyway." She heard the complaint in her voice and wondered if she was remaking the truth to comfort herself for failure. "An hour and a half by bus each way for not enough pay, and Madison Rochester worked there."

"Who?"

"You have to remember. Blonde in our English class. Always had the guys drooling over her."

Gray looked perplexed. He went silent for a moment, then came back. "The one who looked like a tall, skinny doll with a pink bow?"

Echo paused to think about that; she often had to translate Gray's observations. "Probably." She shrugged. "Anyway. I was almost glad not to get the job, but I'm getting desperate."

His elbows were on the table, and he leaned over his arms. "A long beige hallway going nowhere."

Echo nodded, blinking back tears. That's exactly what her life looked like right now.

Gray took a deep breath and let it out again. "Something will come along."

"Enough about me." She straightened her posture. "I'll find something. Maybe I'll get a job in a diner, and somebody will leave me a million-dollar tip." She tried to laugh, but Gray didn't think it was funny, and neither did she.

"Well, Quig got me an internship." He sounded like he thought it might be a prison sentence.

"That's great." She tried to express happiness rather than envy, but it felt like another brick in the wall rising between them. He had a secure future, and she walked a curved and slippery bridge over a bottomless chasm. "Tell me about it."

He gave a smile that lifted only one side of his mouth. "It's an autism charity."

"Oh, Gray." People always started with the assumption that he was autistic. Apparently blind, but seeing everything in a way no one else did, he was *something*—weird, funny, sometimes maddening—but autistic wasn't it. "Quig did that?"

"I understand it," he said. "It opens the door to me. He didn't *tell* them I was autistic, but he didn't correct the impression. So hiring me fits their mission statement." He drummed his thumbs on the table. "I'll feel like a performing monkey."

"What are you going to do?"

He shrugged. "Start tomorrow. What else?"

"Your impressions aren't always right."

He cocked an eyebrow at her.

"It could be a great opportunity." *Listen to me making happy talk*, she thought. *I'm standing on the dock, and Gray is in a boat that's pulling away.* "Did I tell you Aunt Doris found a two-bedroom house in Woodburn? If I can't afford an apartment close by, I'll have to take her up on her invitation to live with her. But Woodburn is hours away by bus. We won't be everyday friends. We'll be sometimes friends and then 'how've you been' friends and then 'it's been ages' friends. And I'll be alone in the boonies forever."

Gray sat up straighter and focused on her face. He grasped his cup and downed the last of his coffee, as if he were preparing to leave, but he sat with his hands spread on the table, his fingers dancing. He took a deep breath. "There's something I've wanted to say to you for a long time." He brought something out of the watch pocket of his jeans and put it on the table with his hand covering it, like a magician. "Echo, I want to share my life with you."

She laughed. She couldn't help it. "Marriage? For misfits like us?" Would their children be the sighted blind like him? With the nice kids scared of them and the mean kids trying to trip them up in the hall at school? And herself—her scars couldn't be transmitted genetically, of course, but there are scars no one can see that can be passed down the generations more surely than a genetic condition. Being part of a happy family was a life she didn't deserve and would never have.

He pulled back his gift and put it into his pocket again. The hope that had hovered around his eyes turned to despair. He pushed his chair back.

She wanted to say something kind, but couldn't think of anything. She reached out and put her hand over his.

His eyes widened—while remaining closed—and his hair, thick and dark and wavy, seemed to lift itself off his head. He pulled his hand away and sat back as if she had slapped him.

"Sorry, sorry, sorry," Echo said. Another blunder. And another reason the whole conversation was ridiculous. If he recoiled at her touch, how could he ask her to marry him? "How could we possibly?"

"It's all right." Gray was recovering, but still breathing hard. "It's not your fault, and it's not what you think. I'm—" He didn't finish. He just got up and left the cafe.

"Gray—" Echo turned in her chair to watch him leave. Should she get up and go after him? She had hurt him often enough in their friendship to know it was better to give him space and apologize later. But apologize for what? What had she said that was untrue? She turned back to her cold coffee with her stomach sinking. She would give him time to come around.

A man at the next table set down the newspaper he was reading. He was old—in his late thirties, maybe—and movie-star handsome in dark sunglasses and an expensive blue suit with a crisp white shirt open at the collar. After checking his phone, touching something in the leather book-like case, and putting the phone back into his pocket, he took off his sunglasses, revealing cobalt-blue eyes. He leaned across the gap between tables to speak to Echo. "I couldn't help overhearing your conversation. It seems that you could use a job." He gestured to the chair Gray had abandoned. "May I?"

She shrugged. "Sure."

He moved to her table. "It just so happens that I'm looking for some-one with a special set of skills to do some work for me." The man's voice was as resonant as a YouTube hypnotist's. "The initial gig will pay well and could turn into a permanent job if things go as I expect."

"Special skills." She sighed. "I've just finished my first year at Portland Community College, and I'm a beginner at everything."

He smiled. "I said special skills, not advanced education."

"I'm not good at selling." She focused on his eyes, watching his reaction. "For obvious reasons."

He shrugged. "I don't see any obvious reasons, but the job is about research, not selling. And I have a sense that you would be very good at that."

"What kind of research?"

The man took a business card from his pocket and handed it to her. "It's a special project. Confidential."

"Nothing illegal?"

The man laughed. "A mission of mercy." His face turned serious. "I do reputation management. I get people out of trouble, not into it. But I also don't reveal secrets to outsiders. I'll tell you the rest if you get the job."

Echo looked at the card. Jephthah Blackthorne III • Success Transformation • Reputation Management, address, etc.

"Call me Jeph," he said. "Interested? I'm holding a group interview at my office at seven this evening."

"This evening?"

He nodded. "It's a game. Gives me an idea of how you work with other people."

"Uhh."

He laughed. "Seriously. Nothing kinky. But something about you tells me you'll find it intriguing—and enlightening."

She looked at the card again. "The US Bancorp Tower?"

"Twenty-seventh floor."

"But—"

"No pressure. I actually came to ask your friend, but he left abruptly, and I think you would be even better. And as I say, the pay is quite generous."

"How generous?"

"I don't like to talk specific figures in public, but let's just say you could cover your rent for at least six months. Enough to get you on your feet. And if it works out, the job would be permanent. I'm looking to expand my business."

She thought about it. Aunt Doris would say there were more questions than answers. Gray would say— But his brother, the judge, had already found him a job.

Jeph pushed his chair away from the table. "Can I expect you?"

The questions didn't matter. The ground was breaking under her feet, and this was a leap to the next step. She tapped the edge of the card on the table. "Yes."

Jeph smiled. "See you at seven, then." He left the cafe.

Echo sat there awhile, feeling new possibilities burbling around her. She finished her coffee and carried her and Gray's cups to the tub for dirty dishes.

She walked away without looking back, excitement running through her body like electricity, unseen wonders fogging her view, and the world like a living map far below her feet.

GRAY LEFT THE CAFE WITH THE DOGS OF FRUSTRATION AND HUMILIATION snarling and nipping at his ankles. Echo had laughed. She had called him a misfit. She couldn't imagine grownup life with him.

But it wasn't grownup life he was offering, but *his* life, in Ytilaer, the world seen through the lens of meaning, instead of the shiny deception most people see.

I want to share my life with you, he'd said. The Doberman of humiliation jumped up and bit his ear. He could have said something normal, like *Let's go to the park. I want to show you something.* The German shepherd of frustration ran up behind him and bit him in the butt. Echo would have refused to go with him until he explained why, right there in the coffee shop. He was breaking rules by even mentioning Ytilaer, but to tell all in a public place? Just no. He should have waited until they happened to be walking somewhere quiet.

His brother Quig and the rest of the Srelevart had told him Ytilaer had her own time, but he didn't trust their judgment. They were too rigid. The time was *now.*

What a beautiful dream it was while it lasted. Ytilaer had lured him into his rash move. The bouquet of roses seemed like a guarantee of success.

And then—the humiliation gripped him again like canine teeth sinking into his calves—catastrophe.

Echo wasn't wrong about his intentions, just the timing, but he wanted to show her the doorway into this reality, to show her how he saw the world. He wanted to see her eyes.

He sighed, fighting back tears. Maybe Quig was right: It wasn't Ytilaer's timing.

CHAPTER 3

An Opportunity

ECHO OPENED THE GLASS-INLAID FRONT DOOR of Aunt Doris's house and went inside. Cooking smells wafted from the kitchen—garlic and herbs, chicken, onions, and love. The fragrance curled around the framed portraits and knickknacks, soaked into the worn upholstery of the genteel furniture, spread a coat of home on the out-of-date wallpaper.

Oh, that's right. Aunt Doris had promised a celebration dinner and a classic movie after Echo's interview. Comfort food. "I'm home." She threaded her way through the small dining room into the kitchen at the back of the house. Aunt Doris was there on the phone, wearing a pink-and-teal jogging outfit, with the afternoon sunlight shining through her short silver hair like a crown.

"I've got to let you go, Clarice. Echo's home and I want to hear all about her interview." She listened a while longer, smiling at Echo and rolling her eyes. Then, "You take care now. Bye."

She set the phone on the table. "How did it go?" She looked at Echo with pleased expectation.

"Terrible. A complete waste of time."

"Live and learn is all you can do." She lifted the lid on the pot and gave the stew a stir. "It's almost ready. Why don't you clean up for dinner?"

"I need to change our plans. I have a sort of interview this evening, and I need to catch the bus."

"Sort of interview? For a sort of job?"

Echo leaned against the counter. "An opportunity."

Aunt Doris set down the spoon and went to the table. From long experience, Echo knew that meant nothing would happen without further conversation. "You don't sound very sure of it."

Echo pulled out a chair and sat across from her. "It's hard to be sure of anything when it comes to finding a job, but it sounds good. I was in the Ugly Mug, and a guy sitting at the next table asked if I would like to apply for a job."

"I thought you were meeting Gray there."

"He was there, and he almost asked me to marry him. I laughed at him. It hurt his feelings, and he left."

A sharp intake of breath, and then Aunt Doris mastered her face.

"We've been friends forever," Echo said. Somehow Aunt Doris always made Echo see the opposite side of the argument. "Maybe it would be a good idea, but not now."

"You could do better."

Echo got up and walked around the kitchen. "Could I? He's weird, but he's kind and funny, and—"

"Sweetheart, you and that autistic boy—"

Echo sighed. "He's not autistic." She spoke the words with none of the enthusiasm of the thousands of past attempts to make that correction. These little traditions just didn't seem to matter anymore with everything falling apart.

But Aunt Doris kept going. "You and that autistic boy have been protecting each other from the need to deal with life ever since . . . . ." She stopped with her mouth formed around a word and then just closed it. "You can make other friends."

"But there's never been anyone else, and there never will be. It's just—marriage—I can't."

"I understand. You're both too young. And you shouldn't give up the idea that you'll find someone more—normal. Clarice says you could be pretty if you fixed yourself up a little."

"Clarice sells makeup for an MLM company."

"No need to be snippy."

"You don't know what it's like," Echo said.

"I've lived long enough to know all kinds of things."

"I've seen your photos from when you were my age. No one has ever looked at you with the horror that crosses their faces when they see me. It's like they're afraid my ugliness is contagious."

"My dear, every teen-aged girl thinks she's ugly. When I look at you, I see someone sweet and smart—impulsive, but that's not necessarily a bad thing if you keep it in check. When you give people a chance to get to know you—"

"That's why this job is such a great opportunity. Jeph does reputation management. I'll have co-workers—"

"What about college?"

"He said I need special skills, not advanced education."

Aunt Doris examined Echo with a skeptical half-wink and a raised eyebrow. "Pardon me for asking, but what special skills do you have?"

"I don't know, honestly. It's a research project. Confidential. I'll get more information if I get the job." She saw her words going through Aunt Doris's mind. She couldn't explain the excitement she felt about the chance she was taking, and it probably wouldn't persuade Aunt Doris if she tried.

"And the interview is at night?"

"At seven. Sundown isn't until nine thirty."

Aunt Doris gave her a stern look. "There used to be people on college campuses who promised jobs to students. Got them all hyped up and took them away from home; then nobody ever saw them again."

Echo returned to her place at the table. "It's not like that."

"What's it like then?"

"Well, there's no selling, he said." Echo tipped the sugar bowl and watched the tiny avalanche slide toward the edge.

"Nobody pitches job interviews to complete strangers unless there's selling."

Echo sighed and pushed the sugar bowl away. "I don't know. It feels like the beginning of something."

"Oh, honey. A feeling and three bucks will buy you a cup of coffee."

"Everything is changing. It's like I'm standing on a surfboard in the middle of the ocean. I love you, Aunt Doris, but I don't want to move to Woodburn."

"It's a nice town. It is a ways outside Portland, but you can use my car to get to work when you find a job and there's an annex of Chemeketa Community College right there in town. You'll make friends. You'll be able to save some money and get your feet under you."

"I don't want my feet under me. I want to step off a cliff and see where I fly."

"That's what I'm afraid of. Most people don't fly. They crash."

She looked at this woman, her last family in the world, and for the first time since she had taken Echo in after her parents and sister died, defied her. "I'm sorry. I have to."

Aunt Doris sighed and gave a quick nod. "Well, you're of age, and I won't tie you up and lock you in the basement." She got up and went to the cabinet and pulled down a soup bowl. "At least take a bowlful before you leave." She filled it and set it and a spoon on the table in front of Echo. "Where does this interview happen?"

Echo dug the card out of her purse and slid it across the table.

Aunt Doris took the card, looked at one side, then turned it over and found his photo on the other. "My, my. He's quite a looker."

"Right?" Echo said. "Everything about him screamed respectability."

"Well, be careful. You're not going to meet in a bar or anything?"

Echo smiled in spite of herself. "The address is right on the card. The US Bancorp Tower downtown. Very stable and reliable."

Aunt Doris turned the card over and looked at the address again. "Twenty-seventh floor." She looked up and caught Echo's eye. "If the floor is under construction, don't get off the elevator."

Echo laughed. "It's totally legit."

Chapter 4

The Game

When Echo stepped off the elevator onto the twenty-seventh floor of the US Bancorp Tower, she almost hoped to see drop cloths and ladders—they would give her an excuse to leave—but there were none. To her right, the hallway was unlighted and empty, but the office to her left sent late-afternoon sunlight flowing into the passage. Windows of greenish glass were set into mahogany-colored frames around the door, and attached to the glass door was a bronze plaque that read:

Jephthah Blackthorne III
Success Transformation
Reputation Management

She stood there a moment, taking in the graceful curves and metallic solidity of the letters in the sign, when a movement caught her eye. The man from the cafe, wearing sunglasses, stepped out of the glass-walled conference room and walked toward her.

Behind him, six people sitting around the mahogany conference table had all turned toward her. They seemed to react to her with surprise, curiosity; one even looked indignant. But not one looked horrified at her scarred face the way most people did. And all six had their eyes closed.

A thrill ran from the top of Echo's head to the soles of her feet. Six people *looking* at her with closed eyes. Was Gray like them, or were they like him? Everyone—even Echo—considered that Gray had a "condition" or a "disability," but what if it was something else? What if this was a community of people as strange and fascinating as Gray?

And then the man, Jeph, was there, sliding his sunglasses into his pocket, crinkles of amusement bracketing his closed eyes. She stepped back.

His smile was warm enough to crack her reticence. "You'll never find out if you don't come inside."

All this time she had wondered why Gray was the way he was, berating herself for even wanting to ask a question that would make him feel awkward. And now an answer stood in front of her? Her curiosity was so strong that she would have climbed over drop cloths and ladders—even walked across an I–beam being swung into position by a crane. She crossed the threshold and followed Jeph into the conference room.

"There's a chair for you." Jeph pointed to the foot of the table, then returned to his place at the opposite end, flawlessly navigating past chairs pushed out, leaned back, turned sideways, at the whim of each of their occupants. "I've been explaining how the game works."

"She's late." A woman with her hair cut close around her face turned toward Echo with a tight mouth and scrunched eyes. "We have to follow the rules."

Jeph gave Echo an apologetic smile. "Don't worry. You'll get the hang of the game." He passed an object the size of a box of kitchen matches down the table. "You'll need to cross over before we can begin."

A man sitting to Echo's right, in wire-rimmed glasses and a salt-and-pepper beard, handed her the dark wooden box that felt and smelled ancient, though how she would know the smell of ancient wood wasn't clear even to herself. It was carved with strange symbols like an alien language, and it caused her fingers to tingle. She glanced up at Jeph, who nodded at her, and she opened it.

Inside, resting on a cushion of embroidered silk, was a mirror. She reached a finger to touch it, and the man who had handed her the box leaned over and whispered. "Focus on your reflection and then touch the rorrim. Breathe out before you touch it and then breathe in. It will be easier."

The woman with short hair, who had complained about Echo's tardiness, looked sour, but Jeph waited with the beatific smile of a man who sees his children behaving well.

Echo held up the mirror. She saw her eyes, wide with awe and wonder, and the scars on her face like the shards of a broken mirror. The image rippled like wind on water, and she touched the surface of the mirror.

She was falling, falling, falling. Falling like Alice down the rabbit hole, like Dorothy in her house, like Jonah or Pinocchio through the ocean. She had done the breathing all wrong, and now she felt like the time, the summer before her father's death, when she slid down a winding water slide, landing in the pool without knowing which way was up. The water was shallow enough to stand up in, but she didn't know where her feet should go. Before she could panic, her father's arms caught her, pulling her upright and lifting her head out of the water. Now she heard a whisper in her ear like her father's voice. "Breathe. You're not under water. You can breathe and you can see."

She breathed out the last gasp of breath she was holding. There was no sound of bubbles, so she breathed in, and light flowed into her. She looked around, and there was—something.

But what?

Human shapes around a table, three on each side, the bearded man on her right, dressed in an absurd costume of gold and brocade, looking at her, eyes open, with friendly concern. Jeph, now in a purple zoot suit, stood at the far end shuffling cards like a casino magician. He smiled and said, "Come, my children. Let's have some fun. There's a key, there's a key, not hidden on me. If you mind it, you can find it. You can wind it. You will bind it. Will it shake you? Will it wake you? It will make you one with the key. And the one with the key is the one with me. And the one with me is one with the key."

He tossed cards face down around the table, one in front of each person, including himself, and one in the middle. "Can I hear everybody say yes to the question?"

Echo said, "Yes," and the others turned to her and laughed.

Jeph laughed, too, but not derisively. "For the Fool, the question doesn't matter. The answer is always yes. But for the rest, let's ask before we answer."

And they all, except Echo, said together, "May I come into your house?"

"We need everyone," Jeph said. "Again, please."

And they all, even Jeph, even Echo, said, "May I come into your house?"

"And the answer is 'Please come in.'"

They all answered, even Echo, but not Jeph, "Please come in."

Then Echo felt alone at the table. All the others sat very still, the way Gray sometimes did when he checked out during a conversation. She would be in the room with him, and he would be there, but gone. She had tried to understand, but it irritated her. She would tell herself it might be a seizure or something, and she would feel guilty for being angry. Sometimes he would come back. Other times, she would leave before he returned. He always shrugged off questions about it. A worm of irritation had grown slowly over the years, but she kept it enclosed in a thick glass case.

Now that there was obviously no medical explanation, the worm grew quickly, and the glass around it broke.

A voice—Jeph—whispered to her. "Turn around."

She spun her chair to face the other direction—she couldn't see anything. Black shadows, thick as smoke from burning tires, poured around the edges of the room.

Jeph laughed. "Put the table in front of you."

She turned the chair toward the table.

"Put your hands on the table."

She did that, too. It felt cool and smooth to her fingers.

"Now stay there and turn inward."

She turned inward; she didn't know how she did it. Her body didn't move, but something that was not her body, partly contiguous, partly overlapping, turned toward its center, and she stepped into a space as familiar as a recurring dream.

The room was long and narrow with an arched ceiling. On one wall, a black iron woodstove held a steaming teapot brightly painted with old-fashioned roses. Lining the walls were shelves with brass railings around them to keep dishes, books, and knickknacks from falling off. At the far end of the room, maroon velvet curtains were tied back to reveal a table scattered with sketch books. Across from the wood stove, a bench with red velvet cushions invited her to sit among its embroidered silk pillows. Both the forest-green roof beams and the Chinese-red shelf supports were ornamented with gilt decorations, and a narrow Oriental rug lay on the floor.

The room was busy and colorful and would drive some people mad, but for Echo it felt like home.

A wide window over the bench showed a floor of darkness outside, with seven illuminated doors arranged in a long oval. Occasionally, a door would open, and a bucket of light would spill out, and then the door would close again. The game, whatever it was, had started, and curiosity drew her to find what was behind those doors.

A door creaked, and light footsteps tapped behind her. Jeph had come into the room, still wearing his purple zoot suit, his eyes open. He glanced around the place, not as if seeing it for the first time, but as if refreshing his memory. He smiled at her. He reached past her and opened a door she hadn't noticed yet. When she stood back to look at it, he stepped out and motioned for her to follow him. From just inside the doorway, she saw him let down a porch that folded up against the side of what she now saw was a wagon.

She took one step out onto the porch and looked around. At the front of the wagon, the end with the raised dais and its table, was a beautiful black horse, standing patiently and swishing his tail. Below her feet, the ground fell away into a deep chasm with a flashing ribbon of a creek that seemed miles below. Her stomach turned as she looked over the edge. "This doesn't look stable."

Jeph walked further along the porch and gestured for her to follow. "In this world, the laws of physics are more like suggestions." She followed and stood beside him, reveling in the feeling of fear turning to excitement in the pit of her stomach. His eyes were as blue as the impossibly blue sky, and he was smiling as she imagined someone might smile if he thought her beautiful.

"I want you to win this, but I'm not going to give it away." He gestured to the door and followed her inside. "I'll at least tell you the rules."

Inside, a door opened, and a man's voice said, "Hello? Hello?" Jeph opened a door that hadn't existed before and went out, leaving no trace of himself or the doorway he had just walked through. The man who had been sitting to her right at the table came in through a green wooden door at the opposite end of the wagon from the table.

He was dressed in a suit of sparkling white and rich gold brocade. Under his jacket was a red velvet vest, and the jacket had matching red patches on the elbows. He wore a gold hat like a beehive and carried a staff with its upper end curved like a question mark. His salt-and-pepper beard now hung halfway down his chest.

"How did you get here?" she asked him.

"You invited me," he said, "and I'm right next door."

"I mean how?"

He looked at her with delight in his eyes. "I recognize you. You're that friend of Gray's."

"You know Gray?"

He moved in closer to her and whispered. "I'm Edward Paladin. Gray and I are members of the Srelevart."

"The what?"

"Shhhh! Jeph doesn't approve of the Srelevart." He looked around the room, continuing to speak quietly, though absently, as if he wasn't quite listening to himself. "He thinks they're too rigid. I'm inclined to agree about some things, but it's a small world among the Ytilaer community in Portland, and when a mutual friend saw a notice about this game online and asked me to see what it's about, I couldn't refuse. I've seen your picture in Gray's esuoh."

"His what?"

"Esuoh. Everybody has one. This is yours, apparently."

Echo threw herself onto her bench and was surprised at how comfortable it was. "Really? How come I don't know about it?"

He examined her with a half-amused gaze. "Are you sure you don't recognize it?"

Echo was about to say she didn't, but it wasn't true. "It's mine?" was all she could say.

"The front room is always your favorite, because your ego would like you to stay here. Your memories are upstairs, and the monsters are in your basement."

"Upstairs?" She looked around at the tiny space.

Edward caught her gaze and looked with her. "There's a ladder or something somewhere." He spoke with utter confidence. "Every esuoh is different, even though they're all the same."

"And monsters in my basement?"

He looked up and down the central aisle of the wagon, then bent down and flipped a corner of the rug aside, revealing a trapdoor. "You won't see them unless you go looking for them. Mostly."

"That's a relief."

"But if you don't look for them, they find you," he said.

"What?"

"I was going to tell you about the game."

"I knew it!" Pru entered wearing a long, obvious wig like the ones judges wear in British courtroom dramas, plopped on top of her severe bangs, which peeked out from under the wig like children hiding under covers. "Telling a late player the rules is against the rules."

Edward Paladin gave an apologetic shrug and squeezed past Pru to leave by the door she had just come in.

"Did you find anything?" Pru asked.

"I don't even know what I'm looking for," Echo said.

"That can't be. Pretty things like you always get the attention."

Echo laughed out loud.

Pru looked hurt. "It doesn't cost a nickel to be nice." She straightened her flowing black robe.

Echo was nonplussed. For anyone to call her pretty had to be a joke, right? On an impulse, she parried with a compliment. "That's a very impressive outfit."

Pru's face softened a little.

"Can you tell me how to go to other people's sesuoh? Would that be breaking the rules?"

Pru thought about it for a second. "I could do that."

"I guess I would go out the door you came in by."

"That should be obvious. When you go outside, you'll see another door." Pru nodded in the direction she had come from. "I can see that you don't know anything. I should go now. I need to win this game."

Echo nodded and followed her to the other end of the wagon. The last of Pru's robe disappeared through the door. Echo examined her own clothing and found it to be rags and tatters, a patchwork tunic over torn leggings. The patches clashed, and the base cloth had been worked upon by warring forces of dirt and fading until the color that remained had no name. She laughed again that Pru had called her pretty and went out the door.

In the darkness, the door behind her and the one before her glowed like iPads. The door in front of her was three-paneled, made of dark wood covered with peeling and chipped white paint. It had an embossed brass doorknob. On the top panel was the remnant of a rough painting of two dogs howling at the moon with a lobster clicking its claws at them.

The door to her own esuoh was rough-cut boards, painted green and covered with yellowing varnish, with a small painting of a hobo in a funny hat, carrying a walking stick and a bag over his shoulder, and a dog leaping behind him, ripping his pants.

As she reached for the other doorknob, she heard someone wailing in the distance.

She looked around, her hand still stretched toward the door with the dogs and the moon. The darkness outside the cylinder of light between the two doors was as thick as velvet, but the sound was so sorrowful that she had to go see if she could help.

She stepped carefully, expecting holes or tripping hazards and waving her hands around to locate obstacles. The only thing she found was a door off to her left, lost in darkness. Its unvarnished wood felt cracked and dry, and its rusty door handle rattled at her touch but didn't open. The wailing recommenced, recalling her to her mission.

The lament grew louder as she walked, and she came to another lighted door with a grayscale image of a skeleton wielding a scythe. She stopped for a second, her hand on the doorknob, debating whether to enter. Dogs and lobsters were one thing. This looked like death. She heard another heavy sigh from inside and opened the door.

Inside the esuoh, the walls were red and the furniture black. Artistic black-and-white photos of decrepit houses and abandoned factories decorated the walls. A tall scythe stood in an umbrella stand near the door. A man sat on one of the leather sofas with his face on his arm in an attitude of misery. Just as she walked in, he looked up at the ceiling and howled like a lonely dog.

"Are you OK?" Echo asked.

He raised his head. He was older than Echo, mid-twenties maybe, with wire-rimmed glasses and straight brown hair that looked like it would ordinarily be combed back but now fell over his forehead. "Did you come here to torment me?"

"I heard you crying. I thought you might be hurt."

"You're not that Pru person, are you? So judgmental."

"Do I look like I have room to judge anybody? I'm Echo."

"The one who got here late." His face lightened to a pleasant smile. "You upset the apple cart."

"The bus—"

"Don't tell me. When someone congratulates you on a good deed, just say thank you."

"Uh, thank you. But why were you crying?"

"I just get tired of it. It's 'Evolve this' and 'Disrupt that' until they get what they want. Then they're all 'Aiiiiiihhhh!' because they are afraid of losing anything. You don't know what it's like."

"I know what it's like to have people scared of me. But you don't have to stay here alone. I'm not afraid of you."

"You're not?"

She started to say no, but the situation demanded honesty. "I guess I am, a little. But who cares? Why don't you try to win the game?"

"I don't know why I even came. I got a call from a guy Jeph knows, and he said they need seven people for this game and they only have six. But I'd rather be home watching serial-killer comedies."

"Sounds like loads of fun," Echo said.

"Thanks for trying to make me feel better." There was no sign that he had caught her irony.

He got up from the sofa and straightened his black vest. Combed back his hair with his fingers. Straightened his red tie with little black skulls embroidered on it. Checked the pocket watch whose chain hung neatly across his vest. "I need to accept myself and be who I am."

"Who else are you going to be, right?" Echo said.

A smile crawled across his face. "I like you. I think we're going to be friends."

Echo wasn't sure what that might mean. "Well, uh—"

"I'll tell you what you need to know about the game."

Echo felt a smile forming. "You'll tell me how to win?"

He shook his head and waved his hand like a fly was in front of his face. "Winning, losing. It's the same thing. But here's what you need to know—" His voice dropped nearly to a whisper, and he sat on the sofa and leaned forward. He looked around as if expecting someone to be listening in. "The game doesn't end when you win it." He smiled as if he had said something comprehensible and leaned back with his arm flung across the back of the sofa and one leg crossed over the other.

Echo pulled up a black wooden chair and tried—but failed—to frame a question. "I don't understand."

"It's games within games, going back as long as there've been humans."

She was silent for a while, trying to join the pieces of the puzzle she had already been given. Patterns formed, but not a picture. She looked around the room—the colors, the scythe, the skulls on his tie. "I guess you've seen it all."

"I'm not the Archetype, not even a prototype. Just an iteration with a role to play, like you. Outside of *this*—" he gestured in a way that pointed to more than the room "—I don't even see how I'm playing *my* part most of the time. But here it becomes clear—and I hate it and love it at the same time."

"That's why you were crying?"

"Tears of joy and sadness. When you came into the game, it all made sense."

"Me?"

"We're natural allies—a blast of chaos that disrupts the flow. We break things, sometimes even things that need to be broken."

Now Echo felt like crying, but she refused to go to that memory. "I thought you were going to tell me how to win."

He smiled. "You've already won, but I'll tell you what Jeph said at the beginning of the game. You're supposed to find a key." He spoke with animation, his earlier sorrow entirely gone. "If you find it, you win. If you think you found it, and it's not really it, you lose."

"A key."

"It doesn't look like a key."

"Then how will I know it's a key?"

He laughed as if she had finally figured out the trick. "They didn't tell us."

"What does it open?"

"I don't know that either. Maybe that's how you know it's the right key."

"This is a weird game."

"I'm finished. It's time for me to go."

"You're not going to play anymore?"

"The deal was that I could leave any time after the game started." He turned back to her. "I'll reward you for your kindness," and then he shouted, "Let me out!"

Suddenly he had the box with the mirror in his hands. He opened it, touched the mirror, and Echo found herself outside in the darkness, between two doors. She felt uneasy about the promised reward.

The next door had a watercolor of a naked woman under a starry sky pouring the contents of two pitchers onto land and water. Another door, where Death's had been, had a line drawing of a man in a beehive hat like the one Edward wore, holding a staff with three cross beams and making a gesture with his other hand. Echo had met Edward already, and his door would take her back toward her own esuoh, so she opened the starry door.

The room smelled like patchouli oil, and the walls were hung with colorful fabrics. A fabulous long-tailed bird sang in a cage, and elsewhere a water feature poured a continuous stream over polished stones, making a merry sound as it dripped and splashed into two bowls below.

No one else was there at the moment, but Echo liked the place and walked over to the window for a look. The Milky Way was a blaze of light and color in an otherwise pitch-black sky. Echo envied the woman whose place this was.

"If you really wanted it, it would be yours," a voice behind her said.

"What?" Echo turned and found a woman, six feet tall or more, wearing a long, simple dress that looked like linen with threads of silver running through it.

The woman smiled. "I saw what you were thinking. It takes work not to be transparent, and you may never develop the knack."

"I—"

"Don't worry about it. I'm flattered."

"Well, OK—"

"Don't go. I wanted to talk to you."

"Are you going to let me answer or just read my mind for the whole conversation?"

The woman laughed. "I'm Estelle."

"Echo. What did you want to talk to me about?"

"I just wondered what you think about all this." She seemed to refer to more than the boho-chic style of herself and her esuoh.

Echo thought about the question for a second before answering. "You mean how to play the game or what the game means?"

"The first, obviously." The woman's manner was both inviting and superior. Echo was torn between liking her and feeling dismissed as inadequate. "I'm sure you have an opinion about the meaning, but mine is more relevant. What do you know about the key?"

"Less than you do. I was late, remember?"

"Yes. I remember Jeph didn't throw you out. So you must be important, possibly the whole reason for the game."

"I only met him a couple of hours ago. He showed up in the coffee shop where I had been talking to my friend and offered me this interview."

Estelle stood eyeing Echo while she was speaking and for a few seconds after. Then she nodded and turned to her front window again, which showed a flat black surface with glowing doors scattered across the landscape. "I can see that you're telling the truth, but it doesn't rule out the possibility that you don't know what you know."

Echo sighed. "Do you people do this stuff all the time?"

"What stuff?"

"Visit each other's s esuoh, read minds, solve puzzles, come into—this—whatever it is."

"Well, Pru, Dennis, and I are coaching clients of Jeph's. I don't know where Jeph came up with the others. He seemed to think it was important to have seven in the game."

"OK. So what is the goal?"

"First, find the key. Then find the lock it opens."

"What does the winner get?"

"I think it depends on who wins."

"He told me this was an interview for a job."

Estelle shrugged. "There's more to Jeph than meets the eye. Maybe it is a job for you, if you win. Is that something you want?"

"Well, yes."

"That explains it then."

"Actually, it doesn't explain anything."

Estelle gave a half smile and looked toward the ceiling. "I don't know. But the only way to find out is to win."

"OK, back to the beginning, then. How do you win?"

"Find the key."

Echo sighed heavily and sat down on one of Estelle's chairs. "How do you find the key?" she asked, conscious that her tone was like talking to a stubborn child. "I mean, what's the process? What gives this key its keyness? What do we know about it? Treat me like someone who doesn't know anything."

Estelle gave her a quizzical look and sat in another chair. "OK. I'll play. A key is a connection between two places or states of being. The key might take you through a door or into a feeling or a memory. If you find a key, try it on a door. We don't need keys to the others' sesuoh for the game because we all invited each other in. It's like a block party."

"Except Jeph didn't say the invitation."

Estelle went over to a shelf and picked up a box with seashells and sea stars on it.

Remembering Death with the box, Echo asked, "You're not leaving, too, are you?"

"What? Leaving? No." She looked down at the box. "Oh, that. It's my short-term memory. Some people have books, some have photo albums, I have this box." She opened it and rifled through the contents. "Here's something." She picked up a seashell and listened to it.

A tinny little voice came out that resonated in Echo's mind as Jeph's words at the beginning of the game. "'Not hidden on me,' he said." She put away the shell, closed the box, and returned it to its shelf. "And then a bunch of other stuff that may or may not be relevant."

"If it's not on him, who is it on?" Echo asked.

"That's a good question," Estelle said, looking at her steadily.

"Don't look at me. The only thing I got from him was a business"— now Echo was thinking about it, even as the word flowed out of her mouth—"card."

"That might be it," Estelle said.

"I wish you would stop that," Echo said again.

But Estelle had already left the room.

"So you got one, too," Echo said to the empty room. "I left mine with Aunt Doris." She left Estelle's esuoh and proceeded to the next door.

CHAPTER 5
We Have a Winner

THE NEXT DOOR WAS DECORATED with an artful half-drawn illustration of a magician in a cape holding a wand, with a table in front of him, on which sat a top hat with a rabbit, a deck of cards with strange pictures, and a cage. The door didn't open at her touch.

She knocked, and Jeph came to the door. He wasn't wearing the purple zoot suit now, but khaki slacks, a Hawaiian shirt with parrots in tropical forests, and huarache sandals. "Echo. This is a surprise."

His esuoh was huge, with a wide glass wall revealing sparkling lights in the distance looking like fallen stars.

"Is it the girl?" Another man's voice called from inside the esuoh.

"Yeah," Jeph said over his shoulder. To Echo, "Hadn't you better get back to the game? I said I don't have the key."

"Wait." The other man got up and came to the door. He was a little older than Jeph, with a scraggly black beard peppered with white. He wore tight jeans, a black T–shirt, and red cowboy boots, and he held a squat glass of brown liquid. "Bring her in. I want to talk to her for a minute."

Jeph rolled his eyes. "She needs to get on with the game."

"Relax. We'll make it worth her while." He looked Echo over with a smile that made her uncomfortable. He felt dangerous in a way that said there's more than one way to fall off a cliff. She took a step back. He laughed out loud. "My name is Cain Timrod. Did Gray ever tell you about me?"

"Gray? What do you know about Gray?"

He stepped in front of Jeph and held the door open for Echo. "Can I get you a drink?"

"No thanks," Echo said. She walked through the door.

Some unspoken communication passed between the two men. Cain gave Jeph the side-eye, and Jeph looked annoyed and amused at the same time. "Gray and I go way back," Cain said. "I just wonder why *you're* here." He cast a quick, questioning look at Jeph.

"I need a job." Echo looked to Jeph for an explanation. "This is a strange interview."

Jeph stepped into the conversation, speaking to Cain. "I told you, the boy turned me down, and the girl looked even more promising."

It was disconcerting to discover she was second choice, and being referred to as "the girl"—not to mention Gray as "the boy"—made it worse. "What do you know about Gray?" she asked again.

Cain looked amused and thoughtful. "I just wondered if you've known him long."

A deep prompting inside Echo told her—for no obvious reason, unless it was just that this man was *too* interested—that she shouldn't talk to him about Gray. She shrugged. "A while."

"His mother and I used to go out together. He was about seven at the time."

"That was before I knew him."

"And you never knew about . . . ." He waved vaguely around the room, the game, the world.

"Not a thing."

"Too bad. I think a friend would tell you." He let that sink in for a moment. It plugged into a chorus that had been spinning in her head: *Why didn't Gray tell me?* "Are you two close?"

"Friends."

He smiled. "Young love. So complicated."

"Are you and Jeph . . . ?" She let it drop deliberately.

"Business associates. I procure antiquities."

"Like the mirror?"

He smiled as if she had shown her ignorance. "They're quite valuable."

"I can imagine."

"It's why I'd like to get in touch with Gray. I bought one as a gift for his mother. But we had a falling-out, and she died suddenly. Did Gray tell you how she died?"

"It seemed to be something he didn't care to talk about."

Cain nodded solemnly. "It would be. Anyway, I wanted to give the mirror to Gray after she died, but I couldn't find him. He went into foster care, and I lost track. It would have paid for at least a year at a top university. But privacy laws for foster kids are ridiculous."

"He doesn't need money. He's fine."

He pulled something out of his pocket and held it out to her. It was a playing card, the Jack of Clubs, apparently, but there was no J on it, just one medieval soldier in full armor with a battle ax and a shield, and the club in the corner was so clumsily painted that it almost looked like a spade.

She took it to look at it more closely, and Cain walked away. "Wait. What am I supposed to do with this?"

He turned back. "Give it to Gray, of course."

"Is this the gift?"

"When you cross back over, you'll see what it really is. A business card. My name and contact information. Have him call me."

Jeph was there, waiting by the door, holding it open for her to leave. Echo stopped beside him on the way out. "I left the card you gave me with Aunt Doris. Can I get another one?"

He shrugged. "All my cards are in my other suit." He gently but firmly closed the door behind her.

"Hey!" A voice came out of the darkness. "Hey! Don't let them close the door! I want—"

But Echo found herself outside Jeph's esuoh, in a space lit only by the magician's door. Another door shone nearby, but not at arm's reach as the other doors had been.

A dark-skinned man in his early thirties strode up to her, panting. "How did you get in?" He wore a navy-blue suit jacket over a crisp white shirt with the collar unbuttoned.

"I knocked, but Jeph didn't want to let me in."

"I saw you come out."

"He had a creepy friend with him. Trust me, they didn't help at all."

"Come into my esuoh and sit down. I want to go over it all."

Echo wasn't sure why she owed him "going over it all," but she was on her way to his esuoh anyway. There was a glass door with a curved metal push handle, like in an upscale mall. The door had a logo imprinted on the glass, but it took Echo a minute to figure out what the image was. First she saw a blue oval with a figure in the middle of it, which, when viewed upside down, turned out to be a naked woman.

"Never mind about that," the man said. "They installed my logo wrong."

His esuoh had simple furniture in neutral colors, with a huge bank of computer monitors on the far wall. Another wall held row upon row of certificates from almost-familiar names such as Ogle, Faceplant, Flutter, Blink.Inc, and Instaglam, in bright primary colors.

The man sat on a long beige sofa with a glass table in front of it. "Have a seat. Do you want a beer?"

She sat in a chair and looked around again. "This is a lot like Jeph's esuoh. Is that a coincidence?"

He pulled a dark bottle and glass out of the air and poured. "Jeph is my mentor," he said. "My name is Dennis LeMonde."

"Echo Shearwater."

He leaned forward, elbows on his knees. "What did you find out?"

"Jeph just wanted me to go away. I left his business card at home and wanted another one, but he said they were in his other suit."

"Business card?"

"I mentioned to Estelle that Jeph gave me a business card. She seemed to think it might be important."

He looked thoughtful at that, patted his suit jacket pocket and pulled out a card, more than twice the size of a business card. Echo couldn't see it well from the distance, but it was colorful and might have been the same as his logo. He turned it over and slid it back into his pocket. He patted the pocket. "Could be it."

"That doesn't look like the card Jeph gave me."

"Well, it wouldn't, would it? Things don't look the same here."

"Maybe you can help me with that. Where is *here*? Is this a different world?"

He looked at her with a puzzled expression. "It's more an alternate view than a world." He continued to analyze her, as if he had just discovered she might be from another planet. "Don't you have a rorrim?"

"Rorrim? I've heard the word."

He nodded, as if she had settled the question. "Mirror, the special kind you use to get here. A lot of the language is ordinary words spelled back-wards. A little trick I've noticed."

"Thanks. This is my first time here."

"Really." There was an edge of irony in his *"really"* and a hint of intense competition.

Echo suddenly realized that she was unlikely to win. "I'm not making much forward motion with the game."

"What do you want to win?"

"A job, I guess. That's what Jeph offered me. Same for you?"

"No." His eyes closed, and he took a deep breath. "A franchise."

Echo had a general idea of what a franchise was, but she couldn't un-derstand how it would apply here. "What is that?"

"I want to be a certified Jeph Blackthorne Reputation Consultant. Using his methods, working with his overflow clients, I have a vision to change the world by spreading this view throughout the population."

"Everybody living in this—view? That's . . . ." Echo couldn't think of the words to express what a bad idea that seemed like.

"Amazing, I think, is the word you're looking for." He took a sip of his beer. "Not everybody, at least not yet, but a lot more of us. Some won't be ready to make the leap. Some won't be able to afford it. Some will fight tooth and nail to stop us. But enough will want in that it will be the equivalent of the Gold Rush."

"Ambitious."

"Powerful, I think, is the word you're looking for."

"I just want a good-enough salary to rent an apartment in Sellwood," Echo said.

"If you've got the power, you don't even need to 'rent'—you just receive."

Echo felt a bit of Aunt Doris's skepticism creeping in. "How does that work, exactly?"

"The energy of the world flows through you, and some of that energy sticks to you. So you live where you want, work the way you want, travel, have experiences—all that."

"Is that how it works for you?"

"Since I got my rorrim." He pulled it out of his pocket and showed it to her. It was the size of a shirt button. "It used to be bigger, but I've taken off pieces trying to reverse engineer it. My sources say it has interesting properties, but they don't understand it."

"Oh, really? What properties are those?"

He looked over his shoulder and winked at her. "Secret. I'm going to get a patent when I crack the code."

"Huh." There didn't seem much else to say. "I guess I'll get back to the game now. Is Pru next door to you?"

"Wait. I've got an idea." He rubbed his hands together. "It'll be a win-win."

Echo waited, unable to imagine what he might have in mind.

"Let's work together. If we win, I'll be the certified consultant, and I'll make sure you get your apartment in Sellwood. You can work for me. I'll teach you my system."

"Sounds tempting," Echo lied. "Let me think about it."

"Don't think too long. There's a countdown running, and if I find the key without your help, you can't hold me to any deal."

Echo would be surprised if he could be held to any deal that didn't include a four-thousand-page contract and a phalanx of lawyers. "If I don't get back to you in time, it will be my loss."

He nodded solemnly.

"Is there any way to get past Pru's esuoh?"

"Walking off into the dark, maybe. I wouldn't try it myself."

Echo had tried it before, and it turned out OK. She waved goodbye and left through the door. Standing between Dennis's door and one with a black-and-white drawing of a woman holding a balance scale and a sword, she heard a hinge squeak and stepped out toward the middle of the table, hoping to elude both Pru and Dennis.

She wondered about the shape of these houses that seemed to have whole worlds attached to them, but took up only the space of a door. "Bigger on the inside than the outside" was the refrain from a television show, and this place took it to the limit.

She took long strides in the darkness, confident she was walking across a flat and polished table and not a landscape of rocks, roots, and other obstacles—except the door she had seen. But when she had found the door before, she was going in a different direction. She was counting on it as a landmark. Would she find it from this angle?

Her foot caught on something and she fell, painfully banging her knee and tearing her outfit.

She felt around for what had tripped her, but found only the smooth surface of the table. She widened her search. Nothing. She stretched out on the ground and made a circle, running her hands and arms over as much of the area as she could reach. She found something. Under her hip. Too small to trip her, but the only thing she found.

The item was a couple of bangle bracelets, attached to each other with a jewelry chain. They were heavy for their size, but she couldn't really see them, so she put them into a pocket of her tunic, then went in search of light to examine what she had found.

Suddenly she was back at the door with the drawing of the woman with the scales and sword. Wonderful. All that and still at Pru's esuoh. She sighed and opened the door. Immediately noticeable on the first wall she came near was a sign: WERE YOU INVITED? IF NOT, GET OUT.

Pru's esuoh was stark and uncomfortable, with square corners and hard chairs. On every surface, there were signs: DO NOT SCRATCH THE FURNITURE. ALL FOOD AND DRINK MUST BE CONSUMED IN THE KITCHEN. NO TOYS IN THE TOILET. A sign on a door out of the kitchen said MANAGEMENT ONLY.

Echo felt that she had seen everything here. She turned to leave.

"Just a minute." Pru's voice caught her. "Don't you think it's rude to leave before greeting your host?"

"Maybe you should put up a sign."

"Look at the door."

Sure enough, the door had a sign: IT IS EXTREMELY RUDE FOR AN INVITED GUEST TO LEAVE WITHOUT GREETING THE HOST.

Echo obeyed the sign. "Hi, Pru. How's it going?" She turned back to the door.

"Very well. Won't you join me for polite conversation?" Pru sounded like *polite* was a concept she had read about but hadn't tried.

Echo didn't want to come in. She had had enough of Pru already and wanted to go out and meet the last of her fellow players.

But Pru stood there with her hopeful smile, and Echo didn't have whatever character trait it took to say no. She turned back into Pru's front room and sat down.

Pru sat across from her and took off her wig, smoothing it and draping it over the arm of her chair. "Did you find anything?"

"I don't know what it is." Echo pulled the thing she had found from her pocket. She held it out on her hand toward Pru, at the same time getting her own first look at it.

It was a pair of bangles that would slide over her hand, with small sparkly stones mounted around them. Maybe glass, maybe diamonds. Pru walked across the room for a closer look, but she didn't touch them. She walked away with her hands clutching each other like friends watching a horror movie.

"What's the matter?" Echo wasn't much for jewelry, but she thought the bracelets were pretty.

Pru didn't answer. She shivered.

Echo found Pru's reaction confusing. The woman had been so eager to win. "Could this be the key? I've heard it might not look like a key."

"If it is, it's yours, not mine."

"Why?"

"There's more than one kind of bracelet." She took another step away from Echo.

"More than one kind of bracelet?" Echo looked them over more carefully. Simple silver bands with sparkly stones. She slid them onto her wrist and held her hand out. They jingled cheerily. "Don't you like them?"

"Now you've done it. You can't blame anyone else for what you've chosen for yourself. You'll be arrested tonight."

Echo slid the bracelets off and put them back in her pocket. "Arrested? Why? I found these. I thought finding something was the point of the game."

"Arrested. Interrogated. Tried. Judged. Weighed in the balance. Everything you are, everything you know, everything you believe."

Echo felt the first burning of tears. Would she be found out? "But I haven't done anything."

"That may be the core of your crime."

"This is a joke, right? More of your impossible rules?"

"The rules protect you only as long as you follow them. Keep the key. You've won, and all that's left is to cross the finish line. Later, you'll know if that's a blessing or a curse."

Pru stood up and shouted, "I want out!" The box appeared. Pru touched the rorrim, and Echo was again in the darkness between Dennis and the door with the moon, the dogs, and the lobster. Estelle was walking into Dennis's door, and Echo turned toward the house of the one person she hadn't yet met.

In a tiny room with barely enough space to move, a man in his thirties wearing an old-fashioned suit sat at a tiny desk and chair set before a small front window. It was dark outside, and moonlight blazed into the room through a skylight above him. He pounded away on an ancient manual typewriter, stopping now and then to vomit into a bucket on the floor beside his feet.

"You're sick," Echo said. "Can I get you something?"

"No." He kept typing. "I've been waiting for you." He looked at her, then back to his typewriter several times, as if writing his impressions, then he pushed his chair back and turned to face her. "I can't stand this."

His face was lean and pale, and his round glasses magnified his eyes, which seemed to take in some unspeakable horror. His brown suit, which he wore with an orange tie, had a rumpled appearance, and his hair, although combed straight back, stood out around his ears as if it had a mind of its own.

Echo wasn't sure if he meant he couldn't stand the world or the writing. "Why do you do it?"

"Just show me the key."

"What makes you think I have it?"

"I've seen the others, and the shape of the story is that you have the key."

"I'm not sure . . . ."

He grabbed his stomach and turned to the bucket again. Then, rising: "Please."

She dug the bracelets out of her pocket and held them out to him.

He took one look at it and turned back to the typewriter.

"You can have it," Echo said. "You people are making me think I don't want it."

"Ha ha! You can't dump it on me." He ripped the page out of the typewriter and shoved it into his inner coat pocket. "I want out!" The box, the mirror—and he disappeared—

Leaving her alone, again, in the dark between her own esuoh and the esuoh of Dennis LeMonde. She went into her esuoh and found Dennis pacing. "Did you get it?"

"Seems like. But I'm not sure. Want to see it?"

"Yes." He spoke fast and urgently. "Show me."

She held it out to him. "Do you still want your franchise?"

"That's not a franchise. I want out!" and soon she was standing alone in her esuoh. She stepped outside into the darkness between Estelle's door and the one with a man wearing a beehive hat like Edward, the friend of Gray's.

The game seemed to be winding down fast, and she hadn't been to Edward's esuoh. The door led into a low-ceilinged, arched passageway, which opened into a room full of bookshelves, with soft lighting and thick carpets on the floor.

Edward was sitting in a comfortable chair among his books with a light shining down over his shoulder. "Here you are. I'm so glad you decided to pay me a visit."

"I suppose you're going to drop out now that I've found the key. Everybody else is."

"Yes, probably, after I see it."

She pulled it out to show him.

He looked it over carefully without touching it. "I suppose congratulations are in order."

"Doesn't sound like it, judging from the others' reactions."

"Don't judge by the others' reactions. You came for what you wanted; they came for what they wanted. What you found isn't for them."

"Does it have to be for me? Pru said—"

"Interrogation, trial, judgment, right? That's Pru's way of looking at the world. Dennis ran away in terror? You wanted to run when you heard what Dennis was looking for. Maan throwing up in a bucket. He always does that in Ytilaer. I don't know why he comes back."

"So you don't think there's anything to worry about?"

"If you were inclined to worry, you wouldn't be asking."

"My Aunt Doris worries for me."

"And always will, I imagine. In the meantime, I'm going to go home and let you start your adventure."

"Tell Gray I'm fine."

"Next time I see Gray, I'll tell him you got your wish." He shouted, "Out!" and then only Echo and Estelle were left.

Estelle was standing outside her esuoh, waiting. "Let's go open the other door."

"Are you disappointed?"

"I knew you would find it. But the game isn't over until we see what happens at the door. It can still turn out differently."

"And the door—"

"The one you found is the only one left," Estelle said simply.

"But nobody invited us in."

"That's why you need the key."

"Whose esuoh is it?" *Echo asked. It must be someone important to the game who wasn't here.* Echo wished she had time to ponder that.

"Let's find out."

They walked confidently through the darkness. There were no more obstacles until the door loomed before them, now faintly lighted in the darkness. Echo could just barely make out a design—a tall rectangle with an upside-down man in the middle of it.

Echo knocked first. No answer.

"Might as well try the key," Estelle said.

"Just in case someone was home."

Estelle shrugged.

Echo pulled the bracelets out of her pocket. She didn't know what to do with them. They didn't fit any lock or slot on the door.

"You don't need to make it more complicated than it is. Just push."

Echo laid the bracelets against the door and pushed. The door swung open to a dark corridor with a musty smell.

"Well, I'll be going." Estelle turned back toward her esuoh. "I think we'll see each other again sometime."

"Could you walk with me?"

"No. You'll be fine, and it would look like I'm challenging the outcome. I'll wait here until you open the door at the other end."

Echo walked the long passageway in utter darkness and bumped into a doorway at the end. It opened at the touch of the bracelets, sending a shaft of light back through the corridor. She stepped through the doorway, where Jeph was waiting, in his purple zoot suit, his eyes closed. He handed her the box with the mirror.

After she crossed over, she saw Estelle on her way out. She was not as tall as she looked in the game, and she wore a lavender dress that was nice but not stunning. She waved without looking back as she went out the door toward the elevator, leaving Cain and Jeph sitting at the table with Echo. Jeph still wore the suit pants and white shirt she had seen when she arrived; Cain wore faded black jeans, white T-shirt, and red snakeskin cowboy boots.

"What do you think?" Jeph asked.

"Did I win?"

Jeph laughed. "You passed with flying colors."

Echo pulled her phone out of her bag. She had a missed call from Gray and a text from Aunt Doris. Nearly nine thirty. She put the phone away. "Is there anything else to do tonight? I need to catch a bus home."

"No. That's enough for an evening. Come in at nine tomorrow, and we'll take care of the paperwork."

C H A P T E R 6

Echo Alone

W HEN ECHO WENT INTO THE HOUSE, she found Aunt Doris watching *Magnum, P.I.,* on Netflix.

"How did it go?" Aunt Doris asked without turning from her show.

Echo leaned against the lintel and tried to keep her voice casual. She couldn't contain a smile, but she had an instinctive reticence about sharing the events of the evening. "Well, I start tomorrow."

Aunt Doris turned to look at Echo, happiness and concern battling for dominance on her face. "Well, that's—good, I guess."

"I need to be there at nine."

The music on *Magnum, P.I.,* rose to a crescendo, and shots were fired. "No drop cloths or ladders on the twenty-seventh floor?"

Echo gave a laugh that to her own ears seemed a shade unhinged. "Nothing like that." Aunt Doris didn't seem to notice. "I think I'll go to bed now."

Aunt Doris turned back to the show. "I'll want to hear all about it in the morning. Good night, my girl. I love you."

"Good night, Aunt Doris. See you in the morning."

ECHO SIGHED WITH RELIEF AS SHE CLOSED HER BEDROOM DOOR behind her. She threw on her pajamas, turned off the light, and flopped on the bed. She was wide awake, with snippets of the evening's conversations going through her head like a merry-go-round.

Then she remembered Gray's call. She picked up her phone from the night table and listened to his message. "I start my internship tomorrow. See you at UM before seven fifteen?"

She put the phone down and flopped over on her pillow. *Oh, Gray. How I would love to tell you how it went. You're the one person who would understand. But why didn't you tell me?* But that would be an all-night conversation, and he apparently had an early morning tomorrow, and she was suddenly very sleepy . . . .

And then she was in a picnic shelter on the Oregon coast, overlooking the ocean, a place she and Gray had gone one Saturday with Gray's brother Quig and his family. While Quig, Julia, and the kids walked and played down on the beach, Echo and Gray walked a trail along the bluff and came to a picnic table with a shelter built over it: uprights made of rough-hewn logs, open walls, a concrete floor, and shingle roof. They had sat on the table with their feet on the bench and looked out over the long bluff of dense salal bushes and coastal pines leading to a beach far below, where Quig's family played in the sand.

"There's an eternal ocean," Gray had said, looking out at the horizon, where, that day, a band of slate-blue clouds divided the sharp, sparkling blue of the ocean from the soft, smooth blue of the sky. She couldn't remember his exact words, but she *felt* his description of as a great bowl where everyone's dreams, wishes, fears, and memories—both remembered and forgotten—slosh together, separate, combine into new forms, and break apart again.

Now, in her dream, she was alone in the shelter in twilight's last remnant, and far below, ocean waves, luminescent in the moonlight, washed calmly over the empty beach.

Echo heard a noise, like a scratch on stone, and found that Gray had just entered the shelter.

"Did you call me?" He eased into the space, as if he were trying to rescue a stray cat.

"How could I call you? I think I'm sleeping."

Gray took a step forward. "I thought I heard you. I was listening."

She turned away from him toward the ocean. "Are you part of my dream?"

"I'm sharing your dream. It's like—"

She patted the table where he had sat before. "Come sit beside me. I want to ask you something."

He sat beside her and looked out over the ocean. He looked different in the strong light of the overlarge moon. There was a dark shadow on his cheek, a sharper cheekbone than she remembered, a stronger jaw. His eyes were open, the first time she had ever seen them, but the moonlight washed the color out of everything.

"Tell me." He reached out and touched her hand. A shock went through her, like a high-voltage current. Gray felt it, too; she could tell by his wide eyes, his rigid body that—

Grew longer, thinner, and suddenly was not Gray, but Jeph's "associate," Cain, standing beside the table, still holding her hand. Echo jerked her hand back and jumped away from the table.

He looked around the shelter in its clearing in the forest. "Nice place. I should get one." He turned back to Echo. "You didn't give Gray the card." It was a statement, not a question.

"I didn't have a chance to. I'll give it to him tomorrow after I wake up."

He smiled at her, amusement on the knife edge of maliciousness, and raised one eyebrow in skepticism. "I think it will take longer than that. But then most people never do wake up." He leaned against a wall. "How did you end up in the game? It was supposed to be Gray."

That irritated her for a reason she didn't quite understand. "I'm the one who needs a job."

He took that as an answer, although if she were under oath, she would have to admit that it wasn't one. He looked casually at his fingernails. "How did you like the game?"

"It was weird." She continued, more to herself than to him, "I'm beginning to wonder if it really happened."

He looked at her with a steady, evaluating gaze. "Most of the time, I find these doubts and hesitations funny. But there's too much at stake here. This is more real than the sunshine and daisies you're used to. Sometimes it meshes with the world you know, but the time to pay attention is when it doesn't."

"That's interesting, but what does it have to do with the game?"

"You think it's over?"

"I won."

Now he did laugh. "Yes, you won. And your prize is being able to stay in."

"Isn't that a good thing?"

He put one foot on the bench and looked at the ocean. "It's the only thing that has any value."

"But they said there are monsters and disruption and death, and nothing is what it seems."

"Oh, the monsters are real, all right. But it's only in this world that you can see them. Why do you think Gray stayed in all these years?"

"How do you know Gray?"

"I told you. I knew his mother." He took a long step forward and seemed to stare down at her from a great height. "And as for nothing being what it seems, the only thing you need to know is that *everything* is exactly what it seems."

She stood there, an arm's length away from him, feeling a vortex of something she had a hard time naming. Danger, yes. And excitement. Freedom. And danger.

He leaned in closer and whispered. "You don't need to act innocent with me. Why did you kill your family?"

She gasped, feeling the memory on the verge of flashing into her dream again, and then she was out of the picnic shelter, walking into Jeph's conference room, where she had been earlier, but different—the colors more saturated, the lights outside the window like Van Gogh's *Starry Night*. Jeph, alone, sat at the head of the table, leaning back in the chair, his tie loosened. Echo took a seat in the chair next to his.

"Don't mind Cain." Jeph spoke casually, as if the conversation had been going on for hours. "He has some strange ideas, but he's harmless."

Harmless. Echo had trouble believing that. But looking into Jeph's intense, earnest blue eyes, she believed he believed it.

"Anyway, here's your quest. Cain tells me you're too inexperienced to carry out the assignment. So I'm giving you a bonus round. There's another key, down on the beach somewhere. You need to find it and bring it to my office tomorrow."

"Is this another game?"

"Same and different. Everything is a game. Dead serious, but still a game."

"So I'll be knocking on people's doors again?"

"Not this time. Walk down the beach and find the key."

"But it's night, and the beach goes on forever. It will take days, weeks, if I can find it at all."

Jeph smiled. "You've got all the time in the world."

Then she was back in the picnic shelter where she had started, alone, with the moonlit ocean far below.

Walk down the beach and find the key. She stepped outside the shelter, looking for the path that would take her back to the parking lot and join another path down to the beach. But there was no path out, only dense woods, and she had forgotten how to get to the parking lot. Anyway, she didn't want to go to the parking lot, which had become a synthesis of every beach wayside parking lot, along with all the malls, schools, offices, and streetside parking—the Universal Parking Lot—where people came and went, a quality infinitely distant from the beach. It made perfect sense in the logic of her dream.

The way to the beach was down the bluff.

She stepped out of the dimly lit picnic shelter. She stood next to the DANGER DO NOT GO BEYOND THIS POINT sign at the edge of the waist-deep salal bushes. The spiky little bushes, cousins of the blueberry, didn't have thorns, but they did have stiff, interlacing branches that only a bird could get through easily. In the moonlight, they formed an impenetrable cloud down the sharp slope of the bluff.

Which would it be? *Walk down the beach and find the key?* Or *Do not go beyond this point?* What's the worst that could happen? If she didn't find the key, she might not get the job. If she fell off a cliff in her dream, she would wake up and be no worse off than before.

She plunged past the sign into the bushes that held her back at every step along the way. The ground under her feet was steep and uncertain, sometimes rocky, other times dropping into muddy ruts she couldn't see. The branches she grasped to keep her footing scratched and gouged her hands. They tore her clothes—the ridiculous outfit she had worn at the scavenger hunt—and her legs and arms as well. When she looked behind her, she saw the empty picnic shelter on the hillside, at the top of the bluff, a small, isolated thing, its outlines barely visible in the darkness. She turned down the slope again.

She arrived at the bottom of the hill, climbed over the boulders and driftwood logs at the edge of the beach, stumbled through the deep dry sand, falling to her knees a few times in her hurry to get to the water.

The waves that had seemed so placid from above now smashed the wet sand with a rushing roar and a splash of foam, then withdrew leaving jetsam in their wake—waterlogged books, jewelry, a paper in her childish handwriting with a teacher's red "B-" on it, a toy she barely remembered, skeletons of dead cats and dogs. They were things left behind and until now forgotten. She rushed into the waves to catch a stuffed purple octopus she had lost, but felt something grasp her ankle. She screamed, the sound muffled in the thick night air. Forgetting the toy, she dashed out of the water. She looked back but saw nothing but the heaving waves. The grip had felt like a hand, but, she told herself, maybe it was just a bit of trailing seaweed. She turned inland and walked at a distance from the surf.

She was cold, and her cuts and scratches were stinging. The waves lapped at her feet as if begging her to come back. She walked along the firm, packed sand at the edge of the waves, her eye on the ground for lost treasure, but finding nothing worth carrying. The picnic shelter had disappeared in the distance behind her. A jetty rose above the horizon in front of her. Over it, colored lights painted the sky. She found no bracelets lying in the sand, but still she walked.

Change occurred— process without time, if that's possible—and now the beach was bathed in the blue half-light of early morning or late evening, but there was no sunrise or sunset in the east or west. In fact, she only assumed she was walking north with the ocean on her left because of her orientation to the Pacific. This could be a place where north, south, east, and west pretended to aid navigation but really pointed to something far deeper and lost to human memory. She knew only that light flared out from the jetty in front of her, and the place where she started was too far behind to see.

She came at last to the jetty—rugged, broken boulders quarried somewhere far from the sea—where lights from the other side painted the sky pink, green, and yellow. The world was entirely silent except for the insistent rush and return of the waves.

The lights called to her like a friendly voice. She had been alone so long that she ached for human interaction, and colored lights suggested people would be there. She looked for footing to climb the rocks. In the sand at the base of one boulder, in a tiny tide pool, she found the key. Or maybe not. It was another bracelet, this time a thick herringbone chain made of silver.

She picked it up and knew—the way she knew her own name—it was the key she was looking for. She slid it into her pocket and began to climb the jetty.

The rocks were the size of doghouses and tumbled together. The climbing took effort, but there were handholds and footholds, and the rocks were solidly packed, so she made progress. As she scaled the boulders of the jetty, she gradually emerged from the shadow. Lights filtered through openings among the rocks, making it sometimes easier to see her way, sometimes harder. And she began to hear mechanical pounding and screaming and music.

When she reached the top, she found an immense blacktop wharf with a carnival on it. Rides, jugglers, a cacophony of competing music, games of skill and chance, and over on the right, away from the ocean, a row of somber, substantial buildings with a few of their windows lighted, sneered at the carnival. Everything outside the lights was a wall of darkness.

Jeph had told her to deliver the key to his office tomorrow. How would she get home? How would she keep the key when she woke up? And *when* was tomorrow? She didn't know. She had been walking for hours and hours—it seemed like days—but it also seemed that no time had passed at all.

She felt hungry, and now the booths and stands that stood out for her were the food booths. They sold fair food—corn dogs, potstickers, sushi, gyros, elephant ears, more corn dogs. Their signs proclaimed "Tasty!" and "Delicious!" and "Fried!" and lines of people waiting for them wrapped through the aisles and pathways like a maze.

And then there was a little out-of-favor shop with a painted sign that said, "Food for the Journey." No exclamation point. No queue.

She walked up to the window and found an old-fashioned hotdog vendor in white shirt and pants, wearing a white paper hat that looked out of place with his trim professor's beard. "Ah! So you're the one who brought me here." It was Edward Paladin from the game. He bent down to look under the counter and came up with a paper tray holding a piece of dry bread and five lentils. "This must be for you."

The food reminded her of her mother's kitchen. A professor of classical literature, she had been more interested in experimenting with ancient cuisine than feeding a kid of the twenty-first century.

Paladin caught her expression. "It may not look like much, but it's what you need."

"Wait. What? This is a dream, right?"

"Are you still in Ytilaer?" he asked.

"In what?"

He looked at her with his head cocked for a moment, like a bird examining a mystery. "No, you're dreaming. Impressive."

"Am I ever going to wake up? It seems like hours and hours."

"Maybe days?"

Panic rose in her throat. "Days?"

"No. Just seems like it. Are you sure you want to leave?"

She looked around. It was an interesting place, with much to explore. "Eventually."

"Then don't eat the food."

She looked down at the tray in her hands.

"You can eat my food." He sounded a little offended. "Don't eat the junk food. The stuff with exclamation points. It's like . . . ." He paused for a few seconds. "Do you know the story of Hades and Persephone?"

"Of course."

"Then you understand. Don't eat the food. Or drink anything. Not even a pomegranate seed."

"But I'm thirsty."

He handed her a plastic bottle of liquid that looked like cranberry juice. "I've got to —" He cut off his words when he slammed the window shut. The lights went off, and the booth was empty and derelict.

CHAPTER 7

The Never-Ending Carnival

ECHO SAT ON A BENCH between pizza and hamburger stands. She tried to chew one of the lentils, but it was as hard and tasteless as she had expected, so she swallowed all five, then turned to the bread. It was dry and crumbly and left a feeling of dust in her mouth, so she opened the bottle and took a sip of the juice. She almost spit it out, not because of the flavor, but because of the surprise. It was wine. Sweet and watered down, but an improvement on the bread, so she ate the rest of the bread, drank the wine, and considered whether she trusted Paladin's guidance over the smell of mouth-watering hamburgers and fragrant pizzas.

A man in black T-shirt and jeans and Birkenstock sandals, his hair tied up in a manbun, sat beside her on the bench, awkwardly juggling an apple, a notebook, and a pen. The item he wasn't using at any given moment he held between his teeth, usually the apple or the pen, but once it was the pad, which left him looking at the two items in his hands in bewildered abstraction, as if he wasn't quite sure what to do with them. Then he recovered himself, set the pad on his knees, wrote a note with his left hand and took a bite of apple from his right.

Echo stared at him in curiosity. For one thing, he looked familiar, but she wasn't sure where she knew him from. She was running through a mental slide show of people she had known, going back even to childhood, but nothing came up. The other thing was that the apple smelled delicious—not the Delicious variety of apple, which she hated, but crispy, sweet, and tart, so juicy that it splashes your face when you take a bite. The kind of apple that appears in television commercials, eaten by ecstatic models, with slow-motion wind blowing beads of water.

The food she had gotten from Edward Paladin had not filled her up, and now the experience of the apple drowned out even the call of the pizza and hamburgers. Her stomach growled, loudly.

The man looked up at her in surprise, and she recognized him. The clothes were different, but he was the writer from Jeph's game.

"Oh, hi," Echo said. "I didn't recognize you. You must be feeling better."

"Sorry." He wiped his mouth on his sleeve. "Do I know you?"

"Maybe not. We were in a scavenger hunt together this evening. You looked like you didn't feel well."

"Oh, that. No wonder." He took a last bite and tossed the apple core over his shoulder. Echo watched it land on the sawdust. He wiped his hands on his pants. "Maan Nilson. I didn't catch your name."

"Echo—"

Before she could finish, he went on. "I remember now. You won, right?"

She shrugged. "I guess so. I'm not sure what I won, though. Not exactly a trip to Hawaii."

"Did you want a trip to Hawaii?"

She thought about that. About the heat, the bugs, the fabulous women on the beaches pitying her face. "Not really."

"What *do* you want?"

She involuntarily looked over her shoulder at the apple core lying in the dirt. "I thought I knew earlier, but now I'm not sure."

He reached into a bag she hadn't seen on the other side of him and pulled an apple out. "Want one?"

Yes, oh, yes. "Edward Paladin gave me some food. Said it would be enough. Said not to eat anything here."

"Oh, he's just talking about the pizza and elephant ears. That stuff is poison. This—" He held it up in the light. Its skin was a gorgeous ombré of green and red, the stem and leaf were as fresh as if it had been picked only that moment, and the smell was like love. "This is organically grown, fresh from the tree, a feast for all your senses." He held it out to her.

She looked back at the Food for the Journey booth. It was closed and dark. She reached out and took the apple. It seemed to vibrate in her hand. When she took a bite, she had to sit back on the bench for a while to absorb the experience. "So good," she said, still chewing.

He was writing in his notebook in tiny, square handwriting. She tried to read over his shoulder, but the letters were unfamiliar and seemed to dance on the page. "What are you writing?" she asked around the next bite.

"Novel," he said. "About a girl who gets lost in the dream world and has to find her way out."

"Dream world. Is that the same as Y— Yt—? Whatever Edward said?"

"No." He was quite emphatic. Then he softened. "You're new here. For me they're entirely different, because Ytilaer makes me violently ill, and in the dream world I'm just fine."

"So I am dreaming."

He laughed and looked around. "Have you ever seen anyplace like this—out there?"

She looked around, taking it all in. The smells of ocean, boat fuel, fried foods, sawdust. The curtain of darkness embracing the lights. The sounds of the rides and people talking and laughing as if a long way off. The crunch of the apple between her teeth, and the distant hiss of the waves against the rocks. The sense of isolation in the midst of the crowd. "But this is so real."

He nodded emphatically. "More real than the other world."

She thought about that. "That's how it feels, but if Aunt Doris came up to my room, she would find me sleeping."

"What does she know about what's going on here?"

"So why am I not waking up? Whenever I've known I was dreaming before, I woke up pretty much right away."

"Ytilaer will do that for you." He capped his pen and clipped it to the cover of the writing pad. He set it aside and leaned back on the bench, taking in the sights, sounds, and smells. "It's why I keep going back, because it gives me this."

"You mean you're really here? If I met you on the street tomorrow, you would remember?"

"Don't ask me. I won't admit it."

"Why not?"

"I have a wife who doesn't know about this. And a job where I'm supposed to be responsible. How could I explain to her that I met a seventeen-year-old at a dream carnival?"

"I'm nineteen. Almost."

"Fine. That would get me out of trouble with the police—except they don't recognize this world—but not with my wife."

"Why don't you tell her?" She was thinking about Gray.

He leaned forward with his elbows on his knees. "I like her the way she is."

"But if this is more real—"

"One of my favorite poets said, 'Humankind cannot bear very much reality.'" He was gripping his hands together tightly.

"So you're basically lying to her, and that's OK."

"I don't want to talk about it." He disappeared.

Echo put her hand over her mouth, but it was too late. She looked around and didn't see him anywhere. Did he go somewhere else? Did he wake up? What time was it anyway?

She stood up and began walking again through the carnival, gnawing around the core of the apple. She could still hear the ocean on her left, and so she was getting farther and farther from the picnic shelter she had started from, but when—*if?*—she woke up, she might never come here again.

She passed a "ride" in which everybody took an elevator up to a high platform, where they pitched into the void—some walked, some seemed to be pushed by invisible hands, some seemed to simply lose their footing and fall. The screams were not the screams of the carnival, but screams of genuine terror. They all disappeared before they hit the ground. That was one way to wake up.

There was another ride called What You Did. It looked like the haunted house rides at the fair, but the outside was decorated with broken mirrors, and the screams from within were, again, real. People went in like sleep-walkers, and most of the cars came out empty. One man came out in his car, with his eyes open and a look of maniacal glee on his face. When he stepped out of the car, she recognized him as Death from the game. He still wore the tie with the little black skulls on it. He caught her eye and gave her a friendly wave, inviting but not quite beckoning. Echo waved back shyly and hurried past.

Panic-stricken people carrying books or briefcases checked their watches and bustled by.

Scattered through the crowds were people who had just realized they were naked. They would stand there a moment, trying futilely to hide their nakedness and looking around to see if anyone noticed them. Most of the others walked casually by as if naked people appeared on street corners every day here. As apparently they did.

Echo looked down at herself—she had to make sure—and found that she was still wearing the ragged outfit from the game, with its additional rips from the trip down the bluff to the ocean.

She joined a rivulet of people going toward a monumental building a block away from the carnival. There was a holiday mood, like touring Broadway play. The street grew dark as they moved away from the pier, and the flood of people grew thicker, stronger. Soon it became impossible to escape, even if she wanted to. But curiosity pulled like an irresistible magnet, and she wondered who could be a celebrity in her dream.

They flowed into a three-story brick building with an imposing facade, and once inside, took their seats in a room as big as a basketball court. She might have gone outside to look at the size of the building again, but there was no swimming upstream against that flow, and she needed to find a place to sit. Every time she tried to sit down, she discovered someone else already sitting there.

After a while, the flow died down, and all the seats were taken except one at the front of the room, at a table facing a raised dais that looked strangely like a judge's bench. She would have left, but the doors had been closed already.

A man wearing a sandwich board with the five of clubs on both sides walked through the room ringing a bell and shouting, "Hear ye! Hear ye! All rise for the entrance of the honorable Judge Prudy."

Pru, with her small tight hairdo and her piercing eyes, still wearing the black robe, but not the English judge's wig, had ascended the dais and now stared at Echo, the only person other than the man in the five-of-clubs sandwich board standing in the room.

"Would the accused please sit down?"

The Five of Clubs rang his bell furiously and shouted, "Would the accused sit down!" All the people around him covered their ears.

Pru banged her gavel. "Would the Five of Clubs please go away now!"

The Five of Clubs hung his head and lowered his bell and wandered through the crowd to the back of the room, found a door, and went out.

Leaving Echo to receive the full blast of Pru's scorn. "Did the accused hear the judge?"

"Are you talking to me? Accused of what?" Echo asked, more in outrage than fear.

"The accused will hear the charges when she sits at her assigned seat."

If she were Alice in Wonderland, it would be almost time for her to wake up. So she went to the table and waited to see what would happen next. The man sitting next to her, dressed in a rumpled, double-breasted, navy pinstripe suit, was Edward Paladin.

"Are you my attorney?" she asked.

He frowned back. "I told you not to eat anything."

"But it was an apple. It wasn't fried food. And I was hungry."

He shook his head. "That's what they always say. I don't know if I can get you out of this."

She shrugged. "I'll be waking up in a few minutes."

"Don't be so sure about that."

"It's just a dream," she said, annoyed that he seemed to be trying to make her worry.

"People who understand dreams never use the word 'just' to describe them."

"Would the accused and her attorney please give their attention to the Court?"

"Of course, your honor," Paladin said.

"Witnesses. We need witnesses, lots and lots of witnesses," Pru said. The crowd cheered, and she smiled beneficently upon them. "Have them tell us stories, beautiful stories, funny stories, stories that make us cry." The crowd cheered again. "If you have to choose between cheating the truth or cheating the story, preserve the story!" The cheering drowned her words as the crowd stood on their chairs and threw their hats into the air.

Echo, looking back at them, saw many familiar faces, but she didn't know them. Maybe she had seen them on the bus or around town or some other time in her past. Maybe the faces were unrecognizable because they were contorted with excitement.

Pru banged her gavel, smiling, and the crowd gradually quieted. "No stories until we all calm down." She sounded like she was talking to kindergartners. There was a rustle in the seats as people picked up their hats, handed the hats that had come to them back to their owners, and sat down. She waited until the excited whispers quieted. "We will call the first witness."

"Sentence first! Witnesses later!" came a voice from the crowd. The cry was taken up by other voices. Not everyone, but a considerable number.

Pru smiled. "Well, since it's late, let's get the boring parts out of the way. The defendant is sentenced to the Dungeons of the Labyrinth."

"What about the charges?" Echo shouted, but the cheering was so loud that no one heard her, except for Paladin, who signaled her to be quiet. "Are you going to ask about the charges?"

"When the time is right."

"Are you an attorney?"

"No, I'm a retired classics professor, but I'm the best you've got."

"That's not encouraging."

He shrugged.

"What does she mean by the Dungeons of the Labyrinth?"

"You don't want to know."

Echo pounded the table. "Why the hell wouldn't I want to know?" The crowd immediately hushed, and Pru looked over her glasses at Echo, but didn't say anything.

"Keep your voice down or you'll miss the stories," Paladin said. "Imagine a cave of deep darkness, lit only by the candlepower of tiny, caged egos separated from their souls. Thousands of branching passages that reshape themselves with every step you take. People who go there never get out."

"And she's sending me there?"

"She has no power to send you anywhere."

"So she is like the Queen of Hearts."

"Just because the Queen of Hearts didn't actually execute anybody doesn't mean nobody ever gets executed."

Pru banged her gavel. "Is Counsel finished interrupting the trial?"

"I was fulfilling my responsibility to my client, Your Honor."

Pru harrumphed. "Announce the first witness."

The voice of the Five of Clubs entered the room far behind Echo, shouting, "Witness for the Prosecution. Justice!"

Pru stepped down from the bench and went to the witness stand.

"Wait!" Echo said. "Is that legal?"

"Oge's rules don't apply here," Paladin said.

Pru was looking disapprovingly at them again, but she waited with some approximation of patience. "I will speak when the Accused is listening."

"Story!" came shouts from the crowd.

"She cheated at the game," Pru said. "She got special help, which was bad enough, and then she went off the path. And that's why she won."

Paladin stood. "Was there a rule that she could not go off the path?"

"There wasn't a rule that she could."

"Would you have gone off the path if you had thought of it?"

"There wasn't a rule!" Pru seemed ready to cry.

"You may step down," Paladin said.

She gave a quiet little harrumph and walked back up to the bench.

"I didn't get special help," Echo said.

"It doesn't matter. You've already been sentenced."

Pru banged the gavel. "Next witness!"

The Five of Clubs shouted, "Dennis LeMonde!"

The businessman who had wanted to franchise Jeph's system strode out. He was still wearing a dark blue suit over a white shirt with an open collar. He climbed into the witness box and sat in an aggressive posture with his elbows on the railing.

"She stole my system and took the place in Jeph's company that should have been mine."

"I did not! I thought your system was ridiculous," Echo shouted.

Pru banged the gavel.

"And slander," LeMonde added. "You can't go around destroying someone's livelihood with impunity."

"I haven't had a chance to destroy anything of yours, but if I ever do . . . ."

"The witness may step down," Paladin said, standing up and walking around the table.

"Where are you going?" Echo whispered.

He walked to the witness stand.

"You're not supposed to do that!" Echo shouted after him.

He sat in the chair and turned to face the crowd, but his eyes were on Echo. "I have to tell the truth. She ate against advice."

"But I was hungry!" Tears sprang to her eyes at the depth of the betrayal. "I thought you were my advocate."

He shrugged and got down from the stand.

Cain slipped out of a secret doorway and took his place in the witness box. "She killed her family."

"I did not!" The dream was coming at her again, like leaves in the wind, leaves with barbed points that clung and stung. She lifted her arm to fend them off, but they kept coming. She took a shuddering breath and realized she was sobbing. She took another deep breath and pulled herself at least partly together. "It was an accident. Diana's fault. Nobody blames me."

Cain looked her in the eye. "You do." He stepped down from the box.

Estelle was waiting to take his place. "Echo is here because she chooses to be." She got up and stepped down.

Paladin stood. "The Defense calls its first witness."

Death stepped up, dapper in his black three-piece suit with the gold watch chain crossing his vest. "Oh, I know the Fool." He smiled at her. "She upset the game, broke the rules. Turned everyone's expectations inside out."

Judge Pru said, "The witness for the defense testifies that the defendant belongs here."

"Wait! That's my *defense?*" Echo shouted.

Paladin ignored her. "I want to present our last exhibit. If I could have Your Honor's assistance?" He bowed with a flourish, and Pru stepped down from the bench, with a pleased and flattered smile.

Together they walked to a box that seemed to have been sitting there forever, but Echo hadn't noticed it before. It was the size of a coffin, black enamel with gold decorations. It stood upright, and Pru held out her hands to it like the magician's lovely assistant, offering it to the audience's attention.

They rolled the box out into the center of the court and spun it around so that everyone could see it front and back. "You can see that it's a complete box?" Paladin asked Pru.

She nodded, smiling.

"Then you may return to your seat."

As she walked back to the judge's bench, Paladin pulled a magic wand out of an inner coat pocket and tapped the box three times. It collapsed into a set of square plates on the floor, leaving a man hanging by his foot from a gallows. A gasp ran through the crowd.

"I present: The man from the hidden door!"

She recognized the design from the door to the empty esuoh to which she had found the key. Fear crept up her spine, because if she had harmed anybody here, it might have been this man when she took his key. Did she cause him to be in this situation?

But he hung there with his eyes staring at Echo, looking less like a hanged man than like a man who happened to be dancing upside down.

Echo pulled the bracelet from her pocket, stood up and shouted, "Is this yours?"

His mouth formed an "O," and he began to make the most godawful scream she had ever heard . . . .

Which turned out to be her alarm as she awoke in her bedroom.

Light flowed in through her bedroom window, and the smell of coffee wafted up the stairs. An enormous bout of shivering seized her, although the morning was warm. She went back under the covers and pulled her pillow over her head, peeking out gradually to assure herself that she was back in her real life. When nothing bizarre happened for a few minutes, she climbed out of bed and looked out the window. Same neighborhood.

She sighed and shuddered in the residue of memory. *It was just a dream,* she told herself.

In the pocket of her pajama pants she found business cards from both Jeph and Cain. She looked at them in her hand, two harmless pieces of paper bearing innocuous words. She didn't remember putting them into her pocket. She shook her head, shoved them into her bag, and went to get ready for her meeting with Jeph.

CHAPTER 8

The Monster

GRAY needed to see Echo at the Ugly Mug this morning. He was still embarrassed about his sudden departure yesterday, when he couldn't bear her laughter. But she had called to him from her dream last night, an action that seemed full of portent. She had said she wanted to ask him something, and then she was gone.

Her unspoken question haunted him as he entered the cafe, which he usually saw as a fairy-tale inn with dark wooden tables and lights powered by magic. The owner, a genial dwarf with a full beard, presided over the place, minding the money box and handing out steaming mugs of coffee. But when Gray opened the door this morning, he stepped into an Old West saloon with scuffed wooden floors and an ornate mirror reflecting liquor bottles behind the bar. He walked up to the counter and asked for coffee. The owner, in a string tie and sleeve garters, slid two mugs down the counter to him and called him pardner.

Something was wrong. Gray surveyed the room—and found who was imposing the perception on him. A cowboy with a black hat pulled over his face was leaning back in a chair with red snakeskin boots crossed on the table where Gray and Echo usually sat.

Gray had seen boots like that before, on the day his life turned upside down and then again and again in nightmares ever since. He froze between the alternatives of running like a frightened mouse, leaving Echo, if she came to meet him this morning, to face the danger alone, or facing a monster with enough power in Ytilaer to change what someone else was seeing.

His heart pounding, Gray finally took a chair at the only empty table, which happened to be next to the cowboy's.

The cowboy sat up, put his feet on the floor, and pushed back his hat, revealing a face of malevolent darkness. Anyone could wear red cowboy boots, but that face proved Gray's suspicions that his day of reckoning had come. He had feared and expected this day since he was seven years old but still wasn't prepared. He pushed down the nausea rising in his throat and fought the urge to run. There was no place to escape. If his mother's murderer could find him here, he could find him anywhere. Gray set down the coffees and waited behind the chair, something in him wanting to die standing up.

"Sit down." The monster's red eyes were open to Gray in Ytilaer, and he spoke quietly with the voice of a man. "Let's talk privately."

Gray bumped the table, spilling coffee, as he sat. He waited for the monster to speak, but it just stared at him, its eyes seeming to focus somewhere beyond Gray's head. And then he *felt* it—a movement inside the space he occupied, not "in his head" as people in Oge might say, but no place and every place, near Gray's heart if he had to give a location. Gray knew what it meant and shivered at the implication.

He went into his esuoh, where he found the monster sitting on an upturned champagne cork looking around the space like a tourist in a foreign city.

"You have no right to come in here," Gray shouted. "You didn't ask, and I didn't invite you."

The monster gave a low chuckle, its black mouth curled in derision. "Cute. I thought you'd be older, though."

Suddenly Gray's esuoh appeared to him the way his home city would if he were showing it to an out-of-town guest—with all the details he had become blind to in their familiarity. It was all humiliating—the space under the bed, with wide wooden boards under his feet, springs and slats above; a table made from a cardboard box, an old fork formed into a lounge chair, and a shelf of postage-stamp-sized comic books holding his short-term memories. When he thought about it, rarely, he might wish for something more—manly, but his esuoh felt safe, at least until now, and Ytilaer gives you the esuoh that fits.

He steeled himself and sat at his cardboard table across from his nightmare.

"It was nice to see you last night," the monster said. "All grown up."

"You saw me? Where?"

"I popped in on your girlfriend and found you there. You were in the way, so I pushed you aside." He reached into the air and produced a cigar box, which he set on the table. "I want to show you something." He opened the box and pulled out a pile of old photos.

"That's mine!" Gray reached across the table to take the box, but Cain pulled it away. "Those are my memories."

"Nope." Cain pulled out a stack of pictures and went through them like a deck of cards. "Though some of them might be the same as yours." He pulled out an image and turned it toward Gray. "This one, for example."

The memory, encased in a faded black-and-white Polaroid photo, was distant but zooming into view as if through a telescope. In it, a man with dark hair and ice-gray eyes, as tall as a building, picked up a toddler Gray knew was himself and threw him into the sky.

"Put that down!"

"OK." The image disappeared. "Who is that?"

"That's my dad."

"*Dad.* I like that. What happened to him?"

"Mom said he was dangerous."

"Truer word never spoken, son. Men are dangerous, and women are liars. Which are you?"

"Don't call me 'son,' you murderer."

"Liar." He spoke calmly, neutrally, as if he had gotten an appropriate answer to his question. He moved more pictures and papers out of the box, stacking them next to it. He lifted out another box, tiny at first but growing until it was bigger than the original. "I think you've got one just like this."

On its lid was a childish drawing of a black-on-black monster shaped like a minotaur with a round head like a black sun, with black teeth and red eyes. "It's not yours. It's mine." Gray struggled to maintain his composure.

"How long since you opened it?"

"I don't need to open it. I remember everything. I remember *you*."

The monster laughed out loud at that. He held up the box beside his face. "It's a good likeness." Then he smiled at it as if he were looking in a mirror. "I've aged a little, like wine."

"Leave it alone! Leave me alone!" Humiliated, Gray felt tears burning his eyes.

"Now, now, little mouse," Cain said in a demeaningly soothing tone. "Don't embarrass me. You don't have to look at it now, but we've got some unfinished business."

"Get out." Gray got up from the box-table and tried to push the monster out of his esuoh. Their bodies sat silent and still at the coffee shop table, giving no indication of the mighty struggle going on in their psyches.

The monster gave Gray the amused smile of a three-hundred-pound wrestler at the efforts of an angry four-year-old. "Jeph told me you belong to some group of 'travelers.' Didn't they teach you anything?"

"Shut up! Just shut up and get out!"

Gray's image of the monster glitched, and he saw an old man, thin and hard and dry, who leaned forward and said, "I could help you make better locks."

Humiliated, Gray sat in his chair again and covered his face with his hands. "I don't want anything from you. Just get out."

The man, monster again, said, "I'll go. I need to be somewhere anyway. But let me ask you something. Why did Jeph invite your girlfriend to the game instead of you?"

That pulled Gray back into the conversation. "I don't know what you're talking about. Who's Jeph? And what game?"

"Just as I thought. That son of a bitch told me you turned him down." He looked Gray up and down. "You're pretty useless, but I hoped not that bad."

"What game?" Gray asked again.

"Jeph and I are working together on a little project. We need someone in the dream world to make a connection Jeph couldn't pull off, and he didn't trust me to do it. I wanted you, but he came here yesterday and picked her up instead."

"Picked her up? Here?" Gray's heart beat faster. Could this Jeph be the man he saw yesterday?

Cain grinned. "Oh, she came of her own free will—although Jeph can be quite *persuasive*, if you know what I mean. She justified his confidence during the game. But I'm not sure I trust him or any of his allies. She's good, for a beginner, but I'd rather use you than someone Jeph found."

"I want nothing to do with you. But *what game?*"

"You don't trust me? Jeph's the one you really need to watch out for—the philanthropist entrepreneur. Don't let the smooth exterior fool you. He's one layer away from this." He pointed with a long black claw at the monster image on the box. "But I'm not so bad if you know how to look at me." He got up, walked to the door, and stopped before stepping through it. "Think about it. I'm sure we'll talk again."

"What game?" Gray shouted after him.

But Cain was gone.

When Gray came out of his esuoh, the cafe was full of malignant ghosts, with gray dust gathered where the wind had blown it and tumbleweeds piled at the door. He left the mugs on the table and walked to the bus stop.

He picked his way through crowds of monsters wearing bright papier mâché masks with red cheeks and big eyes. Their expressions might be cheery or dreamy, greedy or fearful, but in the space between every mask and its face, Gray caught a glimpse of a monster, keeping its appearance hidden from the world.

As he walked, he touched the rorrim in his pocket. It was his ticket back to Oge, back to the illusion that the superficial appearance was all there was. He had carried it since he was eight, the day he let his mother's murderer go free. A man from the crowd—Gray would later know him as Douglas Burroughs, his foster father—had handed the rorrim to him, told him he wasn't crazy, and disappeared.

He had carried the rorrim in his pocket every day since, refusing to use it—even when his first foster families didn't understand him; even when his teachers called him stupid; even when the kids at school ran away from him screaming; even when good things happened, like coming into a community who understood and supported him, like meeting Echo. He stayed in Ytilaer because he knew the monster would come back, and he wanted to be ready. Well, the monster had come back, and he wasn't any more prepared than the day it killed his mother when he was seven.

And it had some connection with Echo.

He tried to phone her as he walked, but got no answer.

Still shaking, he caught the bus to his first day at his new job.

CHAPTER 9

Work

ECHO RAN FROM THE BATHROOM TO HER BEDROOM and checked her phone. Seven-thirty, and last night's voicemail from Gray came back to her like a facet of her crazy dream. He would be at Ugly Mug until seven fifteen. Crap. She'd missed him, and she had so wanted to ask him about what she learned last night.

She sighed and texted back: "Sorry I missed you. Overslept. Congrats on the job. Catch you later," and went downstairs.

She was angry at herself for missing coffee with Gray. Her perception of him had changed last night. Yesterday, she would have said he was funny, kind, loyal, sometimes annoying. But today he had added a new adjective—mysterious. She shook her head, curiosity nagging like a toothache. She would catch him at Ugly Mug after work and demand that he tell her everything.

In the kitchen, Aunt Doris had the phone perched between her ear and shoulder as she poured coffee.

"Good morning," Echo said as she walked into the kitchen.

"Hang on, Clarice. There's a stranger in the house." Aunt Doris offered Echo the mug she had just filled.

Echo accepted it with a kiss on Aunt Doris's wrinkled cheek.

"Missed coffee with Gray." Echo added cream to her coffee and handed Aunt Doris the sugar bowl from the table.

"Oh, she missed coffee with that autistic boy she hangs out with," Aunt Doris told Clarice.

Echo rolled her eyes and sat down at the table. "I need to leave in a couple of minutes."

"I'd better let you go. I've got to find out what's happening here." Aunt Doris hung up the phone, finished doctoring her coffee, and sat at the table.

"I'm off to my new job." Part of Echo was so excited that she couldn't keep still, but another, wet-blanket part was terrified that it was a cosmic joke, like a surprise birthday party that burns your house down.

"What will you be doing?"

"I don't know yet, but it sounds fascinating."

Aunt Doris looked at her with her head tilted a little to the side. "How much will it pay?"

"I don't know. A lot, I think."

"You don't know very much, do you?" She locked Echo in her patented Aunt Doris Gaze™. "If it's too good to be true, it probably isn't."

"I'll tell you what I find out." Echo tossed down a last sip of coffee and dashed out the door before the conversation could get any more awkward.

WHEN GRAY WALKED INTO THE OFFICE of Talking Autism PNW, on the twenty-second floor of the US Bancorp Tower, the receptionist, dressed in a pink tutu and juggling phone receivers, didn't have time to greet him before a kid came out, maybe twelve or thirteen years old, dressed in a circus lion-tamer's outfit and carrying a whip.

"My name is Buzz. I'm your supervisor. I'll show you around."

They walked through the office. The conference room was an enormous Big Top with seating for thousands around the edges. "I've got to report to the C suite here later today," Buzz said, "and you're going to help get the reports ready."

They stopped by the CEO's office, where a man in a top hat sat at a table weighing stacks of gold, silver, and bronze coins. He stood and introduced himself with a sweeping bow. "Jordan Ross. Very glad to have you here. Your brother Quig said you're a wonder-worker with computers."

Gray opened his mouth to say something, but the man had already turned back to his stacks of money. Buzz tapped Gray's arm and pulled him out of the office.

They walked past rooms where acrobats practiced and clowns applied makeup and a tented dining area, empty of people now, with rough wooden tables and a cauldron steaming over a fire. And then they came to a wagon with steps up the back. Buzz led the way in.

It was dark inside, with beeps and buzzes like science-fantasy creatures talking. There were three workstations in the room: black tables with a panel of painted gray wood hanging in front of each. They all radiated energy like a city sidewalk at rush hour. Over in the corner was a small, sad-looking elephant that seemed to be asleep standing up.

In the middle of the room, with hardly enough space to walk around, was an open wooden box, like a magician's prop, reaching from the floor to chest height. Gray looked over the edge, then back at the outside of the box, then over the edge again. He was looking down at a living map of the circus, with people flowing in through various doors and then wandering among the rides and sideshows.

"This is the server room and my office." Buzz pointed to the workstation closest to the elephant. "You'll sit over there."

Buzz waved toward the sign board hanging on the wall above one of the desks. "I keep live web data on this monitor. We can tell who's coming, where they come from, how long they stay, and when they leave. But you've studied analytics, right?" He stared at Gray with his closed eyes, waiting for an answer.

Gray didn't *study* analytics. He *was* analytics. In the web analytics class he and Echo took together, Gray wandered among web visitors as if he were one of them. He would ask what they liked and didn't like. Sometimes someone would tap him on the shoulder and ask how to find something. Echo learned spreadsheets and coding; Gray told her what the numbers meant in the lives of the people walking through the site. "Yes."

Gray watched the people in the box. They didn't pay to get in, but they sometimes dropped coins into a donation box by the door. When they did, lights would flash as in a game, and a tally appeared in bright lights above the doorway.

Gray walked among the people on the midway. There was a flashing billboard that said, "Give Now!!!" and he noticed that the visitors were startled by it. Many would suddenly disappear, leaving no coins in the exit boxes.

He turned to Buzz. "I see that your 'Give now' popup is scaring some people away. Have you tested routing visitors deeper into the site or waiting until they're starting to leave before you fire it?" He leaned back over the map again and pointed. "Some of your visitors seem to bounce right there."

Buzz cracked the whip. It didn't hurt, but the sound of it startled Gray into giving Buzz another look. He was a small fellow on platform shoes, and he had a pinched and angry face. He reminded Gray of one of his first foster brothers in the home where he learned to disappear in plain sight.

"I'm the web analyst; you're the intern," Buzz said. "After you've established that you know what you're talking about, I'll consider letting you make recommendations. For now I need to get my reports ready for the meeting this afternoon. Get me a cup of coffee—black, no sugar—and when you come back, I'll show you what you need to do."

Gray went out and retraced his steps to the commissary. A woman in a gray leotard did stretching exercises in front of a mirror. A man in clown-white makeup opened his jaw and made an O of his mouth as he painted high arching eyebrows over his eyes.

In the commissary, the long wooden picnic tables still stood empty. On a shelf on the far wall was a big coffee pot, and next to it cracked mugs stood upside down on a wooden tray. Gray took one and filled it with the thick brown stew and carried it back to Buzz.

Buzz accepted the mug, then turned to Gray with the whip raised. "Do I look like Caroline to you? I assumed you could read."

Gray shrugged, embarrassed. Another thing Echo helped with. Sometimes the letters spoke to him and other times, if they weren't important, he didn't see them at all. "They all looked alike."

Buzz rolled his eyes. "Last thing I need is Caroline pissed off today. Here." He went to the workstation he had said would be Gray's. "I've logged in for you. I'll give you the information later. Find the document called '0618-meeting.' Print twelve copies, and I'll show you how to bind it when I get back."

Buzz left the room.

Gray sat at the desk. His fingers brushed across a dusty keyboard and then reached the smooth glass of a computer monitor, which he perceived as a rough wooden signboard.

When Echo helped him with this stuff, she said they were like partners in a three-legged race. He had an image of two three-legged aliens racing somehow. He didn't understand how it described Echo and him, but it made him laugh, even now, and the laughter reminded him of Echo's presence and gave him hope.

But now she was gone, and darkness hovered over their future. How could he survive?

He fingered the rorrim in his pocket, asking if now was the time to come back into Oge. But he had never used a computer the way most people did and would probably be even more confused.

Instead, he put his hands on the screen and felt the energy flowing into his fingers.

He put his attention into his hands, as if they were all that existed for that moment. He went deep into the files, finding stories of triumph and pain, fear and hope—an employee caught stealing and let go; an award for service; Buzz being told he needed to produce more results. Gray realized he had gone too deep into the files and pulled back.

Then he found something that felt like a report for the C suite. It was bursting with numbers and had Buzz's energy of fear and resentment. Gray tapped the screen and routed its energy to the printer.

The elephant in the corner groaned and started spitting out pages.

Buzz came back with a mug chipped at a different place than the other one. Gray tried to peg the placement of that chip in his mind so he would find it next time, but he was distracted when Buzz strode angrily over to the elephant and demanded, "Are you kidding me?"

"Maybe?"

"I said '0618-meeting,' not 'report-notes.' You think you know what you're doing?"

"Yes."

"I thought I was getting help, but I'm saddled with a moron."

Buzz cracked the whip again, sat down at his desk, and clicked a few keys. The printer groaned again, and nothing came out.

"I can't deal with this. I'll be right back. Don't touch anything."

Gray listened to the elephant sighing as if in pain. He walked over and rested his hand against its side. He felt cool, flat plastic instead of the wrinkled, hairy skin. He held the elephant in his mind and moved his fingers until he found the problem. The elephant groaned at his touch.

He opened the access panel and felt around inside, avoiding the delicate or dangerous organs. He found a bit of crumpled paper and coaxed it out of the mechanism.

At that moment, Buzz and the ringmaster walked through the door. "What the hell are you doing?" He turned to the ringmaster. "See? He's just not going to be helpful to us."

Gray held out the paper that had been caught in the printer. "Try it now."

Buzz looked at the top-hatted CEO, who nodded at him. He clicked a few keys, and the elephant sighed and released a stream of leaves.

"Well—" the CEO smiled at Gray "—it seems to work."

"He could void the warranty—" Buzz's voice rose in pitch "—or—or get hurt or something."

Jordan turned to Buzz. "Here's what I propose. Get to know this guy a little better. Find out how he can help you."

He headed for the door, then turned back. "Tell you what. Take him out to lunch, my treat. Come back as friends."

Buzz smacked his whip against his leg. "Will do."

"Just be back by one for the meeting."

As Echo stepped off the elevator in the morning light, the twenty-seventh floor was stripped of its magic, now in the possession of well-dressed staffers carrying files, briefcase-toting professionals on their way to consultations, and late-arriving admin assistants in athletic shoes. Echo's anticipation wavered between elation at the new job in a new world and terror of discovering it was an elaborate joke before being laughed out of the office.

But, no, she told herself, she had won, and she had earned the opportunity to know her prize.

She pushed open the glass door into Jeph's office suite. Through the conference room windows, Portland's West Hills glittered in sunlight. The room was empty of people now, its long, dark wooden table surrounded by eight rolling chairs with faux leather upholstery. A speakerphone squatted in the middle of the table, and carafes stood at attention on a credenza at the end of the room away from the big flat-panel screen.

A pretty blonde receptionist at the front desk glanced at Echo as she entered the office suite while speaking into her earpiece. "Marlo will be with you in just a minute."

Echo hardly had time to ask herself, *Marlo?*, before a striking dark-haired woman came into the reception area. "You must be Echo."

"Yes."

"I'm Marlo Enright. Jeph told me to expect you at nine." She smiled, but her smile didn't reach her eyes. "I'm the one who takes care of the mundane details of Jeph's visionary inspirations."

What would Echo know of Jeph's visionary inspirations? She was just a girl the boss had found in a coffee shop, who applied for the job by means of a scavenger hunt, which involved finding a key that didn't look like a key and had to be found again in a dream. "I guess we left out the part about the resume and application," Echo said.

"That's right. Follow me."

They left the reception area and passed an enormous glass-walled executive office, obviously Jeph's, with thick white cotton drapes defending its privacy. Toward the interior of the building was a cluster of cubicles. She wondered if one of those would be hers. She might bring knickknacks to sit on her desk, chat with her coworkers around the coffee pot, go out to lunch with them, and gossip about the boss. An overweight man with a ponytail got up and walked away from his desk, but no one looked at Echo.

Marlo's office was straight ahead, next to Jeph's but not nearly as large and without the exterior windows. Open vertical blinds gave passers-by a glimpse into her small office, with a row of white file cabinets and large framed photos of downtown Portland.

Before sitting down, Marlo picked up a folder and handed it across the desk. Echo stood on the other side, flipping through the forms to apply for the job, to sign up for insurance, a criminal background check, and a nondisclosure agreement.

Marlo leaned forward with her forearms on the desk and her fingers interlaced. "I don't suppose you brought a resume."

"I didn't know I needed one."

"Jeph has his own way of doing things, but we have to dot our i's and cross our t's. Bring one the next time you come into the office, please." She pointed to a low table with two chairs in a corner of the room. "You can fill those out there."

"Uh, OK. But a criminal background check? Nondisclosure agreement?"

Marlo gave her an appraising look, then rolled her eyes and sighed. "This is your first job, isn't it?"

Nodding, Echo felt she was admitting something shameful.

"Do you know what Jeph does?"

"Not exactly."

"Do you know what he wants you to do?"

"Research, I think he said."

Marlo pinched the bridge of her nose between her thumb and forefinger. "His bread and butter is reputation management. He helps entitled people get out of situations they create for themselves. It often involves— persuasion, of a special kind." She looked at Echo significantly. "You played the game?"

Echo nodded.

"You talk to people and find out what they know." Something in Marlo's manner told Echo she had played it before herself.

That wasn't exactly how it appeared to Echo, except now that she thought back on it— "OK."

Marlo gave Echo a hard look, an are-you-stupid look. "You can find out a lot."

Could that be why Maan didn't want to tell his wife about the dream world? "Oh."

"You can see why we don't want anyone with a criminal history. Or a big mouth."

"OK."

Marlo sighed again. The pendulum of Echo's expectations swung toward despair again. "Jeph is not in the office just yet, but by the time you're finished with those forms, I'm sure he will be." She sat at her desk and began typing on a computer.

Echo filled out the first application and then looked up at Marlo. "Excuse me?"

Marlo gave her the blank expression of someone drawn from concentrating on something else. "Yes?"

"Do you know what I'm going to be doing?"

"He said he has a special project for you."

Marlo's voice conveyed irritation, but she hadn't answered Echo's question, so Echo asked again. "Well, do you know what jobs need filling?"

Marlo folded her arms across the papers on her desk and gave Echo a steady gaze. Echo couldn't really tell if it was hostile or just inscrutable. "As I said, it's a special project. I don't know what skills you have that Jeph thinks we need."

"Oh." Echo filled out a few more blanks then looked up again. "I mean, the game was fun, I guess, but I don't see how anybody can make a living from it."

"Fun is not a word I would choose to describe it, but I think playing the game in that world would make it very clear how you can use it in this one."

Echo thought about that for a while. Running house to house to find a key. Walking across a dark tabletop to find a passageway. "It's not something I've seen listed on the job hunt sites," she said mostly to herself, but loud enough for Marlo to hear. Then, "Have you been Jeph's assistant long?"

"Not assistant." Marlo's voice carried withering sarcasm and a tinge of weariness. "Partner. And yes, very long. I'm the one who makes sure Jeph can pay the salaries of the ditzes he brings in for special projects."

Echo took the hint and didn't ask any more questions until Jeph walked through Marlo's door.

"Oh, good. You've helped Echo get the paperwork out of the way." He turned his startling blue eyes on Echo. "How's it coming?"

"Just finished." It was a lie. She had spent the past ten minutes fidgeting with the pen and looking at a photograph of the Portland skyline on the wall, because she didn't want any more interaction with Marlo.

"Great. We can get to work."

He walked through a door leading from Marlo's office to his own, next to it. Echo gave Marlo a tentative smile as she walked past her into Jeph's office, thinking she didn't want future problems with this formidable woman. Jeph, who remained a step behind, gave Marlo a look that seemed part knowledge and part defiance. He closed the door, shutting her out.

CHAPTER 10

Echo's Eyes Are Opened

Jeph's office was filled with reflected light. Sunlight bounced off the West Hills and skittered across the windows of the buildings far below. To the north, it glinted off the ribbon of the Willamette River running through the city. Inside the office, most surfaces were untinted white wood or glass. The floor was covered with Berber carpet just a shade more beige than pure white.

He led Echo across the room to his desk, with creamy white wood grain and almost as large as Pru's judge's desk from her courtroom dream. Echo sat in a chair in front of it, feeling like a small petitioner. He turned to a hanging display of mirrors on the wall behind his desk and reached out to touch one. The movement set its flashing surface swaying, sending barbs of light around the room. He slid a pair of sunglasses onto his face as he took his chair.

"Did you just—" Echo didn't know what to call it.

"I crossed over." He spoke in a tone of friendly correction. He took the sunglasses off and looked at her through closed eyes. "I wasn't trying to deceive you." He tossed the glasses onto his desk. "These are a habit. I find that being in the dream world improves communication, but sometimes people don't understand about the closed eyes." He turned to her with Gray's blind gaze that nevertheless took everything in. "But I was forgetting your friend is in the dream world, so you're used to it."

"Will I—" She glanced up at the mirrors and made a rolling gesture with her hand.

"Soon. There are some matters to attend to first." He came around and leaned casually on the front of his desk, standing like an executive clothing model.

"What's the job? Marlo didn't have much information."

"You'll find a key for me." His voice was light, casual.

"Like in the game?" Echo imagined another meeting with a different set of strangers, asking questions and finding the key where no one else thought to look for it. "Did you hide it somewhere again?"

He shook his head. "Last night was a game in the same way wolf cubs' play is a game. There are no real stakes, but the skills they develop serve them in the hunt."

Wolf cubs grow up to be wolves. "So I'll be hunting somebody down?"

"No, no, no." His manicured hand brushed aside her idea like a leaf on an imaginary table. "You just need to bring me somebody's key. I'll do the rest."

"One of the people from last night?"

He shook his head. "A guy I know." He turned toward the window. "A friend from high school. It's been a long time since I saw him, but I want to help him get back on his feet. Find out what he needs and give it to him. He just got out of prison after twenty years."

Echo's breath caught. This might be a bit too real. "Prison?"

He smiled indulgently, looking down at her again. "Not like that. He made a big mistake, drunk driving accident. He never meant to hurt any-body, but it made a mess of his life. You don't need to see him. In fact, I don't want you to see him. Just get his key from a friend."

Echo stared up at him. "You realize I didn't find that key; I just fell over it."

He laughed out loud. "Nobody else fell over it."

"I'm still not sure why me." He was too close; looking up at him was uncomfortable. Echo got up and walked to the window. Microscopic people swarmed the sidewalks, each living in a separate little dream, with a separate little house—esuoh—that nobody else could see without special equip-ment. She looked back at him. "Do you do this all the time with people?"

"What do you mean?"

She turned and leaned her back against the window, seeking his eyes behind those closed eyelids. "Going into people's minds, looking at their esuohs?"

"It's part of what I do, but not all. In a few minutes, you'll cross over into the dream world, and I'll teach you a few techniques you'll use to get at the truth."

"Marlo said you do reputation management, helping people solve problems. Is that what I'll be doing?"

He walked over and stood beside her, again just a bit too close. "That's what I do for paying clients. This is similar in some ways, but not the same. For one thing, this time, no one is paying me; it's just an act of mercy for someone who might be too proud to accept charity. I want to remain anonymous. If it works out, I'll take you in as a permanent employee."

She felt a shiver of excitement at the phrase "permanent employee." Looking out the window, she saw herself as the junior detective being shown the ropes, making mistakes until her unique abilities shone through and she became an indispensable member of the team. She returned her attention to Jeph and found him examining her face. "You really think I can do it?"

He leaned in, so close she thought he might kiss her. "I can teach you the techniques in a couple of hours."

He was handsome, desirable, but so old. Echo went back to the chair she had been sitting in. She turned it to face him, silhouetted against the window. "Who's the guy?"

He looked outside, then spoke over his shoulder. "His name is Lazar Kyrillovich."

"Sounds Russian. Who has the key?"

He came back and took the other visitor's chair, turning it so that they could speak face to face. "My high school girlfriend, Cali Zielinski."

Cali Zielinski. Echo had heard that name before. It seemed like something from the news, which she didn't follow much. "Who's she?"

"Up-and-coming state senator. Rumored to be thinking of running for governor."

"I'm going to get a key from a politician?" Echo heard incredulity dripping from her words.

"Relax. I've got a cover story set up for you. It's right up her alley. And Marlo has already made the appointment."

Wait. This was coming fast. *What happened to being shown around and learning the ropes?* "Why don't *you* get the key?"

He leaned back in the chair and lifted his arms in a "who knows?" gesture. "Mostly for the same reason I don't do my own accounting. It's not the best use of my time." Then a shadow of sadness crossed his face. "But the other reason is that she started dating Lazar after I broke up with her. I tried to warn her about him, but some people can never forgive you for trying to give good advice. Plus, I was seventeen, so probably not as diplomatic as I might have been."

"Well, I mean, if it's been twenty years . . . ."

"You don't forget something like that, even after twenty years. He borrowed my car without asking and then killed someone with it. She said it was my fault. I get it; she was in pain. But if I try to see her and she doesn't take it well, it could throw off the entire plan."

"Then why help him?"

He got up from the chair and walked away. "We were friends—"

"After he stole your girlfriend?"

He stopped and turned back to her, a sad smile flitting across his lips. "He didn't steal her. We were already on different paths. She wanted to go into politics, and I had found my first mirror the summer before our senior year—which was leading me in a new direction."

"And you think she still has a key to this guy?"

"Yes. She was with him the night of the accident. It may have gotten buried in her memories. I'll teach you how to find it."

"Then what will I do with it?"

He came back and sat down again, wearing his radiant smile. "Just bring it back to me. I'll take over from there."

"You and Cain?"

He gave a disgusted snort. "We both collect mirrors. Sometimes we invest in one together. He has nothing to do with this."

That was a relief. She didn't trust Cain at all. "OK. So who's going with me?"

"I know it would be more comfortable if you had help, but this needs to be kept a complete secret, and I don't trust anybody except you."

She searched his face for lies. His eyebrows were high, his facial muscles relaxed, and an easy smile played around his lips. "That doesn't make any sense," she said. "You've known me less than twenty-four hours."

"That's one of the things you'll get used to about this world—you can get to know a person very quickly."

That was a little unnerving. If he knew her well enough to think she was trustworthy, he might know her well enough to know about—her own uncomfortable history.

"I have complete faith in you—" he placed a hand on her arm, and she felt confidence flow into her like warming sunlight "—as someone who can sympathize with the high price of a momentary indiscretion."

Echo's sister's dead body flashed before her eyes, and she felt again the drip of liquid on her forehead that turned out to be blood.

He pulled his hand away. "Of course, it was partly my fault. I was so tired that night that I left the keys where Lazar could find them. That poor family."

His fault. Relief flooded her, wiping out her painful memory and leaving behind the vision of what her life could be with an exciting, interesting, *well-paying* job. "OK. Take me through this. How am I going to get a key from a state senator? Doesn't she have staff and constituents and calendars and stuff?"

He got up from the chair and rubbed his hands together. "She's eager to talk to you. You're a journalist from a website called YouthNow!"

She tried to imagine telling anybody that. "That's lame."

He leaned on the back of the chair and laughed. "You didn't choose the name. You're asking how an Ashland High School student got to be a state senator. What the school did for her and what it didn't. It will give her a chance to talk about her education plan."

"But I'm not a journalist."

"You don't have to write the article. Just get close enough to get into her esuoh."

"Why would she give me permission to go into her esuoh?"

He sat in the chair again, looking at her as if he were the petitioner, holding her attention with his eyes. "This is what's called an exigent circumstance. Like breaking a car window to rescue a dog from the heat. You're doing it to save a life, and she'll never know the difference."

"Then what was all the 'May I come into your house?' about last night?"

He leaned back again. "You were talking to people who would *know*. She won't."

She thought of Estelle, knowing everything she was going to say before she said it. Even that was kind of OK, because they were face to face. "But—"

He walked toward his desk, shaking his head. "It's OK. I suppose your friend—Gray, was it?—has told you about his sect and their strict rules about what's proper and acceptable."

As a matter of fact, no, Echo thought but did not say.

"In the coffee shop, I got the impression that you're under some financial pressure. But I admire your integrity, that you can't be bought with enough money to solve your immediate problems for an afternoon's work." He picked up the phone and pushed a button. "Marlo? You know that other—"

"Wait." She felt she needed more time to sort out her options, but time was exactly what she didn't have.

"I'll get back to you," he said to Marlo, then set down the phone. He looked at her, with troubled compassion shaping his eyes. "I'm afraid Lazar may be suicidal, and I don't want him to believe the world is against him. I want to act before it's too late."

What would it be like to spend time in prison for a momentary mistake? Then you come out twenty years later, and you're old and have nothing in front of you? Echo felt the loneliness and despair. She sighed. "What do I do?"

The sadness in his face cleared. "Interview her. Go into her esuoh. Find the key. Bring it back here. Easy. I'll teach you everything you need to know."

"And I get to be in that other world?"

Jeph looked surprised and gratified. "You liked it?"

"It's a million times better than any theme park."

Jeph laughed. "Not everybody thinks so, but I'm glad you do." He held out his hand to her.

Echo hesitated. Not that she didn't want to, but it was all so fast.

"Are you sure? I don't want to pressure you."

She shook her head, then shook his hand. "I'm going to do it." A rush of adrenaline, mixing excitement and fear, swirled in her stomach, raising the hairs on her arms. It was like being on a ride at the fair.

"Great! Let's get started then." He opened a drawer and came around his desk carrying the ancient box.

Echo's hands trembled as she opened it to the mirror inside.

The mirror shone as if it were in direct sunlight, even though it wasn't. It showed her ugly face, alive with anticipation. The surface wavered like wind over water, and she touched it.

The sense of falling didn't last as long this time. She again felt she was drowning, but she knew it was temporary and waited. Then her eyes opened to the other reality. She was small—toddler sized—and everything was large. Her feet didn't touch the floor below the chair where she sat. She was in her tattered clothes again. The battered leather bag she carried, closed with a leather strap, had grown to the size of a military duffel bag.

"Let's get started," Jeph said brightly, seeming unaware of her reduced stature. "You brought the key, right?"

She reached into the bag and found that her arm didn't touch the bottom. She scooted off the chair and sat on the ground and opened the bag as wide as it went. It was so big she could crawl into it.

Jeph stopped her. "We don't have time for you to go in there. Just think about what you're looking for."

She remembered the keys she had tossed into her bag. The weight of them and how they appeared in both worlds. She pushed her hand into the bag and found the ancient jack of clubs and, instead of bracelets of any description, a small pair of handcuffs. She shivered looking at them, remembering what Pru had said: *Arrested, interrogated, tried, weighed in the balance.* She held them both out to him. "This is not what I saw before."

Jeph smiled. "Don't worry about it. There are all kinds of bracelets. You're just anxious. Understandable." He took the jack of clubs card and threw it back into the bag. "Leave Cain out of this." He pointed at the handcuffs. "These will get you into my esuoh." A door appeared, and he gestured toward it. She pressed the handcuffs against it, and it opened into an enormous room with a blue-enameled grand piano at one end and a set of champagne-colored leather sofas at the other. Glass doors led out onto a patio with a swimming pool and palm trees and brilliant red oleander in bloom. Beyond the patio was a drop-off whose bottom she couldn't see from where she stood.

"Is this your office?"

"My esuoh. You saw it last night."

Echo looked around the room. It was large, but she felt less like a child in it than she did in Jeph's office. "I guess I had too many things to think about to take it all in."

Jeph shrugged. "Let's go into yours to get started." He walked over to a door and waited for Echo to join him. "This is your door." It opened at her touch. "Keep the handcuffs. You may need them."

She dropped them into her bag and followed him like an obedient puppy into the center of cramped and cozy room.

"We were interrupted in the game last night," he said. "I didn't get a chance to tell you what you have here. This is your front room. When you're in the dream world, you can come here any time, to think, relax, organize your memories."

She turned in place, allowing the busy, colorful room to imbue her with its sense of home.

He pointed to the table. "Those books hold your short-term memories, things that happened recently. The ones on the table are the ones you haven't sorted yet."

She walked over to the stack. Lining the walls around the table were shelves of slim sketchbooks hinged at the top and bound in black. When she flipped through one, she found words she didn't recognize, with drawings and marginalia. It conveyed memories of unsuccessful job searches, and the panicked feeling that circumstances were closing in on her. The ones scattered on the table were the same, but they told the events of yesterday—the humiliating job interview, Gray's bizarre marriage proposal,

Jeph's arrival in her life—she glanced at him thinking of it—and the game. She became so engrossed that she forgot why she was here and sat on the velvet-covered bench that ringed the table.

"You can do that later. We have a lot to cover before you catch your train."

Train? Oh, right. Interview with the senator. She gathered up the books and shoved them onto the shelf and resolved to come back and peruse them later.

He went out the door to the outside. "When we saw this last evening, I noticed a ladder." He stepped out and pulled a metal rod and then walked onto the fold-down porch.

Echo followed him out, finding a ladder attached to the side of the wagon.

"Your long-term memories are upstairs."

Echo stood looking up at the top of the wagon and the sky. She looked back at Jeph.

"Go on. Have a look."

She climbed the ladder to the top of the wagon, and at the last step, her foot landed on a scuffed hardwood floor in a sloped-ceiling attic with corridors leading in different directions, and many doors off each hallway. When she stepped back, she was outdoors on the side of the wagon again. When she stepped forward, she was in the attic, looking at more doors than she could count. She felt no particular reason to explore this area now; she feared the unpleasant memories that lurked there. So she stepped back and down the ladder to the porch.

Jeph had already gone inside. "That's pretty much it for your esuoh."

"What about the basement?"

He looked at her with good-natured surprise. "Basement?"

She flipped over the rug and showed the trap door.

"Nasty creepy-crawlies down there. No reason to open that door at all." He flipped the rug back. "Now, the first thing you're going to need to know on your mission is how to get into someone else's esuoh."

"Without permission?"

"We covered that. If you're not satisfied . . . ."

She would have to keep her mouth shut to get through this, hard as that would be. She nodded.

"People who don't know about the dream world have no defense. The first time you step through into the dream world, you get rudimentary protection for your esuoh—you know if someone is there or has been there, and it keeps out people who might jump in by accident—so it takes a key, like the bracelets you found, to get in.

"Later, as you develop more skills and experience, you'll be able to develop stronger locks, and I'm going to show you how to make some simple keys this morning."

Echo waited for something she could do.

"How do you think you might get into a normal's esuoh?" He spoke like a teacher quizzing her on a past lesson.

"I'm not sure how I get into my own esuoh. You told me last night to turn, and that worked, but I don't understand it."

"That's about as much understanding as you can expect. When you were in the game last evening, how did you get into other people's s esuoh?"

"I pushed on the door."

"Since you had permission, there was no barrier. So how would you get into my esuoh?"

"I had to knock on your door last night."

"I know. I didn't say the invitation because I didn't want to throw off the game. But we're standing here, and you have permission—what do you do?"

"Go out my door and look for your door?"

"That will work, and you'll use it when you just want to pop into a nearby esuoh and you don't care whose it is. But what if you know where you want to go and you want to get in quickly, like in a split second?"

Echo sighed. She wasn't sure why she'd want to get into someone else's esuoh in a split second, but she played along. "Run really fast?"

He shook his head. "Everything you see—all the furniture and stuff in your esuoh—you created. In fact, you're creating it all the time. The colors of the paint, the knickknacks on the shelf, the furniture, all of it, are your creation."

Echo looked around, suddenly pleased with her own design sense.

"And you can make more or take it away or change it at will. It will also adjust itself to match your changing reality, but we don't need to worry about that now."

She looked back at him.

"Watch." He sat down, and a chair appeared behind him before he reached the seat. "Try it."

She sat down and fell to her rear end on the floor.

He laughed. "I think you forgot something. Don't just sit. Sit *on the chair.*"

"What kind of chair?"

"Whatever you imagine is what will be there."

She stared at the floor, thinking of Aunt Doris's favorite chair. Her face got tired from frowning.

"Relax. The chair is already there. Just sit on it."

She looked at him perplexedly and then sat on Aunt Doris's leather recliner. She got up to look, and the recliner was squeezed into the small space of her wagon. She looked again, and it was a simple ladder-back chair with a woven seat. Then it was painted turquoise green with yellow flowers on the legs and uprights. Then she changed the flowers to blackberries. She liked the blackberries better. Then she made the green more of a spring green and painted the ladder rungs the purple of the blackberries. Now it fit in her esuoh. She sat on it, and it held her weight. It had just become her favorite chair.

He was smiling at her, but it was becoming a tight smile. "Let's save the decorating for later. I'm confident that you know how to make a chair. And if you can make a chair, you can make a door."

She stood up and hung the chair on a hook that appeared on the wall. She smiled. A door. She reached for the handle and it opened—to the other side of itself in her own esuoh.

Now Jeph was smiling again. "OK. So now you've got the door. By the way, if the chair disappears, you won't lose it. You can bring it back or a different one anytime you want."

She admired the chair. "I'll save it as a souvenir."

Jeph shrugged. "Have it your way. Anyway, once you have the door, you need to think about whose esuoh you want to enter. Try it again and think about mine."

She turned the knob again and walked through into Jeph's esuoh, then turned around and came back again.

"Excellent."

"I'm going to do that with the senator?"

"Exactly."

"But I don't know what her esuoh looks like."

"If you don't know the esuoh, picture the person. But we'll practice on my staff, so let's keep going." He rubbed his hands together and looked around the room. "Now pick something to make a key of."

She looked around. She hadn't had a chance to explore her place. "Any criteria?"

"Something pocket-sized would be best, but it doesn't have to be."

"How about my chair?"

"That's weird, but the principles are the same. Focus on your chair. When you sit on this chair, you'll be in a different place. Focus and store your feelings about that place in the chair."

She held the chair in her hands and focused. "Aunt Doris's kitchen."

He gave her a quizzical look and said, "OK. Sit on the chair."

She sat on it, and Aunt Doris's kitchen surrounded her. There was a tea-pot on the stove, and Aunt Doris in her pink-and-purple track suit walked around setting out materials for cooking. Echo stood up to give Aunt Doris a hug and found herself back in her own esuoh again.

"It's not *her* kitchen, just your memory of it." Jeph was sitting at her tiny dining table at the door end of her wagon. "It's too far away, and that kind of key takes a lot of power. But you've done a good job of re-creating it."

"So now any time I sit on this chair, I'm going to feel like I'm in Aunt Doris's kitchen?"

"Yes."

Echo nodded. "It'll be nice if it gets crowded in here." She hung the chair on its hook. "But I can't walk around there?"

"Just change the key. You can work on that on your own."

"OK. What's next?"

"Put your hand near the chair."

She did, then pulled her hand back and opened and closed it a few times. "It tingles."

"That's because it's a key. Now, while you were with Marlo, I hid a key in here, and I want you to find it."

"You did?"

He nodded, looking pleased with himself.

"Without my knowing it?"

"Silent as a ghost."

"But I was in the dream world last evening."

He smiled. "And I'm really good at this."

She thought about that for a moment. How many people might have wandered through her mind without her knowing it? Gray? But she didn't have time to be deeply disturbed, because Jeph was waiting, and the smile he wore was becoming less playful, colder. She kept her voice light. "Any hints?"

"Nope."

"Bigger than a breadbox?"

"No hints. It's not your chair."

She looked around the room. "Warmer, cooler?"

"You'll feel it."

She shrugged and began at her wood stove. It was warm, but there was no tingle. Down one side of her esuoh and up the other, past the outer door, around the table, and just as she was thinking he had played a trick on her, she felt something. At first, her palm just felt itchy, but she followed the feeling. It was "warmer, cooler," but the feedback was immediate. Up, up, to the shelf above the woodstove, then over the railing that kept the cups and plates from falling when the wagon moved. A little toy dinosaur set her hand buzzing all the way up to her elbow. She was overcome by the urge to laugh. "This is cute. How come I'm still here?" A fit of uncontrollable giggles seemed to rule her. It was funny that the dinosaur had this effect but not this funny, and still she laughed hysterically.

"Give it to me." He held his hand out.

She did, and then it wasn't funny anymore. The laughter vanished, leaving her slightly out of breath but otherwise unharmed. "What was that?"

"A key can take you to a place or a state. That's a sample."

She looked at it with a disbelieving laugh that passed immediately. "So what good is that except to a standup comic handing them out to the audience?"

"You just need to know what keys do. They don't just take you places. They change things, perceptions; they can connect to memories." He held it another minute, his face serene in concentration. Then he came back to himself. "Here."

Echo received it—and found herself on a balcony above a shining city. Jeph opened a door and walked into the space with her.

"What happened?"

He gave her a mischievous grin. "I made it a key to my esuoh." He looked around the room, then back to her. "Let's go out and practice a bit."

He opened a door that suddenly appeared and stepped out, with Echo on his heels. She glanced back as she closed it, and the door was already gone.

CHAPTER 11

On-the-Job Training

THEY WERE STANDING TOGETHER IN JEPH'S OFFICE. Echo was small again, looking up at all the huge furniture. Jeph walked away, and Echo scurried on her short little legs to catch up. He led out past the cubicles to the reception area.

Echo could barely see the top of the receptionist's head over the cliff of her desk. Jeph leaned on the counter facing Echo and whispered, "This is Meghan. Go into her esuoh and find a key."

Echo stared at Jeph's knees for a few seconds, trying to remember what Meghan looked like, who she was. "How do I know she has a key?"

"Everyone has keys," he said. "Normals call them triggers or anchors. They link to good times or bad, memories, all kinds of things. Just find one of hers."

"Where do I look?"

He eyed her steadily.

She nodded and started to go into her esuoh but turned back. "She won't notice?"

"You'll pass like a ghost."

Echo went into her own esuoh, where she created a door and, calling to mind the beautiful blonde she had seen earlier at the reception desk, walked into a spacious, airy, and very feminine esuoh with white carpet, white furniture, and fuchsia accents, and a glass and chrome table. She tried to take it in that she was walking in the most personal space of someone she had never met. She did wonder, briefly, how she would feel if she learned Meghan had walked in hers like this, but she brushed it away with the reminder that she wasn't going to do any harm. On the wall over Meghan's window was a wide, short photo of pink brown-eyed Susans against a blue sky. Another wall bore the motto: "Live, Laugh, Love" written in a lavish script on a distressed board. Echo could feel the key vibrating after only a few seconds in the room.

An orchid with shell-pink outer petals and deeper pink inner ones sat on the glass-and-chrome table, shivering with life. A man's photograph in a five-by-seven frame looked up at it with admiration.

She stole a peek out Meghan's front window. Through Meghan's eyes, she looked down at an Instagram post on her phone and gave a quick glance up at Jeph and Echo, both turned away from the receptionist, not at all talking about her or rifling through her mind.

Echo went to the orchid, but since it was so large and delicate, she didn't pick it up, just lightly touched its stem, and a door appeared right there in Meghan's front room.

As Echo stepped across the threshold, she found herself on a bed, covers tossed in all directions. She was naked and the man from the photograph was on top of her. Meghan made a low moan of pleasure that seemed to come from Echo's mouth, and the man responded. Echo stepped back and closed the door.

She stood for a moment, back in Meghan's front room, breathing hard and feeling her face flush red, her hand resting on the doorknob. Jeph stood near her in Meghan's esuoh, laughing. She let go the doorknob, and the door disappeared. Jeph opened another door, and they both stepped out into the reception area. Echo was sure her face was still red, and Jeph was still laughing.

A tweety tone sounded, and Meghan answered, "Jeph Blackthorne, Success Transformation, Relationship Management." She caught her error, sounding scattered and embarrassed. "Reputation Management. How may I help you?" When she released the call, Jeph walked up to her.

"Meghan, this is Echo. She'll be working here." Echo didn't think she had passed through Meghan's esuoh like a ghost.

"Hi, Echo." Meghan peered over the edge of her giant desk with closed eyes, and Echo felt herself under scrutiny.

The only things Echo could think to say were just wrong for a stranger to know. "Nice to meet you" was where she finally settled, feeling like a spy who had gotten to know the object of her surveillance just a little too well.

Jeph asked for his messages and turned and walked down the corridor toward his office.

"Is it always like that?" she asked, scurrying to catch up to him.

"Like what?" He turned to her, sizing her up with his glacier-blue eyes.

"So—" She felt flustered under his gaze. "So intimate?"

He laughed. "You mean the sex? Lucky break. Most times it's boring. Mom spanked him with a shoe, and now he's traumatized. But you're always in it and not just looking at it, and everything is intimate in this world." He opened his office door and allowed her to walk in before him.

"So in this—"

"I call it the dream world. I think your friend and that group have another name for it, but if you understand that it's just a dream, you'll get on better than if you think it's some mystical place of ultimate meaning."

Mystical place of ultimate meaning? So far it had been fun and fascinating, like being immersed in an amazing book. She wasn't sure she believed in ultimate meaning, so the idea of finding a mystical place of it seemed unlikely.

"Now you're going to need to get around, and you won't see the world the way everyone else does."

"I won't—" Echo's heart stopped beating for a second. "Wait. When you say no one is going with me—" She stopped, the plan hitting harder than before. "I'm taking the train to Salem, alone, in this—this world?"

Jeph gave her an encouraging smile. "You have a gift for navigating the dream world. It's why I picked you to try out for the job, why I'm giving you this training—worth thousands of dollars—at no cost, why I'm sure enough of your success to promise you a job at the end of it."

"But—"

He shook his head and sighed. "I know you can do this. Look how your friend gets around in the dream world—and the people in his sect don't even use it to its full potential. I'm teaching you everything you need to know to navigate it. But I can't give you a mirror. They're too expensive, too fragile."

"Really, I'll—"

"Sorry. Liability. Insurance. Marlo would kill me. You know how it is."

She really didn't.

He gave a little shrug. "I do understand, though, if you think you can't do it. Even though I don't know anyone more qualified than you are—the look on Estelle's face when you aced the game!" He sighed. "I just need to find someone who's not so scared of taking a risk." He turned toward his desk.

"Wait." A shiver climbed up Echo's spine, as she watched her shiny opportunity drift away on an ocean wave. "You'll really teach me how to navigate it?"

He took in a deep breath and let it out slowly, as a smile built on his face. "Of course I will. What do you think of me?"

Echo felt her face flush as she asked herself how she could think so badly of Jeph after all he'd done. "It's just so overwhelming."

He gave a sympathetic smile. "I know. But we're not finished yet. If you change your mind, I'll let you cross over and leave. No pressure."

She couldn't ask for more than that. "OK. Let's do this. Where do we start?"

"With my employees. They're close by."

Echo walked to the glass wall, whose white cotton drapes obscured but didn't hide the cubicles beyond.

"You don't need to go anywhere. Sit here."

Echo clambered awkwardly into the chair where she had been sitting before.

"My accountant's name is Jack. Tell me what he's looking at."

She turned in her chair and craned her neck. She saw the side of a white shirt and dark pants; the rest of him was hidden by the wall of his cubicle. "He's not even in the same room."

"Distance can be a problem, but this isn't far. Stretch yourself."

She slipped from the chair to look out the window.

"No peeking."

She shrugged. She went into her esuoh and collected her attention to an accountant, named Jack, in Jeph's office. She felt the consciousnesses around her. Jeph's was very strong. Marlo's was nearby, a roil of anger, sadness, and jealousy. Meghan's was distant and faint, but familiar. And two more. One was Jack, the accountant.

She created a door and opened it.

She walked into a room only slightly larger than her own esuoh, but more square than long and narrow. A big desk dominated the space, with a huge monitor sitting on it, and a set of shelves holding eleven-by-seventeen binders that must be his short-term memories. At first she thought there was no window, but then she found it, almost completely blocked by the computer screen. She peered around it and found his space in the physical world—a narrow shelf at eye level with a photo of a woman and a small child, a stained cup beside his keyboard, and on the screen of his desktop computer an online job board. Oops.

Echo's mind spun. Getting someone fired was not moving through like a ghost. And Jack had a family. She turned to his memories for an alternative story.

She opened a binder and found columns and rows of numbers, whose labels she couldn't read, and yet as she stared at them, they resolved into images, spoken words, feelings of excitement and greed. A story emerged. The photos of his wife and child were fake. He had an insatiable desire for fun. And it all led to a slow drip of theft from Jeph in amounts small enough not to be noticed but large enough to almost fund Jack's lifestyle.

She slammed the door on the way out.

"What did you find out?" Jeph asked.

"He was looking at a job board."

"Good work." He caught her look. "He's been doing that for weeks."

"OK. Did you know about the other thing?"

He looked at her with one eye half squinted while she told him. "Well, hell." He glanced at Jack and back at Echo again. "I'll have Marlo take care of it. Let's focus on getting you ready now. Anyway, now you know how to look out someone else's window for a view on the physical world. With practice, you'll be able to watch through their eyes while moving your own body where you want to go."

With practice. "When am I going to get this practice?"

He gave her a piercing look. "Getting cold feet again?"

She squirmed under his gaze but didn't answer.

"It's a straight shot down Fifth Avenue to Union Station, and you can head-hop all the way."

"Head-hop—" She'd heard the phrase, but it didn't fit the context.

"Catch someone looking where you want to go, then use the world they see to guide your body through it. You saw Jack's desk, right?"

"Just barely."

"Yeah. Jack watches the world through a screen. He probably can't walk down a sidewalk without getting lost in the physical world. But when you go outside, just step out your front door—not the one with your porch, the one you used to get to other people's sesuoh at the game."

"The way I saw Meghan's Instagram feed?"

He nodded. "Like that." He tapped his upper lip with his forefinger. "But you might need to make them look where you need to go." He sat silent for a few seconds; then his eyebrows went up. "I've got it. Chris is my IT guy. Make him move."

"Like leave town?" Echo had been thinking about Woodburn too much.

"No, make him do something surprising. Something abnormal."

Abnormal? Echo scrambled for ideas. She kneeled in the chair with her arms on the back to get a look at the guy. He seemed quiet and forgettable, a little overweight, short beard, ponytail that reached to the bottom of his neck. *How do I know what's normal?*

Jeph gave an exasperated huff. "Why are you sitting like that? He's not some exotic bird. Go and find out."

She wanted to ask Jeph a question about mind-reading, but his narrowed eyes and tight lips stopped her.

"What kind of movement?" she asked.

"I don't care what. Make him dance, run around in a circle, freak out about something—as long as it stands out as your influence."

"I can do that?"

"I know of someone who used it to put an enemy in the hospital by convincing him that the shower water was boiling. The enemy got second- and third-degree burns, and everybody else just got an ordinary shower."

"That's a terrible thing to do."

"Yeah, it was. So don't put Chris in the hospital. It's not hard. Show me you can do it. "

Echo didn't want to hurt the man, but there had been a few times in middle school when it would have been good to have that skill in her toolbox. Like when somebody put a spider down the neck of her blouse at school. Humiliation still washed over her like a red wave when she thought of it.

Jeph was still talking. She didn't know how much she had missed. "All you have to do is find a memory that caused you to react physically. Focus on it, put the feeling into an object. Make a key." He paused. "Something smaller than a chair."

She hardly heard him, caught up in the memory of the spider. It was her second week at her new school, only a few weeks after the accident that had killed her parents and sister, and the scars on her face were still bright and painful. She had made friends with Gray on the first day and then discovered he was a social outcast, and she was, too—not only hideous in her own face but weird by association.

Sitting in her 8 a.m. math class in the minutes before the final bell, she heard a noise behind her, and then a tickling movement on her neck. She brushed at it, but it moved down instead of stopping. Laughter erupted behind her. She jumped up and took off her shirt to shake it out, sending a medium-sized brown spider running away across the floor.

Laughter, shouts, and catcalls. A boy's voice: "Take it all off!" She ran to the restroom and stayed there a while, crying out her anger, frustration, fear, and grief, and investing all those feelings in that spider. Then she waited for her face and eyes to stop being red. When she got back to class, the teacher looked up at her—she didn't have the courage to meet his eyes—and said, "Miss Shearwater. Are you all right?"

She looked around at the rest of the class—the smirks, the contempt, the rapt attention to something fascinating on their desks—and a new relationship developed with them. It wasn't that she hated them or even that she didn't trust them. Instead, she completely trusted them to be exactly who they had shown themselves to be—cruel, heartless, and craven. They became faceless mannequins to her. She could speak civilly to them if she had to, but they never penetrated the hard shell she built around herself to keep them out. All except Gray. "Everything is fine," she told the teacher truthfully. She took her tardy without objection. The only lasting effect, to be honest, was an irrational fear of spiders.

"Is there a problem?" Jeph asked. He was not smiling now.

Echo had missed a lot of what he had said, but she went into her esuoh and checked her notes. She looked out her window at him. "Find a memory. Make a key." Her voice came to her as if magnified from a distance and a little out of sync with her perception of speaking. "What do I do with the key?"

"Put it in his short-term memory."

Back at her table of memories, a plastic spider was lying there, buzzing with meaning. She created a tissue to pick it up, barely protecting herself from the emotion it carried. She hadn't been able to separate the experience from its emotional load. Was there any other way to do this besides sending that emotion to Chris, the IT guy? At least it wouldn't put him in the hospital.

Jeph crossed his arms. "If you really can't figure it out, come back."

She knew what that would mean. She focused on Chris and "IT guy" and opened a door into a very high-tech-looking room with no windows at all. Presumably the enormous flat screen on the wall was his window on the world. But that didn't matter. All she needed to do was find his most recent short-term memory to put the spider into it.

Unfortunately, he didn't have books like other people she'd seen. All she could find were what seemed to be hundreds of small boxes, each holding dozens of flash memory cards. She found a card reader and inserted a card that seemed to be at the end of the line. The screen flashed from something Chris was writing to a walk past Meghan, who was wearing the same clothes Echo had seen that morning. Echo may have actually found the right box.

She stood over the open box with the tissue-covered spider in her hand, waves of humiliation and isolation rolling off it like a rip current. Was this really kinder than scalding water?

She wondered if there was something else she could do that would achieve Jeph's objective without sharing the contagion she held. The screen before her had gone back to whatever document Chris was working on, something about computer security. The words filled the whole screen, and she wondered if there was something on his desk that would give her what she needed.

She reached out to the screen and moved its focus, like examining a photo on her phone. She was surprised that the view moved. There was nothing above. A shelf of binders to the left. On the right of the screen was a six-inch figurine of Data from Star Trek.

Maybe she could do something with that. It obviously had at least sentimental value. If he tossed it into the trash, that would be evidence of him doing something "abnormal"—*Right, Jeph?* She turned the screen to look over Chris's shoulder at Jeph, whose eyebrows rose, but he gave an almost imperceptible shake of his head.

Yeah, I get it. Not enough. But what about this? Hardly aware of what she was doing, she reached out for the toy. Her arm, there in Chris's esuoh, reached out, but more than that her will to reach out guided Chris's arm as well as her own. It was a clumsy reach on Chris's part, and he almost knocked the doll off the shelf, but recovered and grasped it, bringing it close for inspection.

A humming flowed through the atmosphere, like bees singing. *A key? In the physical world?* Echo processed that, thinking of the power of things to hold memories and feelings—and the objects floating in the ocean in her dream. Feelings of being honored—even loved—and respected flowed through Chris's esuoh, having friends to help him become more human. She moved the screen to look at the trash can and moved to toss the Data into it. But even she couldn't work up the will to do it. It had become beautiful in her sight. She looked to its place on the shelf, and watched his arm put it back.

Echo dragged the screen around to look at Jeph again. Again the subtle shake.

She sighed and picked up Chris's box of short-term memories. She dropped the spider key into it and watched as the spider morphed into one of his cards. She started to feel the anguish and humiliation flow from the spider-key even before Chris began to react to the sensation. She hurried to escape from his esuoh before the emotions washed over her again.

She went through her own esuoh and back into Jeph's office.

Jeph was standing by his window, watching Chris's shoulders twitch. He reached around and brushed at his neck. He stood up and shook himself like someone doing the boogaloo. He looked at Jack, whose eyes were fastened on his screen, then he dove out of the office.

Jeph turned and shook her hand. He pulled his phone out of his pocket. "Excuse me." Echo thought he was going to make a call, but he opened the case to a rorrim he kept there, and when he looked up, his eyes were closed. "I'll be right back with some things you'll need."

She turned in the chair again to see if there was any aftermath from her manipulation of the IT guy. He hadn't come back yet, so she went into Jack's esuoh to look around. She started with herself—her ugly face, high-topped tennis shoes, and a big leather bag beside her. She turned him to look the other direction, and Chris was coming back from somewhere, giving Jack a glare of pain and anger. Echo didn't need to force Jack to turn and watch Chris take his seat. She felt the *What the hell?*—an exclamation without breath—reverberate through Jack's esuoh. But Echo, more than Jack, noticed Chris take the Data figurine from his shelf and toss it into the trash.

What? She stepped into Chris's esuoh to find out why. The humiliation and betrayal Echo had felt at the prank—that she had given to Chris with the key—resonated with similar events from Chris's life. In the swirling reverberations, she heard shouts, things falling, derisive laughter, demeaning words. Echo *felt* Chris's middle-school experience, and it was much worse than hers. In the here and now, both Data and Jack had become part of the laughing crowd. Data—even from the trash—because Chris had thought a plastic figurine of a fictional character could give him confidence. Jack because who else was there to put a spider down his shirt? Echo realized that Chris was haunted by middle school into his thirties, and it was likely he would never escape. It was pain that made a scalding shower seem mild.

What had she done?

She wanted to fix it. Her job didn't depend on destroying this man, just on getting him to move. Could she use Jack to rescue it for him? She went back into Jack's esuoh and guided his vision down to the figurine in the trash can. It wasn't broken, but it would be gone by morning. She tried to guide his hand to take it out of the trash, urging him to put it away, save it for later. But she heard only a sigh like the hydraulics on the city bus, and Jack turned back to his job hunt. She didn't know if the problem was with Jack or herself, but she couldn't get him to pick up the Data. She did get him to glance back at Jeph's office, and Jeph was there, talking to Echo.

She went back into her esuoh and found Jeph holding out sunglasses so big they would fall off her face and a plastic card the size of a dinner plate. "Take these."

She held out her hand for the items. When she looked at them, they were big and awkward, and she was sure she would drop them. When she looked away, her hand felt them as normal size. She stashed them in her bag, zipping the card into the pocket where she kept her bus pass.

"You need to catch the train at one thirty," Jeph said. "You've got plenty of time to walk to Union Station, and you can get used to the world while you're walking. Then you can explore your esuoh while you're on the train. By the time you get to Salem, you'll be all ready to get Cali's key."

"How am I going to get there being so small?"

He looked down at her from his great height—he seemed as tall as a building. "Small?" After a second he pulled out his phone and crossed over, still looking down at her, with his eyes now open. She felt his watchful presence inside her esuoh, and she went in to stand beside him in front of her window, with all the giant furniture outside. "It's the way you perceive yourself." His face registered a preview of disappointment. "You're not planning to fail, are you?"

"No." She heard her voice, high-pitched and desperate. She wanted to believe, but if this was the way she would navigate the world, she didn't think she could make it.

"Calm down. The world conforms to your expectations. It's like they say about the weather: If you don't like it, stick around; it will change." He left her alone in her esuoh.

She was starting to hyperventilate, and then the voice of Death from the game came tinnily from her table of memories, saying that people love change until it happens to them. He was right. It was just a different view of the world.

And then it was better. Her esuoh was the right size, even if Jeph's furniture wasn't. She came out into the overlarge world with a better attitude and another question. "You promised to pay me enough for six months' rent. What if it doesn't work?"

He lifted an eyebrow.

"I'm going to do it. But I'm just asking."

He folded his arms across his chest. "I'm supplying the tools and paying for your expenses, but if you don't solve my problem, I don't solve yours." He stared her down with a steadily neutral expression that gave her a chill. "It's an afternoon's work. All you have to do is find the key. It's an investment of your time with a big payoff. I pegged you for a gambler. Was I right?"

She was still shivering. But he was right: she wouldn't turn down this opportunity. "Yes."

"Your appointment with Cali is at two thirty."

"Got it."

"Yes, you do. There's money on that card, so feel free to get something to eat if you want. Just don't go crazy."

She almost laughed at the idea of going crazy. But it would have come out maniacally, so she swallowed it.

He took her elbow and walked her out of his office and past a room-sized aquarium with seven gorgeously colored fish swimming in it. "Remember, you're a journalist for YouthNow. Just ask about growing up in Ashland. What were her influences? Who encouraged her along the way? How did

Ashland High School provide a grounding for the success she's become? Like that."

She nodded.

"The man you're looking for is Lazar Kyrillovich. If you have trouble finding anything, try mentioning the name. It might shake something loose. It might also cause her to throw you out."

Great.

They stopped at the receptionist's desk, which Echo still couldn't see over. "Don't worry about forgetting anything," Jeph said. "I put all the information on the table in your esuoh. All you need to do is slip it into one of your sketchbooks. You can do it on the train."

"Absolutely."

"You've got this. I'll see you this afternoon." They were at the doors to the offices of Jephthah Blackthorne III • Success Transformation • Reputation Management. "I forgot to ask. Would you like a cane?"

"Cane?"

"Like blind people carry."

She thought before she answered. "I'll just trip over it."

He shrugged. "Suit yourself." He turned and walked back toward his office.

On the way to the elevator, the scale changed, and she felt more like her normal, above-average height. Then the elevator door opened like a spaceship hatch, and she stepped into a transparent bubble taking her down to the ground of an alien landscape, with flat rocks, trees that ended in glowing mushroom tops, a rock formation like a slab that seemed to have been ejected from a great depth, all lit by a bright crescent moon with stars shining through its center.

Stick around. It will change.

She felt alone and, but there was electricity flowing from the soles of her feet up through her head. She was at a decision point between fear and excitement.

She chose excitement.

CHAPTER 12

Ships Passing

THE ELEVATOR BROUGHT ECHO to the ground without stopping, and when the doors opened, the scene had changed again—to something both more familiar and more alien. The bank lobby, which she had seen many times before, was made of painted concrete and colorful plastic, like an amusement-park bank for children. All the people were mannequins, fashion dummies—empty-faced, naked to their matte black plastic, with wrist stubs instead of hands and their feet shaped for high heels or flat shoes, indicating female or male.

She picked a woman standing in line at a bank teller's station. Using the techniques she had just learned, she slipped through the unlocked door into the other woman's esuoh. It was basically all kitchen, huge and well stocked, with a twelve-burner stove and the smell of cookies pervading the air.

Echo looked out into the world through the window above the woman's kitchen sink. The woman glanced down at her deposit slip—*Very nice*—but that wasn't what Echo wanted to see. She willed her hostess to turn, whispering, "Look behind you!" and the woman turned slowly to survey the bank lobby.

People. Just people. Echo breathed a sigh of relief and was about to leave the woman's esuoh when she saw a familiar face. It was Gray, following a man who was a few years older with a sour expression and a posture that said he wanted to get somewhere as fast as possible.

Echo hopped back into her own esuoh and turned for a better look at Gray. He was being pulled like a puppy by a spoiled kid in a sailor hat licking a lollipop. They were the only two people in the crowd of mannequins.

"Gray!" she shouted, waving like a high-school girl seeing her bestie enter the cafeteria. She was excited to be with him in his world. She wanted to tell him all about her job and also that Cain wanted to see him. Mostly she was overjoyed that something made sense.

Gray turned to her, staring, mouth agape and his eyes open. Even though they were still separated by most of the bank lobby, she wanted to be close to him, to embrace their suddenly shared reality. The remnants of her earlier annoyance at not being told flitted away like a dragonfly. Whatever ridiculous reason he had would be explained, sorted out; it would not overcome their friendship. She started to run to him. But he didn't respond with the warmth she expected. Instead, she saw shock and horror. She couldn't understand where it was coming from.

He stood there, dumbstruck, while the kid pulled the leash around his neck. Finally, Gray pulled the leash off and threw it at him. The kid stalked off toward the door, morphing into a mannequin, the transformation starting at his hands and feet and flowing toward his torso like a magical disease, as he left.

Echo waited for Gray to show some sign of the joy she felt at seeing his eyes, but he just stood there. At last, she went to him and would have hugged him if he hadn't backed up.

"Finally," she said, fighting to keep from squealing. "I get it. I'm so excited. Can you believe this? Now I understand about you."

"What happened to you?" His voice sounded like he was choking. Obviously he didn't need to ask. She went into his esuoh to talk to him. It was a small, dark, closed space with wooden beams overhead like the slats of a bed. The furniture was made from odd household items. "It's cute in here. It looks like you." She hardly had time to look around before she found herself bumped out into the field of mannequins, where only Gray was human.

"What are you doing?" He looked furious. She thought it might be the first time she had ever seen anything more than mild annoyance in him.

"I thought we could talk. You can come into my esuoh, if you want. You've probably been there before, right?"

He looked offended. "I would never—"

"OK. This is going to be complicated, I guess. I can forget that you never told me. Can you forget that I found it on my own?"

"Forget?" He sounded as if he didn't know what the word meant. "Found it on your own?"

"Look. I've got to go. I've got a job." She couldn't restrain a little jig at that. "I wanted to tell you some guy named Cain wants to see you. He said he's got a present for you. I didn't tell him anything about you. I don't trust him." She dug in her purse for the card. She was about to crawl in again, but remembered to look for it inside herself, and it leaped into her hand.

Gray accepted the card, then looked at it and reacted as if it were a poisonous thing. He tossed it aside. "Echo, this stuff is dangerous." The card reappeared in his hand.

"Is it a key? He said it was a business card, but I thought it might be a key."

"You know what a key is?"

"Sure." She studied his face. "Don't you? Not that you're—" She stopped, realizing that what she was about to say might not be flattering. "I mean, so many secrets in your—world."

He tossed the card aside again, and it reappeared his hand. "There are reasons for secrets." His face glowed with anger.

"I didn't know it would do that. It never stuck to me." She looked toward the exit, where a steady stream of mannequins flowed through the revolving door like air through a fan. "I need to get moving," she said. "I'm sure you'll work it out." She hopped into the esuoh of a mannequin who was looking down toward the space beyond its truncated wrist as if at a phone. She didn't take the time to look at the esuoh, but just through the window at the time on the phone's screen. She stepped back out into Gray's world. "I've got a train to catch. Let's get together for coffee tomorrow morning. Was that your new boss? I hope you've cooled off by then—I want to hear all about your job."

He stood there, his mouth opening and closing like a fish's, so she turned and walked away.

"Do you have a rorrim?" he shouted after her.

She wasn't sure she heard him. She turned back. "A what?"

"A—a mirror?"

She had heard correctly. He couldn't have a rorrim, or he wouldn't have stayed in the dream world all the time. "No. I'm like you."

"Take mine." He dug into his pocket.

"You've had one all along?" And then the idea struck her as deliciously funny. He'd never felt the need to use it. She laughed, and all the faceless mannequins turned to her, their expressionless faces showing surprise through no obvious mechanism, and that was even funnier. She head-hopped into a mannequin walking toward the door, and with effort brought her body along to follow through the crowd. She spun out through the bank door onto the sidewalk outside.

Gray watched Echo spin out the door as a rare and beautiful fish darting through a tropical sea. She slipped through a school of flashing silver anchovies, past octopuses pushing themselves along like sentient balloons, and behind a whale lazily sculling by with its mouth wide open.

Gray felt like some slow and ugly creature of the oceanic depths, watching his life passing away from him. He set out to chase her, but he was held down by an anchor laden with barnacles.

Cain's key was the anchor holding him back. He dropped it, and it reappeared in his hand. He threw it away, and it circled back like a boomerang. When he held it up to look at it, there was a familiar face on it, a black monster with obsidian teeth and red eyes. It tugged him toward the elevator.

Obviously, the only way to get rid of it was to return it to Cain, and he couldn't follow Echo until he had gotten rid of the key.

He had told Buzz he would catch up with him in five minutes. He knew now that he would not catch up with Buzz, ever. He regretted the effort Quig had put into helping him get the job, but if he had to choose between Buzz and Echo, the choice was easy.

He didn't know who Echo had gone to work for. Cain had used the name Jeph as if he were a common acquaintance, but he wasn't. But the key pulled Gray into a dead submarine, with a bioluminescent jellyfish ascending and descending like a living lava lamp to relieve the gloom. The ship floated across the ocean floor with its door open. Occasionally, the movement stopped, and fish swam in. It stopped again, and fish swam out. It stopped again, and more fish swam both in and out.

All the while, Gray waited in the semi-darkness. And then there was a stop where the key pulled him out the door and onto a beach of wet sand, where a lovely sea turtle sunned herself. He told her he had come to talk to Cain.

But another man entered the scene, in an old-fashioned office, encased in a bubble that expanded to displace the ocean scene entirely. The man's face was vaguely familiar, but Gray couldn't place him in his trim brown suit, stiff collar, and bow tie.

Gray reluctantly accepted the undersea environment Ytilaer had served up to him, but this man was changing it by his will, just as Cain had in the coffee shop that morning. It was a sign that he—both of them—were willing to practice deceit and manipulation, and Gray was uncomfortable being in the same space with it—and in the fact that this man smiling at him with a shark's grin must be Cain's partner, Jeph. And that meant—

"Well!" the stranger said. "It's Echo's friend," confirming Gray's fear.

Gray recognized him now, as the stranger at the Ugly Mug yesterday, who had revealed himself as being in Ytilaer and disguising his true appearance. Now he was controlling Gray's appearance as well—Gray looked down at himself and found ankle boots, knee socks, and knickers. He felt his head and found a soft cap with a narrow bill. "What did you do to Echo?"

"She's working. Let's go to my office for a chat."

Gray followed reluctantly, checking for Cain around every corner. He had to be getting closer, or the key wouldn't let him proceed.

Jeph led him into an office furnished with dark wood, much scuffed and worn. Two used glasses flanked a half-empty bottle of whisky amid piles of paper on the desk. He lounged in his office chair with his feet on the desk and indicated a small chair on the other side for Gray.

Then suddenly, Gray felt the stranger's presence from inside his esuoh, and he ran in to confront him. "Don't you have any manners?" Gray said. "I haven't invited you."

The man looked around at the toys and childish things, his nostrils widening and a curl touching his lip. "I can understand how you might be embarrassed, but I want to have this conversation in private."

Gray tried to stand taller, but he cringed remembering that Echo had said his esuoh looked "cute," like him. "I want to know where Echo is." He heard his voice squeak.

"And I'm sure you will—" the man's indulgent tone made Gray want to climb him like a tree and punch his face. Instead, he balled his fists and fought tears "—as soon as she contacts you. In the meantime, she's working for me, and I have no reason to send you off to harass her."

"She's my friend, and I deserve to know where you've sent her, in Ytilaer, without any training. It's dangerous."

"Dangerous for a mouse, maybe." Jeph lifted a single eyebrow to him. "But her esuoh is on the side of a mountain, and the eagles nest below her. But you've never seen her esuoh, have you?"

"I don't march in without permission."

"And you were just about to bring her into your special world." His voice dripped with sarcastic sympathy.

Gray took a deep breath.

The man gave a little shake of his head. "You say you're friends, but you don't know her, and you don't know yourself."

"I've been in this world since I was seven. I know how to navigate it. Let me take her place."

"To find Echo and then quit? Thanks, no. The truth is, kid, you have nothing I want. Except Echo, and I have her now. So go play." He left Gray's esuoh, and when Gray went out into the world in Jeph's office, he was on a grimy beach with garbage coming up on the waves and Jeph nowhere in sight.

He left Jeph's office and found Cain the cowboy-monster coming toward him.

"Well, well. Look who's here. The shrimp."

Gray made a supreme effort to pull himself up the evolutionary ladder and stood on the beach as a crab, waving its claws at the monster.

Cain laughed. "That's better. I think you have something of mine. Let's talk in my esuoh."

"Just take it back. We have no reason to start visiting each other."

"That's what we need to talk about. Your esuoh or mine?"

Gray thought about it. He might be able to drop the key in Cain's esuoh. "Yours."

Cain smiled. "Good choice."

Gray followed him into a one-room cabin with rough log walls. On one side was a big stone fireplace with a smoke-darkened mantle. A ladder ascended to a dark loft, and over in the far corner was a locked trapdoor that would lead to Cain's basement. Following Cain in, Gray passed a barrel full of walnuts, pulsing with energy.

But Cain was still talking. "Cozy, right?" He pulled up a ladder-back chair and straddled it with his arms resting on its back. He didn't look like the monster Gray had grown up fearing, but rather like the wiry, aging cowboy Gray had seen that morning. "Given any more thought to what I asked you this morning?"

"Did you ask me anything?" Gray took another chair and sat in it with a view of both Cain and the front window. Out the window of Cain's eyes, he saw himself as a boy in tattered clothes in an upstairs room of a frontier whorehouse. The bed was tumbled, with clothes tossed over it, but the woman was absent.

"I invited you to work with me and offered to help you save your girlfriend."

"What makes you think she needs saving?" Gray tried to keep the shiver out of his voice. He didn't want to give this man power by revealing how worried he was.

"I told you. Jeph is a bad guy."

"Says the murderer."

"For one thing, *I* didn't kill your mother. For another thing, yeah, I'm telling you Jeph is a bad guy. That should mean something."

"Aren't you guys partners?"

"Associates. I'm helping him get what he wants. He's helping me get what I want. Turns out it's the same thing. I told him about you because I thought you might be helpful. I said I would come and get you, but I lost track of you."

"Did it occur to you that I might not want you to find me?"

"Well, sure. But I'm still your *dad*."

"After I got you arrested?"

"No hard feelings. Especially after you got me off, too. Genius."

Gray felt mortified at the memory, earnestly telling the jury that the perpetrator was the black-on-black monster sitting at the defendant's table, when all they could see was the pale outer layer, not the depth of darkness that lay within.

"I wasn't prepared to drag a kid with me, so somebody decided to look after you for a while. Anyway, I told Jeph we needed you, and he used his influence somewhere to find you. He didn't tell me what laws he broke, and I didn't ask. But when he got to you, he found the girl hanging out with you. He said the girl had more promise than you did."

Gray gripped the edge of his chair. "Promise for what?"

Cain gave Gray a long, steady look and didn't answer.

Gray slid the key out of his pocket and dropped it on the floor. It fell with a loud thump.

"Keep that. It's the key to my labyrinth, not yours. Go try it. You're not a prisoner. I just wanted to talk."

Gray looked at him with wonder. Cain's face was open, his eyes wide and ice-gray, even though the soul behind his eyes was like the mouth of a cave in nighttime. Gray took the key and pressed it against the trapdoor. It popped open. He pushed it shut again.

He came back to the chair, leaving the key on the kitchen table. "I don't get any of this. You killed my mother, threatened to come back after me, and now twelve years later you're back and—what?"

"That wasn't a threat. It was a promise. You're a mouse. I can make you something more."

A feeling rose in Gray that he had struggled against his entire life. In his first foster home, he had learned to be quiet about what he saw. In the second, he had learned not to speak of what he knew. In the third, he had learned to disappear in plain sight. In the decade of love, support, and understanding that followed, he had not unlearned those lessons. He had learned to make peace, be invisible, go along. Always ignore the stubborn knock on the door of his labyrinth that said, *Stand up. Speak up. Make it stop.* It was knocking now, insistently, and with a force he had never experienced.

He crossed into his own esuoh and found everything broken and scattered as if by an earthquake. Something was pounding, pounding on his cellar door. He piled his furniture against it, but it bumped the things out of the way like the plastic and cardboard they were. The walls were cracking, the bed that had sheltered him vibrated with the pounding. He took a deep breath and stood there for a minute, listening to the noise, borne up by it.

He went to the door of his basement, which led to the labyrinth where his monsters dwelled. Bang! Bang! Bang! With each blow, the wood curved out like a cartoon door and the lock rattled. If he didn't let the monster out, it might go back to sleep. Maybe. But if he ever opened that door . . . .

Bang! Bang! The door formed into a huge fist as the monster banged against it and then went back to its shape.

Everything in his esuoh had fallen to the floor and was breaking into pieces. "Stop! Go away!"

Bang!

He was as filled with rage as the night his mother had died, when he hid under the bed while the monster above him pounded the bed, muffling her screams, until there was silence.

He was also as terrified as he had been that night, when his life had fallen apart and left him beached like a jellyfish in a world he didn't understand, among strangers who hated and feared him. After killing Gray's mother, the monster bent down and looked at him under the bed. Black on black he was, with a mouth like a black hole full of obsidian shark's teeth and eyes that invited Gray to die with his mother. Gray had screamed, a seven-year-old boy's scream. He was screaming now, and it seemed that he had never really stopped since that day twelve years ago.

There was really only one way to get rid of it. This was the wisdom of the Srelevart. They hadn't "made" him a mouse. They had only allowed him to remain one as long as he chose.

Run away. A whisper from the labyrinth rustled under the pounding from the monster. *The beast will stop bothering you. You can put your esuoh back together. But if you open the door, your world will break into pieces again—you will break into pieces. If you keep it closed, you can hold on to your life, your job, the world as you know it.*

The pounding continued as Gray considered. Echo's decision had already torn his world apart. It would destroy him to go after her.

But life without Echo . . . .

She's already gone. The whisper hissed around him like the breeze before a storm. *There's nothing you can do about it now. Jeph has taken her. If she had wanted you, she would have let you show her the rorrim. She laughed at you. She laughed.*

"No." Gray spoke aloud to it, his voice sounding distant in the growing wind. "No, no, no, no, no." He saw the cafe again, the roses turned to dust on the table. "She is my sunlight."

He reached for the door.

You will die. The whisperer squealed in panic.

"I will rise as someone else." Gray pulled open the door.

The monster climbed out. As it stood, it broke the roof of Gray's esuoh. It looked around, turning its head side to side like a curious dog, then bent down and looked at Gray again.

Gray was growing, too. His head hit the top of his esuoh and broke through it. He was in his childhood bedroom, with the same books and toys on the shelves, the pile of clothing on his chair waiting to be folded. Outside his window were the laurel bushes where the raccoons sometimes played. He stopped growing when he was about half the monster's height. The monster held out its hand, and Gray reached to take it. His own hand was black, too, and scaly like a dragon's, and he walked on two legs like a minotaur.

"Son." The monster grimaced down at him.

Gray found himself on the beach again, screaming, and a woman in a red dress with a hat made of fruit was bent over him, telling him he needed to stop.

The woman took his arms and raised him to his feet. He walked with her like a child fallen prey to bullies. He wasn't hurt, and he had stopped screaming, but he had not stopped shaking, and he wasn't sure he ever would. She led him to a beach where the tide was so far out that he couldn't see the ocean. She helped him sit on a driftwood log and sat beside him and waited.

He listened. No voices came from his esuoh. He went back inside. His bed was smashed, the small toys he had used as furniture strewn across the floor. He picked up the matchbox that had been his bed and threw it into a dumpster that appeared there as he threw it. The room looked as if it had been hit by vandals and abandoned. Outside the window he saw only fog. But on the windowsill was the key he'd thought he'd left in Cain's esuoh.

He carried it through his unfamiliar, broken esuoh to a half-door he'd never seen in the apartment where he and his mother had lived before she died. He opened his basement door and tossed the card inside and locked it firmly. He checked all his other locks—they did not give him confidence, but they were all he had—and went out to talk to the woman in the fruit hat.

She was still waiting for him, watching him through closed eyes. He shifted in his seat on the log, and she spoke to him. "Are you feeling better?"

Gray checked and was surprised at the answer. "Yes." Better than a couple of minutes ago, at least, and that was something.

"Did Jeph do this to you?"

"What?"

"I can get one of his damned mirrors if you want to come out."

"Thanks. I choose to be here." And a fat lot of good it had done him.

"You can tell me what that was all about, but I won't ask. You people are pretty private about your magical world, although sometimes a listening ear can help."

"I came looking for Echo."

She gave a sad smile. "I tried to talk both of them out of it, but Jeph doesn't listen to me, so why should the girl?"

"Are you his assistant?"

She jerked her head back. "Partner."

"I'm sorry. He seems—"

She sighed. "I know. He's the visionary; I'm the practical one. It's always worked before, but lately . . . ."

"Cain?" Gray said.

"You know him?"

Gray shivered.

"That's my reaction, too."

"Where did Echo go?"

"She's on a mission, as Jeph calls it. Pretentious. It used to be part of his charm; now it's just his schtick." She stared at Gray for a moment. The red dress had sometime in the past minute transformed into a wine-red suit, and the fruit hat had disappeared. She looked beautiful and formidable, dressed for an office, but standing on the damp beige sand. "Is she your girlfriend?"

Gray shrugged, the truth being too painful to tell.

She nodded solemnly. "Jeph is . . . ." She seemed to weigh her words.

Gray waited, wishing he could go into her esuoh, where communication is so much quicker. He had the impression that the silences of Oge are packed with meaning.

She took a breath and started again. "Jeph is hard on young girls."

Gray's heart pounded as he thought of the ways a man—egam krad—might be hard on young girls. The possibilities battered him like blows of a stick. He wanted to know. He didn't want to know. He wanted to find Echo and bring her home. "She was desperate for a job. What did he hire her to do?"

"There are some things he doesn't tell his business partner. Cain is the one you'd have to talk to for that."

Talk to Cain. Holding hands with his dad, the monster. He shivered violently.

The woman shook her head. "I don't know where she's going. I just know where she went."

"She told me she was going to take the train."

The woman was quiet for a long time. Gray could see that she was struggling with something, like a sea creature caught in a net. Finally, as if clipping the last thread, she took a deep breath and slowly let it out again. "I'll tell you if you'll promise me something."

"If it gets Echo back, I would probably do it without a promise, but in Ytilaer a promise changes your life."

She shook her head. "You've got to stop him. I loved Jeph once, but he's become something else—a beast in a thousand-dollar suit."

"Why don't you just quit?"

"He owns me." She stopped, looked around. "Owned me. We—he had a word for it—"

"Syzygy?" Gray asked.

She nodded and pointed at him. "He said I can't escape, but maybe I just did. I'm wrung out and empty—done with him, but never truly free. Every time he takes another one, I feel more stretched out—like I'm ripped into pieces and scattered on the sea." She got up and went back to her desk. "It's not just kindness that makes me want to stop him from taking your friend. But there's no point in telling you anything if you're just going to go home and forget about it."

Gray considered his options. He could follow Echo to the end of the world or go home and forget about it. The first was a terrifying option; the second wasn't an option at all. "I've been in Ytilaer for a long time, and I've never learned to use it the way Jeph and Cain do. But if you knew Echo better, you'd know I can't forget her."

She leaned back in her chair and stared at the ceiling. Gray almost gave up and left before she spoke again. "She has an appointment to interview Senator Cali Zielinski this afternoon at the State Capitol. Echo is pretending to be a journalist. She plans to be back this afternoon. Maybe she will be."

Gray struggled under a heavy burden as he rose. He stumbled over the doorsill, and the woman got up from her desk.

"Are you OK?" she asked.

"Yes." He thought he was OK, but he was breathing hard. "Can you show me how to get to the stairway?"

She walked him to a side door, and he heaved himself into a vast tower built on the sand with stairs encircling the inner wall. He sat on the first step, beset by images brighter than memories. Echo in a dungeon in Jeph's labyrinth; Echo in syzygy with Jeph, merged soul to soul and never free to be with anyone else; Echo holding prisoners in her own labyrinth; Echo in danger with no one to help her; Echo alone with the dangers of Oge.

He went back into his esuoh. It was tumbled about, and its structure was changing. The mouse house was gone forever. He took a second to ask himself if he missed its childish familiarity. Cain's key, which he had thrown into his labyrinth, was lying on the floor. He stooped to pick it up.

Cain, as monster, opened a door that appeared and disappeared as he walked through into the middle of the room. "I like what you've done with the place."

"How did you get in here?"

"Made my own key. Very handy. Maybe I'll teach you."

Gray felt panic rising again, but something else, too. Something that analyzed what he was trying to do and what it would take to do it. He looked at the monster who had turned out to be his father. It was just as black, but now shades of black, and there was an expression of need as well as cunning in its eyes.

Outside Gray's window, the fog cleared, revealing a collapsing tower, buffeted by wind and flames, its stones falling like leaves in the storm.

Gray returned his attention to Cain, who was now a cowboy dressed in black except for blood-red boots. He looked as if he hadn't shaved in a week, and white threads ran through his hair and beard. "You said you want something from me. What is it?"

"I want a partner I can trust. Someone to watch my back."

Gray took a deep breath to hide the chill that shook him. "I'm looking for Echo. No partnership."

"I won't be able to show you the things I know, then."

"I can live with that. Why did you weigh me down with this key?"

"Oh, that. I want you to find the girl and tell me where she goes."

"Uh, right. Your track record with women—"

"I don't want *her*, I keep telling you. Jeph wants her. I want the guy she's looking for."

"Why?"

"Because he has something I want."

"What?"

"I'll only tell a partner. I tried recruiting an associate, but now my associate is trying to cut me out. So it's partner only. With safeguards." He folded his arms across his chest and stood with his chin tilted upward and his lips tight.

Gray gave a rueful half-laugh and shook his head. "I don't trust any of this. I'm not going to help you, but I'm going to find her."

"That's my boy."

"Please don't call me that."

Cain laughed, raucous, delighted. "I'll call you anything I want."

"Your key makes it harder to do anything."

"That's because you needed to talk to me. It's not holding you now."

Gray stared at him.

"We're connected, whether you like it or not. The key gives you access to my labyrinth. You might need it sometime."

Understanding rose from the floor like the rising waters of a flood. It was as if his feet knew first. By the time it covered his eyes and the rest of his head, he was looking at a very old, very tired, very sad man. "*You* might need *me* sometime."

"Listen here, sonny." The bent old cowboy shook his fist at Gray. "I stole my first mirror when I was ten. I killed my mother—for reasons even *you* would understand—when I was fourteen. You and your mother were the closest thing I ever had to a family, and even at that I was fine when she took you and left town." His age drained away. His body stood straighter, taller. "Am I going to need *you*? You're an embarrassment. With your cute little mouse house and your girl who doesn't know you give a shit. Maybe you *don't* give a shit." He was seven feet tall and still growing. "But maybe, just maybe, you're more like me than you think." He was the monster now, black on black and pounding the air with rage. "You think I'm going to eat your soul? I could have done it the first time I saw you, and every time since. But there's not enough there to make a snack."

The flood of understanding rose again and bubbled up in Gray's throat as laughter. He was like a grownup watching the movie that terrified him as a child and seeing all the camera tricks and special effects. His mother was still dead, and this was the man who had killed her. But his fear was not for himself, and now he seemed to have the key to escape if the man—yes, his father—did capture him. He put the key in his pocket.

"I don't need your help to find Echo." He was growing, too, like Alice in Wonderland, and both their heads smashed through the ceiling of his childhood bedroom. "We're not friends or partners. I guess you're my father, but you're not my dad. Whatever happened between you and my mom, you broke our relationship when you killed her."

Cain the cowboy smiled an "I've got a secret" smile. "Call me if you need me."

Gray shook his head. He'd had enough of Cain's power plays. "Get out."

Cain disappeared.

Gray sat alone in his broken esuoh, feeling the stairs in Oge shake under him. He went out into the world and found himself in the falling tower he had seen from his window. People ran down the stairs, screaming, infecting him with their fear until he realized they were all him—in different clothes, different ages, some men, some women, but all with his face, his dark hair, and their eyes closed. He sat calmly then, watching as an elderly fireman, bent with age and gasping with every breath, ran upward among them, dispersing them as he passed until there were none.

Gray took the rorrim out of his pocket and looked it over. He was afraid to use it, but he was tired of being afraid, so he focused on his reflection and touched the surface. He could barely see, but the first thing he did was to stand up and catch a glimpse of the rescuer. It was not a fireman, but a young woman in a blue jogging suit, and she quickly disappeared on the stairs above. Gray was otherwise alone in a stairwell with cream-white walls and a green sign over the door.

He went out into the blinding light and stumbled through the hallways until he found the elevator.

CHAPTER 13

The Streetside Idol

SEEING GRAY HAD GIVEN ECHO A BURST OF CONFIDENCE. Yes, he was angry, but he would get over that, and his surprise made her feel she was doing better than expected, above average, extraordinarily well. After all, he himself had had a mirror all along and apparently never used it. How hard could it be to get along without it?

She had received an all-expenses-paid trip to the Mystical Kingdom, and she would enjoy every minute of it.

The play bank opened into a city-sized play shopping mall. The floors were smooth, tiled in a checkerboard pattern of black and white. The buildings were caricatures of a city, brightly colored in tile and plastic, but on a smaller scale, like Main Street in a theme park.

The light from above was filtered through translucent plastic, so it was steady and unchanging, immune to the effects of shifting clouds. The smells of cooking that wafted to her were popcorn, candy, hot dogs—like food from the carnival in her dream—not the mix of Mexican, Indian, Japanese, and odd local fusion fare of the Portland she knew. And instead of the usual city sounds—the roar of traffic, the hum of conversation, the dinging of bike bells, and the saxophonist who always played down the block—the air was full of soft, forgettable music, barely audible above the fairground noises of the play city and the clack of the mannequins' shoes on the floor—sidewalk.

The street was wide and flat and shiny black, with yellow tile stripes along the sides. Child-sized buses, trucks, and cars ran along it with adult-sized mannequins driving, their elbows and knees sticking out. The vehicles had headlights like eyes and bumpers like smiles and made no engine sounds, only the pull of their chain mechanism, half-hidden in tracks on the street, and an occasional beep-beep of protest when they collided.

She turned toward the train station and threaded through the stream of mannequins flowing out of the bank as if it were spawning them.

Mannequins crowded the checkerboard sidewalk, doing all the things city people do. They crossed streets, waited for buses, drove cars, begged for spare change. They walked at a pace Echo would have to run to keep up with—and she tended to be a fast walker. They bumped into her, stepped on her feet, pushed her forward. She walked up to one to ask directions, but it kept going as if unaware of her existence. She stepped in front of another, waving her hands at it, but it would have mowed her down if she hadn't moved at the last second. She grabbed an arm. It was rigid enough to be a weapon, but the mannequin kept moving, not reacting to her touch.

She went into a mannequin's esuoh to look around. It was industrial—concrete floor, scuffed walls—and empty. Outside the small, square, dirty window, there were people—about a third human people and the rest mannequins—and the crowd was so dense that she couldn't see sidewalks or buildings. The humans poked along, dragged their feet, impeded the progress of the mannequins, who needed to *be* somewhere and didn't have time for this shit. Instead of the calming music outside, this esuoh had angry, abusive voices screaming together in a cacophony imitating a song, with rhythm like a fast heartbeat. She couldn't understand the words, but they filled her with rage. She jumped out again.

She tried another mannequin's esuoh. It was the same, down to the scuff marks on the walls and the dense crowd outside the window. This time the humans—a smaller proportion of the growing crowd than she had seen from the prior mannequin's window—were *looking* at her, their eyes narrowed in hatred, their mouths contorted with disdain, or *not looking* at her because they obviously felt she was beneath their notice. Here the voices screamed in a minor key, still in rhythm, still unintelligible, but with a slower beat. Echo felt like she had been tragically ill-used and didn't know why. She left the mannequin's esuoh.

What was wrong with these people? The ones inside the bank had seemed normal under their mannequin exterior, but now she was surrounded by empty shells full of destructive emotions.

She tried one more. Again, the room was exactly the same, down to the shape and position of the scuff marks. The number of humans in the crowd had shrunk to very few, and the music had the same voices, with a different energy. The drumbeat was slow and menacing, like the approach of a Stephen King villain, and the voices were high and screeching, like the knife attack in *Psycho*. The emotion was *fear*, but Echo couldn't tell whether the mannequin whose viewpoint she occupied was the perp or the victim.

She jumped back into her own esuoh for a moment of rest, hoping to find the humans—even if only a minority—she had seen from the mannequins' windows. Now her esuoh also looked like an industrial warehouse with the exact same scuffmarks on the wall, but a bent folding chair lay on its side on the floor. She turned it upright and sat on it. She could still hear all the tunes she had heard in the mannequins, forming a unity with the forgettable music—a symphony of rage, self-pity, and fear, with a sugar coating of sweet, sweet strings. Outside her window, mannequins ruled the city, pushing against each other, elbowing others aside, breaking into fistfights that spilled into traffic, bringing out a chorus of beeps from cars whose headlights now looked angry and whose bumpers were definitely not smiling.

Terror gripped her. She ran outside. Mannequins streamed by like an intrusion of roaches. She pushed through the crowds, telling herself that in the train station everything would be normal. A mannequin came her way, its empty arm poised to hold a phone, but it had neither hand nor phone. She tried to dodge it, but it kept coming. She tripped over something and fell. Her bag spilled its contents—nuts and bolts, rusty screws, broken devices that seemed intended to calibrate something, a small socket wrench twisted into a spiral—and the mannequin kicked her and stepped on Jeph's key as it walked on.

"Why don't you watch where you're going?" a voice said.

She picked up the things that had spilled from her bag, even though they seemed useless, because given her way of seeing, it could turn out that a passing mannequin had kicked her wallet or phone into a storm drain.

"Hey!" the voice said again. "I exist here!"

She turned and saw a small nut-brown man sitting in a little wooden booth, with spilled vases of flowers in front of him. He had a scar running vertically across his eye and down the length of his face, as if he were a novice ax sculpture, and his hair and neck-length beard were as white as the ceiling. His eyes had fury in them. In the midst of that forest of mannequins, he gave her hope.

His four glass vases of flowers had spilled on the sidewalk. One was broken.

"Did I do that?" Echo said. "I'm sorry. Did you see that guy? He was so busy with his imaginary phone that he almost ran over me."

"I saw *you* run over me," he said.

She set up the unbroken vases and put the flowers into them. She collected the pieces of glass and looked around for a place to dispose of them. But the flow of mannequins was so thick that she couldn't get to a garbage bin. She put the shards in a neat stack next to the wall.

Then it hit her. His eyes were open. "Wait. You're—" She sat next to him on the sidewalk. "May I come into your house?"

"You may not. I'm still alive because I see monsters and don't let them into my house."

"I'm not a monster. This is my first day in this world. How long have you been here? What do you see? Mannequins or something else?"

"I see a dummy asking me a bunch of stupid questions."

"What about them?" She gestured toward the moving mannequin legs.

"They're all dummies. Dancing to the devil's music. But they didn't knock over my flowers."

"I'm sorry. It was an accident."

The man nodded solemnly. "Sorry don't rebuild the shithouse."

Echo looked into her bag for her wallet. The bag was now full of shiny baubles, costume jewelry, small girly toys. She closed the bag around her arm and felt for the wallet. Having found it, she pulled out a bill and held it out to him. It was a child's drawing of a dead president with black hair sticking out around his head and dot eyes, sharp nose, and a straight mouth with slightly down-turned corners. "Will this cover the damage? I have no idea how much it is."

He took the bill without looking at it. "It's a start." He smacked his hands together and held them up like a magician, revealing that the bill was gone.

Echo got up to leave. "Can you tell me which way is the train station?"

"First, I'll tell you a story."

"But I'm going to be late."

"You need to hear the story."

Echo went into her esuoh, which was her gypsy wagon again. Everything was covered with dust, and cobwebs hung from every corner. It seemed as if it had been abandoned for a long time, but it was hers. She created a chair and sat in it, watching the man through her front window.

"The first murderer killed his brother because God liked his brother best. But when the shard came into the world, he didn't have to kill. He could separate his brother from God till Judgment Day." He sat there, looking at her as if waiting for applause or something.

Echo was wondering how she would explain it if she missed her train. She wondered what had happened to the optimism that had filled her only a few minutes before. Speaking from the behind her window, she made her mouth say, "That's a very interesting story."

"God damn it! It's not a 'very interesting story.' It happens to my people every night. If you're not a monster like them, you need to do something about it."

"Uh—"

"Promise."

"What can I do?"

"First you can come out here and talk to me. I ain't going to bite you unless you deserve it."

Echo sighed and came out into the world.

"That's better," the man said. "Stop them."

Echo had no idea what he was talking about, but it seemed the fastest way to escape was to go along with him. "OK. Can you tell me which way to the bus station?"

"Say you'll do it."

She nodded. "I'll stop them."

"You say you've been in Ytilaer world one day? A promise here is like a rudder on your boat. You think you've gotten rid of a tiresome old man, but you've changed the direction of your journey. You can thank me later."

Losing hope of getting an answer, she got up to leave.

"You were walking in the wrong direction."

She turned back to him. "What?"

"Beyond the mirror, left is right and right is left. What kind of idiot wouldn't know that?"

"A fool, obviously." She started walking back in the direction she had come.

CHAPTER 14

The Dragon Woman

As Echo approached the bank door, the mannequins poured out like stormwater from a drainpipe onto the sidewalk and the street, where they collided with each other and with grumpy-faced vehicles beeping furiously. Echo felt like a salmon swimming upstream as she navigated among them, at first against the current and then, past the bank, with the current, until she came to six lanes of bumper cars and kiddy vehicles with no traffic lights or walk signals.

Not as many mannequins were crossing this street, and there were fewer still on the other side. There were no breaks between the cars, and the mannequins who did cross did so willy-nilly, with no concern for the vehicles. Echo watched for any clue to timing, but finding none, took a deep breath and stepped out. The grumpy cars stopped and beeped at her, the kiddy vehicles made toy siren noises, and only after reaching the other sidewalk did she realize she had heard a real horn and brakes squealing among the ToyTown noises. She gave a glance back and shrugged. It had turned out fine, and she had a train to catch.

On this side of the major street, the mannequins were shabbier, their bodies dirty and worn, with holes that revealed gaping darkness. They zigzagged among their fellow mannequins, staggering, stumbling, or simply unfocused in direction. A male mannequin with a gray metal rod extending beyond broken plastic where its ankle should be limped into and fell over another mannequin shouting silently to the sky, shaking its empty wrist at the translucent plastic ceiling.

They fell together and lay there struggling as other mannequins stepped around, over, and on them.

Echo could hear their voices now, and they looked at her as they passed, expressions of annoyance on their expressionless faces. She still felt the music playing inside her like a malignant ear worm, and she wanted nothing more than to get away from them. She told herself the train station was ahead, and it would be clean and gleaming, either silent or playing smooth and soothing music, and empty of mannequins. The vision pulled her forward.

The scene grew increasingly rundown and neglected. She stumbled in craters on the floor where missing tiles had been and puzzled over the meaning of faded and broken plastic store signs and facades. The music flowed through Echo, pulling her emotions into its wake, and making her more and more afraid she was on the verge of joining the mannequins.

She had no desire anymore to go into their sesuoh and was terrified of going into her own. The voices pursued her, becoming a screeching symphony working its way to its rollicking finale. And then she understood the lyrics of the song they had been singing to her all along.

> You're just like us
> You're one of us
> We see your scars
> We know your crime
> You're just like us
> You're one of us

Panic pursued her. She couldn't see the train station, and she felt she was losing herself among the empty people surrounding her. Despair seized her. She thought of going into her esuoh, but she would not go there, and the decision felt like a patient holding off a terminal cancer diagnosis by avoiding the doctor.

She held up her hand before her face. Her wrist hovered in view—matte black plastic, faded and scratched—with no hand.

She went out into the world and broke into a run. The mannequins were like cockroaches under a spotlight, running in all directions, climbing over each other. Echo was just like them. When a mannequin fell, she ran over or around it, based only on what was easier for her. The music pursued her, the mannequins singing in their hideous voices:

> No one knows you
> No one cares
> You can't escape
> You're here forever
> You're just like us
> You're one of us

The train station appeared. She ran to it, pushed her way inside, thinking it was home base, escape from the mannequins, but they pushed in with her, filling the station to the point that she couldn't maneuver through them at all. Panic pushing her, she shoved them out of the way with the same intensity they had used against her. They deserved it; they were dangerous; they were blocking her way. She had to get through. She had to.

Then she heard her name, adding to her terror. She spun around, looking for a direction to run, but she collided with a dragon who was a woman in a red silk jacket with a dragon embroidered on it. The woman's head, with black hair tied into a bun, was feminine and human in its dragonness—terrifying and no less beautiful. She was as tall as a basketball player, and her eyes were open—red-gold with vertical slits for pupils.

Echo stared at her with awe that drove out her panic. Even the noise of the music quieted around them.

The dragon stretched her neck, making herself even taller, and looked down at Echo, tilting her head left and right. "Did Gray do this to you?"

Echo took a step backward. "Gray? No! What?"

"Where's your guide, then?"

"My— What?"

The dragon sighed mightily in frustration. A faint whiff of sulfurous smoke flowed out of her mouth.

Echo coughed. "You know Gray?"

"He's been nagging the Srelevart for permission to bring you in for years. We finally agreed it was time, so I assumed—"

"I got into this world my own way."

"Well, use your rorrim and get out. This is dangerous."

"I don't have a rorrim. Once I get away from the mannequins, I'll be fine."

"Mannequins?"

"They're—" Echo gestured around the room, noticing as she did that there weren't as many as there had been before.

The dragon gave her a stern look that somehow communicated kindness. "May I come into your house?"

"I don't think you want to. *I* don't want to."

"Then it's the thing you need to do. May I come into your house?"

Echo shivered at the thought. The dragon would hear what the voices were saying. She would *know*.

"The streetside idol said he doesn't let monsters into his esuoh. Because they'll take his soul, I think."

The dragon's lip curled on one side. "So you met Cornelius."

"He didn't tell me his name. He was scared of monsters."

"As he should be, but at least his monsters are outside himself."

"You mean the mannequins are not real?"

"They're real. You made them."

"How do I know I can trust you?"

"How do you know you can trust whoever sent you into Ytilaer?"

That stopped her. Because his eyes were so blue. Because he said she was special. Because she didn't know there was a danger to be aware of. But Jeph had offered her a job when there was no other hope. "It will work out." It *had* to work out. "I just know."

The dragon sighed again, with an even larger cloud of sulfur. "My dear girl. You're enough of a fool that it may just work out. May I help you get rid of the mannequins?"

"I need to catch the train to Salem."

"I won't stop you from catching your train."

Echo sighed with resignation—and relief. The woman now looked less like a dragon and more like someone who might have a dragon for a pet. "I invite you into my house."

Her esuoh was hers again—still messy, but not the industrial horror it had been before—but the music was even louder.

The dragon woman took a seat at the tiny table near the entrance of Echo's wagon.

Echo glanced around her esuoh, noticing the dust on the shelves and cobwebs in the corners, the piles of open sketchbooks on the table at the other end of the wagon. The music played louder here, but the dragon woman didn't seem fazed by it.

"Why don't you get us a cup of tea?" The dragon woman pointed to the teakettle steaming on the wood stove.

"I have to catch the train."

"You seem stressed. Panic is dangerous in this world."

"I was doing fine except for the mannequins."

She cocked her sort-of-dragonish head. "Making tea will help you get rid of them."

"I don't see how—"

The dragon woman gave her a look that reminded her of the one her mother—a formidable woman—used on extreme occasions.

"Tea, then." Echo opened a cabinet, reached into the empty space, and pulled out a box of English breakfast tea. "I hope this is OK. I drink coffee."

"It's the gesture that counts."

Echo made tea, pulling what she needed from the empty cabinet, including a Blue Willow teapot like the one her mother had received from her grandmother. She brought it to the table on a tray with a painting of sunflowers on it.

"That's nice. Thank you," the dragon woman said as Echo set down the tray. The smell of the tea changed from the fragrance of the English breakfast to something sharp with a pine tar vibe. "I should introduce myself. My name is Theodora Greenwood. You may call me Theo."

Echo took the opposite chair, produced a cup of coffee for herself, and sipped. The liquid had the flavor and aroma of coffee, but didn't warm her as it went down. She preferred the experience of physical coffee, but she didn't complain.

"When did you first see the mannequins?" Theo asked.

"When I left— When I first went out into the world alone."

"Why do they frighten you?"

"They didn't at first, but there were so many. At first it was like I was invisible to them. And then I heard their music. It's full of fear and anger and self-pity. They said I'm becoming one of them."

"The music—what's playing here?"

"You hear it? I thought I was the only one—besides the mannequins."

"Turn it off."

"But I can't—"

"It's your esuoh. More yours than any piece of real estate you'll ever buy. Turn it off."

Echo listened to the music. It got louder and filled her with anxiety again. *Shut up! Shut up! Shut up!* she shouted within herself.

"Stop arguing with it. It gives it more power."

"If I can't get them to shut up, how do I turn it off?"

"Listen to it."

"What? It makes me crazy, and listening to it makes it louder."

"I know. Mine does, too. Here's how you turn it off. Hear it. Accept that it's there. Understand that it's not you, because you're observing it."

Echo tried. The rage and sadness and fear flowed through her body. She could feel it in her stomach, her back, her throat. The accusations of the music flayed her, and then she knew it was like a radio. She had brought it into her esuoh, and she could turn it off. She found an old-fashioned radio sitting behind books on an upper shelf, pouring out the music. It had two knobs. One changed the channel, playing fear, anger, self-pity in variations and permutations up and down the dial. The other lowered the volume until, with a quiet click, it turned it off.

And then there was silence.

Echo turned back to the table and breathed. "Does everybody have one of those?"

Theo tilted her head at Echo and answered slowly. "Not exactly the same thing, but yes."

Echo wondered if there might be a way to use that in her mission. "Thank you. Now how do I get around the mannequins?"

"Let's look out your window." Theo set her empty cup on the table, and all the tea and coffee things disappeared.

"My esuoh is kind of a mess."

"That's what happens when you spend more time jumping into other people's sesuoh than you spend in your own."

Echo stopped and looked into the dragon's eyes. "I'm not supposed to do that, am I?"

"It's not just the law; it's a good idea."

Echo led the way to her window. "Believe it or not, it's better than the last time I looked at it."

"What do you see out there?"

"Fog mostly."

"Jeph taught you how to hop into other peoples' sesuoh but not how to clear your vision?"

"You know Jeph?"

"I know of him. How big do you think the Ytilaer community is?"

"I don't know. The way I keep meeting people, it seems like a multitude."

The dragon woman nodded. "Ytilaer has a tendency to bring her people together. But there are factions."

"I get that, but they're loose, maybe?"

"And shifting. I used to be egam krad, so I know where that goes."

"Egam krad?"

"Mirror language for dark mage. But that sounds more airy-fairy than it is."

Says the dragon woman, Echo thought.

"Show me your porch."

Echo released a handle from a clip on the side of her wagon, and the porch dropped into place. It was the first time she'd had a chance to let down the porch herself. She was pleased with the simplicity of the mechanism. She gazed at the unnerving depth of hte chasm. "I was told the laws of physics here are suggestions."

The dragon woman, following her out and stopping to look over the distant hills, nodded. "I understand you've talked to Edward. That's something."

"He told me I didn't need to worry."

The dragon woman looked her steadily in the eye. "That doesn't sound like him. I would think he'd say something like 'You're not inclined to worry.'"

Echo thought about it. "Maybe. I need to sort my memories."

"Yes, you do. They fade if they're left on the table too long. But that's not your big problem right now." A low stool of enameled black wood appeared behind her, and she sat down.

"My train." Echo felt time pressure building, and the fog in the valley grew thicker.

"Sitting on your porch slows time so you can collect yourself. It also gives you rest and focus instead of amping up your stress and dividing your attention; it's the closest you'll get to sleep in Ytilaer."

Echo wondered what would happen if she just left the dragon woman here and went out to buy her ticket.

"Sit down." She spoke like Echo's favorite English teacher that time in tenth grade when the class troll asked the teacher how old she was.

"What am I looking for?"

"Nothing."

That seemed hard. Beyond the chasm and the tiny creek, now obscured by fog, rolled out a vast panorama of hills, low mountains, and snow-capped peaks marking the horizon like a bumpy bowl. "What do I see if I look for nothing?"

"A glimpse of what's there."

Echo worried whether she would catch her train. How would she get from the train station to the Capitol? How could she interview a state senator? What would she see in Cali's esuoh? Would she find the key? What would Jeph say if she found it? What would he say if she didn't? What would she do next?

The fog filled the valley, rolling in thick billows like white smoke, but without any smell.

The dragon woman let out a plume of sulfur-scented smoke. "If you can't look, then listen."

Echo put her focus on hearing. The fog dampened the sound, and there wasn't much to hear. But then it came to her, a high-pitched screech from somewhere far away. "What's that?"

"Good. There's an eagle's nest on the far side of the chasm."

Echo squinted, and the fog opened, allowing her to see a green hillside with a huge tree in the midst of it. Her attention brought it nearer, like binoculars.

"Watch the eagles coming and going."

She watched. She saw only one at first, flying away, following the shining silver river from high above, its huge wings rarely flapping at all, with a tweak of a wing feather adjusting its course. Its flight took it out of sight down the valley, and then it flew back, hovering on an updraft, its feathers glinting golden in the sunlight. It hung there like a mobile, in stillness like an airborne dance.

When it arrived at the nest, the eagle—the same, different one?—went out following in the other's path. "How many are there? Are they golden eagles? I don't see white heads."

The dragon woman sighed again. "Don't analyze. Watch."

"How long? I've got a train to catch."

"As long as it takes. You'll get there."

"Really?"

"Define 'real.'"

That stumped her.

"It's a question that can't be answered without a definition. Watch, and if there's time later, I'll explain."

Silence descended. Echo and the woman sat like two statues, and Echo forgot the train, the strange woman beside her, even herself. The eagle or eagles—she still hadn't seen more than one at a time—rose through the clouds on powerful wings, soared on the updrafts like kites, and dropped into obscurity again. The fog was still there, shifting clouds that dampened the noise and filtered the light and the landscape, and Echo felt that she was part of the picture, neither more nor less, and was content in the silence.

"I think we can go now." Theo stood, and her stool disappeared.

"What?" Echo felt she was waking from a nap. Her worry about catching the train rose and snagged her attention, but she decided there was nothing to do about it now but go and see how late she really was.

They went inside her esuoh, and out her window now was an animatronic jungle scene. The mannequins were gone. A man in a khaki suit behind the counter sold a ticket to a human-sized raven leading three macaws the size of human dwarves, chattering, squawking, and screeching at each other.

"Just the one?" The man typed in something on a keyboard.

"They're just seeing me off," the raven said with a girl's voice. A red, blue, and yellow macaw flew up to the counter and inspected the man's head. "We're just seeing her off," the macaw said in a teen-aged girl's voice. Another macaw flew around the station, blue and gold wings impossibly wide for the space, and yet soaring as if in a clear sky. The third, red like the one on the counter, hopped on the floor, pushing a lost penny with its beak.

"Is that real?" Echo asked the dragon woman.

"Define 'real,'" she said again.

"Is that what other people see?"

"It's probably not even what I see. Do you see any mannequins?"

"No."

"Let's step out, then. It's almost time." The dragon woman created a door and went through it, holding it for Echo to follow. "The mannequins are less real than what you see now. I see a ticket-seller in a tuxedo, and four lovely girls in 1920s' fashion paying their way to a show."

"I see a theme park jungle adventure, and there's a crow or raven with a bunch of parrots."

"They are real people, with their own dream of these events playing for them. Your dream means something, and so does theirs. The segam krad use the dreams and dreamers for their own purposes." She turned to Echo and captured her attention, locking her gaze with her dragon eyes. "Here's what I have learned. Every person you see out there, including the parrots, is on a journey. Seeing that journey doesn't make you more important or more valuable than the people who don't. It's a privilege, with responsibilities."

Echo's attention drifted. She was mentally navigating the jungle of the train station, with its land masses and water channels. A boat pulled up to the dock. "Is that my train?"

The dragon woman sighed again. "Go catch your train. If you want something in Ytilaer, you'll find it, but it's never without a price." She left Echo's esuoh and disappeared into the jungle.

Echo followed her out into the world, heading for the ticket booth.

Panic gripped Echo as she walked up to the counter to buy her ticket. She had spilled her bag all over the sidewalk. What if she lost the prepaid credit card? She couldn't cover the ticket from her bank account. Worse, what if she had missed the train? How would she explain that to Jeph?

She went into her esuoh to collect her wits and found the information Jeph had left on her short-term memory table. When she came back out into the world, she located the card in the side pocket of her bag where she kept her bus pass. She greeted the man at the ticket counter.

She jumped into the ticket agent's esuoh to look at herself. Her ugliness offended her, but she wanted to make sure she was acting normally. But her efforts to "act normal" made her a beat too long in responding. She stumbled over her words, and her smile seemed forced, because it was. She had to ask for directions twice because she wasn't paying attention the first time.

But all she heard in the man's esuoh was a whispered *This is an odd one*, which, all in all, could have been worse. She held her head high as she walked toward the massive wooden boat with the canvas top.

CHAPTER 15

Crossing Thresholds

G RAY STOPPED FOR A MINUTE OUTSIDE THE BANK, leaning against its rough stone wall, seeing spots and swirls and explosions flashing inside his closed eyelids. Reflexively, he tried to go into his esuoh, but he was in Oge, where your esuoh is available only in dreams. He tried to open his eyes, but every glimpse was so bright that it brought tears. What he did see was shiny and solid and chaotic.

Oge was a monster of blinding light. He had no place to run, no framework to understand, and no one to help or guide him.

Feeling like a failure, he took out the rorrim and crossed into Ytilaer again.

He was on a dusty track in a desert, standing next to a road full of rusted vehicles spinning up clouds of soft sand. It was good to be home.

He went into his esuoh and found it under construction with exposed two-by-fours and no furniture. He looked out the window and saw the same dust-impaired traffic.

None of this was helping him find Echo. Gray shook his head and put the rorrim back in his pocket and walked the half mile to Quig's office in the Portland Justice Center.

A MAN IN WIDE-LEGGED WHITE PANTS, blue and white striped shirt, and white cap—all the whites really only approximate—accepted Echo's ticket at the gangplank. "Watch your step." He handed back her ticket stub.

She stepped aboard carefully, feeling the boat rock gently on the dark water. She took a window seat on the side away from the station, looking out across the river into the jungle, where the trees interlaced their branches, promising revelation only to those with the courage to enter. As she watched, a man in a fat-bodied, round-headed African bird costume slid through the branches and stood on the red mud of the riverbank. His old man's knees and lower legs were bare except for cloth wrappings, and he rested one hand on a cane taller than his waist. While he stood there, a snake the size of a firehose glided down from the tree limbs toward his head. He turned in irritation and smacked it away, then faced Echo again.

She was still watching the costumed man when someone asked, "Is anyone sitting in this seat?" It was the raven she had seen in the station, over five feet tall and wearing Doc Martens boots, and speaking in a teenaged girl's voice.

"Uh, no." Echo moved her stuff and looked outside again. The costumed man was gone from the opposite riverbank. A canoe slid by two men paddling mightily against the current. Something huge rose from the depths of the water, broke the surface, and flowed downward again, its show ending with a flash of water at the end of a sharp and scaly tail.

The raven was beautiful, iridescent black, with a fringe of feathers on her black beak and a ruff of black plumage around her neck. The other passengers on the boat looked like theme-park tourists—men in cargo shorts with out-of-town T-shirts and women in sundresses with wide sunhats and bigger purses, leaning out over the water to shoot photos with their phones.

The raven perched on the seat like a human being, her feet swinging above the floor like a cartoon bird's. Echo was speechless.

"Where are you going?" the bird asked.

"Salem. You?"

"Same. Staying with my mom for the summer." The bird stretched her neck upwards and shook her feathers down.

"Not looking forward to it?"

"She's cool. A little *too* cool, if you catch my drift."

Echo shrugged. "Not really. My mother was a force of nature, but never cool. Not deliberately, not even by accident. On the other hand, I was never a raven." She shocked herself by saying that, but kept going. "My sister was a flamingo, so maybe she saw a different side of our mother."

The bird gave a hoarse squawk that might have been a laugh. It reminded Echo of all the times she had laughed at Gray's surprising observations. She thought he was clever; now she knew it was just what he saw. She also wondered what strange animal Gray thought she looked like.

"You don't get along with your mom?" the raven asked.

"My parents are dead. I live with my great-aunt, who is the opposite of cool. I like her."

"Sorry."

"It was a long time ago. If you're staying with your mom for the summer, where do you live the rest of the year?"

"With my dad in Portland. For school."

"Are you in college?"

"I wish." The bird gave a small squawk. "Not that I was in college, but that I was old enough they couldn't tell me what to do."

Echo sighed. "Adulthood is overrated."

The bird didn't answer, just looked around at the other passengers. The boat pushed off into the river and began chugging upstream. Thinking she had survived the introductory chatter, Echo went into her esuoh and sat down at her table to organize her memories.

"Why do you wear sunglasses inside?"

The words filtered in, and Echo had a sense that the raven had asked the question more than once. She went out into the world. "Sorry. I nodded off there." She touched the frames. "I'm blind."

The bird tilted her head to one side and then the other. "You don't carry a cane?"

What would Gray do in this spot? He never tried to pass for normal. He would just say, "I *see* everything." That wouldn't work for her. She had hoped for time to develop a story, but life hadn't accommodated her. "Legally blind. Super light-sensitive."

The bird looked at her steadily. "That's incredible."

"Isn't it?" Echo said, looking off over the water. She waited a space of time, then went back into her esuoh, where she was almost immediately interrupted.

"My name is Galynn." The bird looked down at her with closed eyes.

"Echo."

"Echo. That's an unusual name."

"My parents were classics professors. My older sister was named after a goddess, and I think they hoped I'd be quieter. Didn't work out that way, unfortunately."

The bird raised her head and settled her feathers. "What takes you to Salem?"

"I've got an interview, and then I'll come back this afternoon."

"Looking for a job?"

"No." Echo felt something like pride or a sense of accomplishment rise inside her. "It is my job."

"That's cool. Are you a vlogger or something?"

"It's an assignment for a web publication called Youth Now!" It still sounded preposterous.

"Lame name."

"I didn't name it. I'm just writing for it."

"That's what you meant when you said adulthood was overrated?"

"That and things like making rent."

Galynn said nothing for a while. Echo had the distinct impression that making rent would never be a worry for her.

"Who are you interviewing?"

"A state senator. Cali Zielinski." Echo assumed the name would be as unfamiliar to Galynn as it was to her.

"I've met her at one of my mother's parties."

She had assumed wrongly, of course. "What did you think of her?"

"I wouldn't want to cross her, but she's nice enough after her first drink. We didn't talk long. After meeting her, I had to go to my room and let my mother do her networking. Cali probably wouldn't remember me unless I told her who my mother is."

"Who is your mother?"

"She's an executive with the state development commission."

"Sounds boring."

"She likes it. She was bored working as my dad's office manager, until she found out he was bored with her, too. Then she went to a guy who taught her to have confidence and transform her life. Now she lives in Salem and throws parties for legislators and out-of-town businesspeople. She says she's happy."

Echo didn't know how to respond to that. She felt trauma behind the words, but didn't want to commiserate the apparent happiness of Galynn's mother. She didn't say anything.

"I thought you might recognize the guy who changed my mom's life." She waited.

Echo expected another clue but didn't get one. "Is he famous or something? Maybe Aunt Doris has heard of him. She likes to watch Oprah."

"So you haven't gotten your life transformed?"

That startled her. Yes, as a matter of fact, within the past couple of hours. Was Galynn talking about Jeph? Did she know something about him? About the world Echo was walking in? "What are you asking?"

"Nothing." She turned away and didn't look back.

Echo let out a deep breath, partly annoyed at the apparent rebuke, partly at the unsatisfactory end to the conversation. She went back into her esuoh.

She stood at her table glancing through her sketchbooks. She flipped through the older ones, starting with coffee with Gray yesterday, then focused on her work with Jeph.

The memories in the books were clear and strong, and she added notes to them, connections she made as she browsed through them.

She opened a door into Galynn's esuoh and looked out her window. Galynn was posting a photo of her friends in the station to her Instagram account. Echo checked the time on Galynn's phone and went back to her own esuoh and her table of memories. She needed to prepare for her appointment.

She skipped forward through the journals to review the note Jeph had left for her about her assignment. In handwriting with flamboyant capitals, Jeph's notes looked like a foreign language but still told what she needed to know. Cali Zielinski, State Senator, grew up in Ashland, graduated from Ashland High School in 1999. What influenced her to go into politics? How did Ashland schools help her get started? Does she remember anyone special from her time in Ashland? The last line, in thick, strong letters, read: "Get the key." She shoved the book onto the shelf.

She filed away the rest of the books, assailed by doubt that she could get the key from someone who could win political office. It seemed like a heroic quest, and in the face of it, she felt like a bumbling fool.

She went to her front porch and looked out over the chasm. The wind blew through her hair and an eagle flapped its wings and rose out of sight on its way up the valley. She made an Adirondack chair on her porch and sat looking out over the landscape, forgetting her journey, her job, and her annoying companion, until she felt a jarring thud. She went into her esuoh to see what caused it.

There she heard Galynn saying, "Hey! Are you asleep?"

She stepped back into the world, stretched and yawned. "I guess I was. Is our stop coming up?"

"Soon. I didn't want you to miss it."

"Thanks. I'm awake now." And she was. Awake and rested. And in a new reality. Gone was the jungle boat. Now they rode in a creaking wagon over a rugged dirt track, just emerging from forest into rolling farmland. The other passengers wore woolen cloaks with the hoods pulled up and held long staffs at the ready beside them.

Echo, too, found a wooden staff beside her. "Do you know where this came from?" she asked the girl—still a raven—beside her.

The bird pierced her with its closed eye. "What?"

"Sorry," Echo said. "Dreaming." She tried to ignore the staff, but it sat beside her, manifestly *hers*, and she would not leave it in the wagon, because it was magic. The knowledge of its magic came to her as a visceral truth, and she wondered only how to keep the staff without looking strange to the bird. Maybe the bird would go away soon and leave her to her new magical reality.

Chapter 16

Gray and His Mentors

Quig's assistant, Michelle, a gorgeous long-haired cat with luxuriant black fur, was at her desk reading a document and sharpening her deadly claws with a nail file.

She gave Gray a complacent smile as he entered the office. "Judge Burroughs is in conference. He'll be finished in a few minutes."

Gray sat down to wait, and it really was only a few minutes before Quig walked two leashed dogs out of his office: one a tiny fluffy thing walking with its tail held high; the other a big long-eared dog drooping at both head and tail. When he released their leashes, they nosed open the door and headed in different directions out in the hall.

Gray always saw Quig's office as an image of his esuoh—a throne of carved stone, tapestries of reason's triumph on the wall, and the beige filing cabinets that opened only to his touch. Today, Gray took in only a glimpse before he shut the door and opened his hand to reveal the rorrim he had concealed there. Shutting down the temptation to deliberate, he took a breath and crossed into Oge. He put the rorrim back into his pocket.

In Oge, Quig's office was blinding, not as bright as the outside, but still overwhelming. In the glare, he located a wooden desk and a chair in front of it. He felt for the chair, mostly missed it, and nearly fell.

Quig stood up in surprise, helped him sit down, turned off the overhead light, and closed the window blinds.

The light was dazzling, but it was better.

Quig reached for his phone and touched a button. "Michelle, would you cancel my lunch reservation and order in a couple of sandwiches? The usual for me—" He let loose the button, asked Gray, "You?"

Gray shook his head.

"Ham and cheese for Gray. Thanks."

They sat staring at each other for a while. In the midst of everything was Quig, the way most people saw him. His gray hair was thin and a little crazy on top; his wire-rimmed glasses magnified blue eyes wide with surprise.

Long pause. "Congratulations," Quig said.

Gray squinted at him. "For what?"

"You've actually left me speechless."

Gray wished he could go into his esuoh for a minute to collect his mind. There were so many *things* in this reality. What did they all mean? Why was a paperclip lying on the floor? What was the shape of the pile of papers in the trash container? What did it mean that the hairs on top of Quig's head stood up? "I surprised myself."

"So what brought about this decision?"

"I've lost Echo."

"Lost her? Where?" A note of urgency peaked on the first question, faded on the second.

"Going out the door of the US Bank building."

Quig leaned forward and set his elbows on his desk. "You don't *have* to tell this story, and you don't have to tell it now. But if you want to do it now, you need to come to the point faster."

"She's in Ytilaer and on her way out of town," he said. "Alone."

Quig's eyes scrunched and his lips tightened.

"Did I mention that she doesn't have anybody to help her?"

"I think you did," Quig said. "Start earlier in the story, but maybe not at the beginning."

"I tried to invite her into Ytilaer yesterday."

Quig's eyebrows seemed to gather for a conference in the middle of his forehead. "I knew you were planning to tell her about Ytilaer, but I didn't know it would be so soon."

Gray sighed, humiliated at the memory. "It didn't work out well."

Quig didn't answer. It was a running joke among his family and friends how much information he elicited by simply waiting for a question to be answered thoroughly before going on.

"She thought I was asking to marry her."

Quig's left cheek twitched almost imperceptibly, but he didn't laugh.

"She laughed at me, and I got up and left."

"From what I've seen, Echo is someone who tends to see the funny side of things. I think that's one thing you like about her."

Gray shrugged. "I like it better when I'm not the target."

"I can see that," Quig said. "And so—"

"And so after I left, apparently, an egam krad came and offered her a job."

"Egam krad." Quig's deadpan tone carried volumes of skepticism.

"Which you don't believe in." The congregation, or "pilgrimage," of Srelevart that Quig led tended toward a rational approach, with discussions of Jung, Adler, and Fordham and debates about the efficacy of lucid dreaming. Gray's earliest memories of an Ytilaer community were a circle of extended family, firelight glinting off Great-grandma's gold tooth as she told stories about Ytilaer from ancient times.

"So what makes this person egam krad?" Quig asked.

"Cain Timrod is involved somehow."

Quig's eyebrows went up. "I haven't heard that name in a long time."

"My father."

"Oh, you know about that."

"*You* know it?" Gray had thought this would be new information.

Quig shrugged. "Well, it came up when Dad was going through the adoption." He studied Gray's face. "I guess I should have told you sooner, but it's one of those things that it never seems to be the right time for. I thought Dad would tell you, but then he—" He stopped for a moment, the foster brothers united in their shared loss. Then, "So you found out the hard way. I'm sorry for that, but there's not really an easy way to learn your father was the man you saw attack your mother."

Gray sat with that for a moment, the truth of it putting his anger into perspective.

"But now Cain Timrod is exhibit one in your case that Echo is working for an egam krad." He held his chin in his hand and squinted over his glasses at Gray. "How does that work exactly?"

"He's working with the guy, Jeph Blackthorne, who brought Echo into Ytilaer without any training, and he told me Jeph is a bad guy."

"I've heard of him. Self-taught, doesn't respect the tradition, but—" Quig finished the sentence with a little half-shrug.

"Cain would know he's bad."

"Possibly." Quig shrugged. "But you believe him?"

Gray shivered. "No. But wouldn't he come up with a better lie? I mean, this one has so many twists and coincidences that it sounds like a Dickens plot. He said he and Jeph are working on some kind of project, and Jeph was looking for me, but found Echo instead. Brought her into Ytilaer and then sent her down to Salem on the train, without anyone to go with her or help her."

"Troubling, if true."

"She jumped into my esuoh without an invitation."

Quig's mouth tightened and his eyes narrowed. "That's disturbing. But it *is* Echo. You'd have invited her in anyway."

"Not the point." Gray felt that he was dashing his arguments against an impregnable fortress. "She gave me a *key*."

Quig sat back in his chair, then leaned forward. "May I see it?"

Gray fished it out of his pocket and held it up. In Oge, it was a simple business card.

Quig held out his hand. He looked at it closely, turned it over, and handed it back. "Looks like a business card."

"Echo knew it was a key."

"She had the full picture of what she was giving you?"

"How could she get the full picture of anything in a couple of hours in Jeph's office?"

Quig waited.

"*If* that's all the experience she's had. She called me in a dream last night. At least I think it was a dream—post-Ytilaer dream." He shook his head. "But keys, dreams, calling to someone? How could she learn all that in such a short time? It makes me wonder how well I know her."

"So you think she's been in Ytilaer before?" Quig asked. "Never told you about it?"

Gray shook his head. "This is Echo we're talking about. She can't keep a secret about a birthday present, much less a dark conspiracy." Fear clutched at his heart. "Theo said she might be a prodigy. Jeph saw it, and I didn't."

Quig seemed to weigh that possibility. Gray noticed a bronze lady holding a set of balance scales sitting on a shelf behind Quig's shoulder. When he finally spoke, he didn't answer Gray's question but asked another. "What do you know about the project?"

Gray tried to collect his memories. It was hard without going into his esuoh. "Cain said it was something about a guy Jeph knew in high school. He wouldn't tell me more unless I accepted his deal."

"What's his deal?"

"He wanted me to join the family business."

Quig looked at the card again. "Antiquities." He handed it back to Gray. "Egam krad."

Quig rolled his eyes. "Back to that again. Let's stipulate that I'm skeptical and go on with the story."

Gray pocketed the card. "Echo gave me the key and left. The key wouldn't let me follow her; it kept pulling me back to Cain. I had to go talk to him. He told me—" Gray shivered. "He told me who he is. Anyway, Jeph's assistant—no, partner—said Echo had gone to Salem to interview a state senator, and Cain told me Echo's in danger."

Quig stared toward the window for a moment. There were pictures of the room on his glasses, even Gray with his arms crossed over his chest and his hair as crazy in its way as Quig's was. Gray combed it back with his fingers, but it didn't help much.

"What do you want to do?" Quig asked, returning to his customary detachment.

"Can you send the police to arrest them?" Gray heard the panic in his voice but couldn't control it. "Bring Echo back?"

"You know I can't do that."

"Can't or won't?" *Panic, meet frustration.*

"What would you make me? I could be judge, jury, and executioner for everyone who walks into my courtroom. Then everyone who walks by me on the sidewalk. I can become the same monster he is."

"Echo could become that if we don't stop her."

Quig patted the air with the flat of his hands. "I still think Echo's innocence may protect her."

"They're teaching her the stra krad."

"The police can't go after them unless they break a law of Oge. Ytilaer has its own structure, more a pattern than a law. The enforcement is not external but internal. And it is relentless."

"So I'm just supposed to sit down and wait for it to work out?" Gray put a hand over his eyes.

"I never said that."

Now he looked at Quig again. "What can I do?"

"Your first idea, sending the police, will not work. Ytilaer is outside their jurisdiction. Again I ask, what do *you* propose?"

"They have to be stopped," Gray said.

"Maybe your heart is telling *you* to stop them."

"What?" The words made Gray's stomach turn over. "Me? I'm just—"

"You're just the man who cares enough to change the outcome. That makes you more qualified than anyone else."

"They called me a mouse."

"They would, wouldn't they? Especially if they were afraid of you. Especially if they should be afraid of you but don't know it yet."

"I don't have any power. I can't drive. I don't know how to find her."

"You could get help."

"The Srelevart?"

"That's one possibility. Go into your esuoh and see who's waiting."

Gray stared at him open-mouthed.

"It was your principle never to enter Oge. Is it now your principle never to leave?"

Gray had chafed against the rules of the Srelevart at times, but not crossing over had never been one of them. That was his rule.

Quig waved his hand in a circle. "It's OK. I'll wait."

Gray pulled his rorrim out and crossed back into Ytilaer. It felt like going home. Quig's office was more majestic than ever in its heavy medieval furniture and anachronistically weird filing cabinets. Quig looked more like a warrior king and less like a surprised high-school teacher. But Gray stopped looking around the room and went into his esuoh.

It had aged since the last time he was there, but was still unfinished. The wood framing was darker and had a coating of dust. There was still no furniture, only a ladder leaning against a wall. He checked the ancient door into his basement; it was firmly locked, and he left it that way.

Turning back, he found a knight in armor with rust around the edges. He was perched on the ladder with his head bowed and his visor down as if he were asleep or in deep thought.

Gray came out and found Quig waiting. "Did you do that?"

"Did I do what?" Quig asked. "You know I didn't."

"It was the Blue Knight."

Quig waited with a quizzical expression on his face.

"The detective who handled my mother's murder. I never saw him in Oge. In Ytilaer, I saw him as a knight in shining armor. It's not shining now, but it's the same armor, so it must be the same man."

"That's an interesting idea."

"I haven't seen him since I was eight. He's probably forgotten. After I got Cain acquitted, I couldn't face seeing the Blue Knight again."

"Well, which is it? Did he sit around being angry at an eight-year-old boy for eleven years or did he forget?"

"I don't know. I don't want to know."

"I don't blame you." Quig leaned back in his chair with his fingers laced over his chest. "I mean, Echo's just a girl, and she's working for an egam krad, so there's nothing you can do about it. You've got a job. You can go back to work and get on with your life. You certainly don't want to take the risk of talking to the man Ytilaer deposited in your esuoh as a recommendation."

"You're right. I have to call him. Maybe he can tell me something. Anything." The thought hit him. "How can I call him? I don't even know his name. If I call the police and ask for the Blue Knight, they won't be helpful at all."

"I *can* help with that." Quig caused an old-fashioned, fancy phone to appear on the arm of his throne. He dialed, holding the handset to his ear. He waited a space, then said, "Let me speak with Matt Wilkerson in the detective bureau. . . . Yes. Judge Quigley Burroughs. . . . Thanks."

He nodded at Gray.

"Matt, good to talk to you." He lounged in his throne. "I've got a personal favor to ask. I hope it's not too much trouble. . . . You know that homicide investigation about twelve years ago, when the victim's son was the witness? . . . It made the news when the kid blew up the trial by describing the attacker as a black monster when everyone in the courtroom could see that the defendant was white. . . . Yeah, that one. . . . My dad became the kid's legal guardian. . . . Yes, he was. But here's what I'm wondering. Gray, the kid—well, he's an adult now—would like to talk with the detective in that case. Seems they had a bond, and he'd like to explore a personal matter with him."

He leaned over and wrote something on a notepad. "Really. I'm sorry to hear that."

Gray froze in his seat. *What? Dead? Moved?*

"Well, do you have a phone number for him by any chance?"

Gray breathed again. *Not dead.*

"Sure, I'll wait."

He turned to Gray, his hand over the mouthpiece of the phone. "He's retired—" Then back to the conversation. "Yes, I'm still here." He wrote on the notepad again, muttering as the figures danced across the page. "Yes. This is exactly what he needs. Thanks so much." He hung up.

"His name is Travis Rankin." He read off a phone number, which Gray committed to memory. "He took early retirement because he had some sort of nervous breakdown, Matt said."

The bones of Gray's legs felt like they were made of jelly. "He may not want to talk about the case."

"That's true."

"It's all I've got." Gray now spoke more to himself than to Quig. "It's the next step." Gray got up to leave.

"Wait. I've got something for you." Quig opened a desk drawer. "Are you going to be traveling in Oge at all?"

Gray shrugged. "I guess so. It takes some getting used to."

"You'll need these." He held out a blue crystal.

Gray hesitated. Cain's key had made him suspicious of accepting anything, but this was Quig. His hand clasped what felt like a fragile cluster of plastic pieces.

"Why don't you cross back over and look at them."

Gray did and laughed when he found thick black sunglasses that wrapped around the side of his eyes.

Quig's eyes crinkled at the corners. "Don't tell the Srelevart."

"What?"

"That I sometimes go into Ytilaer during my lunch hour."

"You?"

"I go onto the front porch of my esuoh and think. The glasses hide my eyes."

"But I've been going around in Ytilaer for years. No one who matters is surprised that I've got my eyes closed."

"You might need them for the light. You ought to see an eye doctor after so many years in Ytilaer, but you're not going to listen to my advice about that. The sunglasses will make it easier to get around."

Gray slid them on his face. Instantly, the light was much more comfortable, and the pictures were gone from Quig's glasses. "Thanks."

"Don't wear them indoors. People think that's strange."

Gray laughed in spite of himself. "After all these years, I don't want anyone to think I'm strange." He got up to leave. "Thanks for the sandwich, but I think I'll get going."

"No problem," Quig said. "I'll find a home for it." He tore a sheet of paper off his notepad. "Take this. It might come in handy."

Gray stepped into the outer office and found Michelle typing something on a computer. She was, of course, not a cat, but a plump, dark-skinned woman between Quig and Gray in age. She looked up at Gray as he stepped out of Quig's office. Her eyebrows pushed close together, making lines between her eyes, and her nostrils were wide open. When she saw him, her face relaxed, and she went back to her work. "Nice shades," was all she said.

Gray sat on a bench in the first bus shelter he came to after leaving Quig's office. He spent a few seconds studying the interface of his phone; then, with a feeling like that of an Egyptologist reading a mummy's tomb, he cracked the code. He punched in the Blue Knight's phone number and—looked for an excuse not to press the call button. The distraction of people going by on the sidewalk, the noise of traffic, his disorientation in this world—any one of those would have been enough reason to procrastinate on any other afternoon, but not when he had seen Echo swirl into Ytilaer with no one to protect her. He touched the green button at the bottom of the screen.

After four rings, he got a recording saying that the voicemail box was full. He pulled up the number and pushed "send" again.

On the third ring of the fourth try, a scratchy male voice answered. "Yeah?"

Gray couldn't see who he was talking to. He should have expected that, but it caught him by surprise and left him feeling out of his depth. In Ytilaer, it took effort not to go into the other person's esuoh on a phone call. The flow of connectivity carried more than sound; it brought your energy into direct contact with the energy of the person you were talking to. Douglas, Gray's foster father, had spent many telephone calls with Gray between rooms in his home so that the boy could learn to stop outside the esuoh door, to be present with the person but not barge into the esuoh on the other end.

In Oge, the phone wasn't a magic portal. It was just a glass box with a disembodied voice and a frustrating feeling that Gray was missing important information.

"Travis Rankin?"

"Who wants to know?"

"Gray Birdsong. You handled my mother's murder in 2007."

"That's a long time and a lot of murders ago."

"I used to call you the Blue Knight."

"That kid." A flow of breath surfing the electromagnetic waves. "Let me guess. You've got new evidence or you want to sue me for screwing up the case."

"It's too late for new evidence, and I'm the one who screwed up the case. I want to talk to you about something else."

"So talk."

"In person."

Long pause. Gray looked at the phone to see if it was still connected. Finally the man said, "It's the maid's day off."

"I'm not interested in your housekeeping. A friend of mine is missing, and I want you to help me find her. I'll pay."

"I don't have a PI license."

"I just need you to drive me and maybe give me advice if I need it."

"It'll cost more than you think."

"I'm raiding my college fund."

Another exhalation, a wind that carried weariness, resignation, and despair. Then the address.

Gray found the stop for buses going to Travis's neighborhood in East Portland and got on the next one.

Chapter 17
Disaster

Riding the bus to East Portland, Gray sat in a side-facing seat looking around at the strange and exhausting world he had entered.

Everything was light-reflecting surface in this world, from the cars to the signs and sidewalks along the street to the bald forehead of the man sitting across from him. The light hurt Gray's eyes, and even shop windows showed only images of what was outside, not the truth of what was within.

Aside from the light, there were too many *things*. In Ytilaer, everything *meant* something. But Oge was a dizzying complexity. A boy running down the street with an iPhone in his hand. A man in a vibrant yellow vest directing traffic. A car slamming on its brakes at a stop sign. How could they fit together? And if they did fit together, how could anyone take it all in? It would be madness.

And the words! Conversations, signs, books, newspapers. Words, words, words. How did anyone know what they meant when they related to inconsequential, passing things? Outside in the street scene and inside the bus, the surfaces of everything were plastered with signs. Because of his "disability," Gray had been excused from learning to read. Echo had saved him by reading to him, starting in seventh grade, and he had talked with her through what she read, and the two of them passed their schooling well enough. He remembered learning the letters during his first couple of years of school. But the myriad shapes and combinations were like a desert windstorm.

Worst of all were the words in his head. *This is stupid. You shouldn't have left Ytilaer. You're not ready. You're losing your chance at a job. How do you know Echo wants you to find her? You should have at least waited to get off the bus before crossing over into Oge.* And on and on and on.

In the noise and confusion of Oge, he yearned to retreat to Ytilaer, even if just for a few minutes. To sit in the quiet of his esuoh, to find out how the construction was going, and to see who he was becoming.

"The rorrim is valuable," Douglas Burroughs had told him. "You can keep it, and I hope you use it, but when you do, choose a still and quiet place where you're alone."

The urge to go back to Ytilaer was like a hungry thing growling in his chest.

But the bus was not still or quiet, and he was not alone.

And then the bus stopped. Out the front window, a man in a bright yellow vest was holding up a stop sign, and the bus waited. After a moment, Gray felt that he had found external stillness even on the bus.

He perked up. Was this a gift from Oge? An invitation to go back to Ytilaer for a short visit? He was not "alone" alone, but he had dark sunglasses and no one paying any attention to him. In fact, if he did go into Ytilaer, he knew how to be more or less invisible to people looking at him. Wasn't that isolated enough?

The hungry thing leaped inside him. He saw his opportunity passing. He pulled out the rorrim and crossed over.

Home. Still unfinished. Frame walls he could walk through, bare boards on the floor. But it was quiet and there was an upturned bucket in the corner where he could sit and collect himself.

He wouldn't stay long. Just enough to calm the hunger for significance. Not so long that Echo would notice, if she were here.

But she wasn't here, and her absence made his esuoh seem dim and pathetic. It was time to go back, anyway.

He was crossing over when he felt the bus move. Just in time. He gripped the rorrim, and then the cataclysm happened. Screeching tires, a crash further back in the bus, squealing metal, flying glass.

He found his Oge vision just in time to see a glint of light as the rorrim flew from his fingers into the midst of screams and shouts, jostled bodies, and flying bags.

"Stay in your seats, please," came the voice from the driver's loud-speaker. "There's been a collision. Is anyone hurt?"

Answers from further back in the bus. The bus driver pressed some buttons on a box near his seat and went back to see. As soon as he passed, Gray got down on the floor trying to find the rorrim.

He saw something shiny and reached for it, but it was only a quarter, and another hand was grasping for it, too.

There were newspapers, candy wrappers, gum, a bus card, a book lying open face down. With growing panic, Gray searched.

The bus driver came back. "You need to get back in your seat."

Gray pulled his head out from under the seat across from where he'd been sitting. "I lost something."

The driver looked down at him from what seemed a great distance. "You can look later."

"But . . . ." He got up and sat down again.

The bus driver got off. The rest of the passengers gathered near the windows, watching. "What an idiot!" "Did you see that?" "He must have been going fifty." "Just plowed through the fucking red light." "Is he dead?"

Gray got on the floor again, crawling under other seats, until he came to a forest of legs. When he tried to push them aside, they lifted heavy feet and set them down again in the same place.

A female voice came at him through the crowd above. "Go fuck yourself."

He shimmied until he came to a thick pair of legs in shredded blue jeans. A woman looked down at him. "What the hell are you doing?"

"I lost something in the crash."

"What?"

"A   " What could he say? "A piece of jewelry."

"Get out of here, you pervert."

There was no place else to go. He slid out, looking everywhere as he went. *It's not just valuable. It's dangerous. You've really lost it this time. You'll never get another one. I hope you enjoy Oge because you'll never get out. Quig will throw you out of the house when he finds out.*

He sat down with his head in his hands. He had seen people like him on the bus before, clouds of black threads hovering around their heads like snakes. He hadn't known what it felt like, because he had been able to lose the snakes—the thoughts—by going into his esuoh or, if they were really bad, out onto his porch. But his rorrim was gone—*and you'll never have another one*—and his esuoh was empty—*how could you be so stupid?*—and the chance of finding it diminished with every passing moment.

The bus driver came back. "Would everyone take their seats, please? I'm going to hand out cards. Please write your contact information so we can get in touch with you. Sign the back if you're not injured." He went down the aisle handing out the cards, answering questions, adding to the mind-boggling sum of words in the world. Gray stared at the card for a few seconds, waiting for meaning to flow out of it, but nothing came—only letters in incomprehensible combinations, accusing him. *You can't read. You thought you were so smart, and you can't even read. What will you say? It's a miracle. They let me off the hook because I was disabled, but now I'm OK again. I was blind and saw everything; now I can see everything, and it all means nothing.* Gray put the card in his shirt pocket.

A siren sounded outside and an ambulance came. The side door of the bus opened, and people began to shuffle out.

"Once the injured are out—" the bus driver's voice came from the loud-speaker "—the rest of you can leave. The next bus should be here in about twenty minutes, and the tow truck should be here in about ten."

The injured from the bus stood outside with the emergency techs, gesturing and pointing to where it hurt. A crowd of firefighters surrounded the other vehicle, adding the discordant whine of saws to the overall din. Most of the other passengers picked up their stuff and left the bus, going to stand in small groups at the next bus stop.

At last only Gray and a young woman with a hoodie pulled over her eyes remained on the bus, crawling around, searching. "What did you lose?" she asked. "I'll give it to you if I find it."

Should he tell her? He took a risk. "A mirror, the size of a nickel."

He saw a glint of her eye from the depths of the hoodie. "That's strange. Is it valuable?"

"It was a gift from my dad. He's dead."

She went back to looking.

"How about you?" Gray asked. "What are you looking for?"

Teeth gleamed at him: a grin. "Whatever I can find."

Whatever she found, she didn't tell him, and Gray didn't find his rorrim. There were cracks it could have slid into, open windows it could have flown out of, and there had been laps and shoulders and shoes it could have landed on.

The driver came back onto the bus. "You'll need to leave now. The tow truck is here."

Gray went out to look where it might have flown outside, but the police shooed him off the street.

At the bus stop, men with clipboards collected cards from the passengers, listening intently and taking notes. The girl with the hoodie walked up the street toward the next bus stop, and Gray followed her.

They stood side by side outside the bus shelter.

"Did you find your mirror?" She spoke from deep inside her hoodie; only a fringe of hair and the curve of her nose were visible.

"No. Did you?"

There was a movement of her face, mostly hidden. "What was so special about a mirror?"

Did she have it? If he were in Ytilaer, he would *know*. But now he was in Oge, and he knew anyway. Without speaking a word, without seeing her face. But what could he do? Call the cops and have them search her? Knock her to the ground and search her himself? Tell her a lie? Tell her the truth?

She was small, and the sweatshirt hung from a thin frame. There was a restless and defiant energy about her. Maybe the rorrim had chosen her. Not that the rorrim has will, of course, as the Srelevart would point out, but in the old stories, things sometimes did. "It left me because I wasn't careful with it," he told her. "Or maybe I wasn't careful with it because it was time to go to you." He took a deep, shuddering breath. "I give it to you. It's yours now. If money is what you want, you can sell it. It's valuable." He tried to look into the depths of the hood. He thought he might see a glint of eye. "Don't use it. But when you do, be careful. Everything is real and everything matters. The way in is the way out."

The bus pulled up, nearly full from adding the other passengers from the wrecked bus.

He touched her arm as they were about to board. "If you need help, google 'weird mirror.' Go to the very last search result. It's a crummy-looking website. There's contact information."

He saw it this time—the hood revealed her face for a fraction of a second—a smile of dismissal, derision even. She took a seat at the far rear, and Gray took a seat in the side-facing area near the front. She sat with the hoodie pulled down, looking at her lap. Sleeping? Playing with the rorrim? She might have crossed over already for all he could tell, or she could be counting her fingernails.

Gray looked out at the multiplicity and wondered what Ytilaer had in store for him now that he could no longer see it.

CHAPTER 18

The Chosen One?

THE WAGON CAME TO A SQUEAKING, JOSTLING STOP on the rutted road, and Echo followed the raven down the aisle of the wagon. Uncertain about the exit, Echo hopped into Galynn's head to see the train, the conductor in his uniform, the steps from the train down to the sidewalk.

Once on solid ground, she left Galynn's esuoh. The bird was giving her a sharp look, a very sharp look, even with her bird-eyes closed. *Does she know? How could she know?* A wordless prompting served up Marlo's stern face and the nondisclosure agreement, as well as Jeph's confidence that she would keep his secret. Whatever all that meant, it was probably just as well that she and the girl raven had arrived at their destination and would be parting ways now.

Echo turned away and leaned on her staff, which had acquired a glowing stone at the top. *Nice. Maybe I am the chosen one.*

People were already pushing Echo aside to board the wagon as it prepared to depart on its journey south. Echo let Galynn slip into the crowd and concentrated on the landscape as she followed the departing passengers away from the wagon.

The ramshackle buildings of a decrepit city surrounded a gray-stone castle on the hill, with a gold figure on the top. A maze of narrow streets and footpaths zigzagged up the hill toward the castle. She and Gray had visited the Capitol on a school field trip in seventh grade. In the ordinary world, the gold figure perched on top was a pioneer, facing the front of the Capitol, head turned toward the northwest. Now the figure was a woman with a child on her back, in a flowing robe with wide sleeves, standing atop the highest tower of the castle, pointing toward the southwest.

Echo stared at it for a moment. Everything was different in this reality, but that detail about the statue, the direction she was pointing, felt like a prophecy, even from this distance.

I may as well find out. She set out walking in a straight line for the imposing stone building on the hill. A dog howled and a hawk screeched.

"Are you crazy?"

Echo felt a hand on her arm and turned to find Galynn beside her, her wing extended.

"You'll get yourself killed. I'll walk you over there."

Echo hopped into Galynn's esuoh again and got a glimpse of the parking lot, the car sitting with its bumper just inches from her legs and the driver fuming, other cars barreling past on the street, the irregular intersection with its complicated walk lights. She hopped out again, her heart pounding. "I guess it's harder than it looked. Yes. Thanks."

Galynn didn't look at her, just started flying. Echo hurried to follow.

THE PATH LED THROUGH A MAZE OF ARBITRARY RIGHT ANGLES among stone buildings with sagging rooflines and eccentric architecture. Echo followed the bird until they entered the castle walls and she landed in the building's cavernous entryway.

"You're going to see Cali Zielinski?" the bird asked.

Echo still felt like the heroine of an epic fantasy, and *I need to speak to the Wise Woman of Shalom* was the first thing that came to mind. But it wasn't what someone in the ordinary world would understand. "Yes. I've got this now. Thanks for your help." Echo turned and began walking toward a stairway up to the Queen's Council Chamber.

The raven landed in front of her. "That's the wrong direction. The senate offices are up that stairway."

"Oh." The glowing stone on Echo's staff had become a round, gray river rock. "Fine. Lead the way."

The raven hopped, with Echo following, down a long stone hallway with a series of doors on one side.

A woman in a shimmering robe of peacock colors stepped out of the first chamber. "Can I help you?"

Echo opened her mouth to speak, but the bird answered for her. "We've got an appointment to see Senator Cali Zielinski. Do you know where her office is?"

We? When did Echo and Galynn become "we"?

The woman pointed, awesome in her shimmering colors. "Right down this hallway. Second from the last on your right."

The second chamber from the end had a young man dressed like a Shakespearean page sitting at a table outside the closed office door.

The raven landed. "I'm Galynn Powell, and this is Echo—" Galynn looked over at Echo, prompting her.

"Shearwater."

"Senator Zielinski is expecting us."

THE RAVEN AND THE FOOL who might be the chosen one followed the page into the presence of the Wise Woman of Shalom, beautiful in power and authority and appearing to be about seven feet tall. She wore a long, black woolen robe and a wide-brimmed hat and stood on a dais behind a low table bearing implements of alchemy—a mortar and pestle, a small burner, glasses and bottles in strange shapes and sizes, metal spoons and stirrers, and a large open book, handwritten in brown ink with colorful decorative sketches on one visible page. In her left hand, she pointed a sword at Echo and Galynn as her assistant escorted them into her chamber.

"These are the two reporters from Youth Now," the assistant said.

"Two?" Her voice was imperious but not threatening; perhaps she was letting the sword speak for her.

He shrugged.

She looked them over, then nodded at him. He left the room. She slid the sword into a scabbard hanging on the wall behind her. "I was told *one* reporter."

"I brought my friend—uh, assistant—" Echo felt a burning glare from the raven's closed eye and dove into her bag of words, coming up with one she got from Cain. "Associate."

"Have a seat." The senator gestured toward a couple of stools in front of her. Galynn perched on one; Echo on the other.

Echo stared at the woman; then, realizing her mouth was open, she closed it, then opened it again because she was expected to speak. Nothing came out. Jeph's jotted description had conveyed a downstate politician with a knack for speaking the language of bureaucracy. But this woman had majesty, power, and a sense of mission. Echo couldn't remember the questions she had prepared, and all she could think about was the puzzle Jeph had given her: *Where is the key to Lazar?*

Galynn was glaring at Echo with her closed raven's eye. Finally, she turned to the senator and asked, "Tell us about your educational initiative."

It was like pressing the "speak" button on a talking doll. "Yes. Oregon ranks—"

Echo left Galynn with the details and went into the woman's esuoh, a grand blend of medieval and modern, like an updated Italian palace. A book hovered next to a bookshelf, and its pages turned by themselves, phrases rising from the sheets and each joining the others like a train moving on invisible tracks through the air. Echo couldn't understand any of it. There was no energy of a key about it. She needed to derail the conversation.

She jumped into her own esuoh and looked at the notes Jeph had left for her. She went to her window and looked out at the impressive woman, with her theatrical speaker's gestures, and interrupted the flow. "When did you first become interested in politics?"

Echo went back into the senator's esuoh and found the train of words falling into piles of letters on the floor and dispersing. She began to recount her childhood. This was better. Echo saw Cali's father, an attorney; her mother, a member of the Ashland school board. And then another book from the shelf opened, and the train started running again: Public service was a family tradition, and she believed blah, blah, blah.

Echo heard a buzzing noise from the mezzanine that wrapped around the upper level of the room and went up to find it. The sound came from a side door that opened into a curving hallway with many doors, one of which vibrated like the muffled ringing of an old-fashioned telephone. She opened it and found two children, fifth or sixth grade, maybe, sitting next to a creek arguing in a lazy, friendly way.

Then Echo was in Cali's experience, sitting beside the boy who was Jeph, his face rounder than the adult Jeph's, but his eyes the same piercing blue. He picked up a rock and tried to skip it over the face of the water. It bounced once and then sank like a stone. Cali laughed and picked up a nice flat stone and side-armed it across the water. It skipped six times, and she felt pleased at its track along the creek.

Jeph picked up another and threw it for maximum splash. "My dad says politicians are all owned by people with money, so it's money that runs the world." Echo felt Cali's rage at the insult, as a blow against her clan of sacrifice, history, and investment. Cali threw a handful of water at Jeph's face. "My dad says your dad knows the price of everything and the value of nothing." She got up and stalked off, leaving Echo outside the door.

Echo ran down the stairs to look outside the senator's window. Galynn, a black-haired girl with a nose stud, wearing black clothing and, yes, Doc Martens boots, glanced at Echo, staring off into space. "She's autistic," Galynn said. "That's why I have to help her. What are your long-term plans for public office?"

Echo had dropped the conversation. How could she do this? How could *anyone* do this?

She needed a question that would lead to Lazar. Jeph said they knew Lazar in high school. She opened a door out of Cali's esuoh and stepped out into her own point of view. The magician was leaning against her table, explaining that people were asking her to run for governor, but she thought that was premature. Again, it all seemed canned and didn't get her any closer to the key. Echo interrupted again. "How would you say your experience in Ashland High School helped prepare you for your career?"

Cali blinked twice, then said that losing an important election as a high-school senior something, something, something. Echo made a door into Cali's esuoh and felt a buzzing from upstairs again.

This time, behind the vibrating door was a hallway with the reverberating ambience and musty smell of an empty school. Cali and Jeph, older teens now, looking like stars of a 1990s *Grease* remake, stood nose to nose gazing furiously at each other.

Echo, as Cali, felt anger and betrayal. She had come back from a trip with her dad, and Jeph was different. Taller for one thing, but not the important thing. "You knew I wanted to be student body president since grade school. You never cared about it. Now you're buying votes to take it away from me?"

"Your dad always called me a slacker." Jeph spoke with quiet rage, his eyes narrowed, and his mouth tight and rigid. She didn't understand it; last year he was proud that he could get away with being a slacker. "But when I come back to school and want to make something of my life, you don't like it. Maybe you like slackers?" An innuendo in the last two words revealed the whole mystery.

"Wait. You're still mad—and you would take away my goal—because I talked to that new guy?"

Echo felt a punch on her shoulder that ejected her from the scene. *What?* She left Cali's esuoh again and found Galynn glaring at her. But she needed to understand what she just learned. *Jeph. Something about Jeph. And the new guy. Could that be Lazar?* "What about friends?" she asked. "Did they support you in your journey?"

She concentrated on the corridor of memories upstairs in Cali's esuoh and opened a door into it.

"What are you doing?" Cali's voice was far away, but angry, like an altercation outside her esuoh.

Echo didn't have the time or skill to deal with that. And another door was buzzing.

She opened it into a school bathroom.

Cali's reflection in the mirror revealed a stunning beauty, despite the floofy blonde hair and the floofy blue prom dress held up by one shoulder strap.

Another girl in a lollipop-pink dress with sleeves that poofed out like water wings came out of a toilet stall and shrieked at her. "God, Cali! Awkward! Did Jeph tell you he was going to ditch his date for you? Ashley left *crying*!"

"I didn't come with Jeph. I can't help his behavior." Cali kept her voice cool, serene, sophisticated, to hide the growing dread that Jeph was not finished with her. She left the bathroom, striding toward the table where she had left her date, Lazar. She could see him from across the room. Brown hair, soulful eyes. She wouldn't admit it to anyone, but his low, scratchy voice, like black coffee, and his shade of a Russian accent made her heart beat faster just to think about it. She imagined taking his hand, telling him she wanted some air, and they would kiss under the moonlight, and the musky smell of his skin would intoxicate her. She was smiling at him as she walked, but he wasn't looking her way. She rounded a cluster of dancers and saw Jeph sitting at their table.

The chill grew colder, and she walked a little faster.

"Cali!" Jeph's voice portrayed friendliness, but she didn't believe him. "I brought you and my friend Lazar a couple of Cokes. No hard feelings, right?"

He reached over and shook Lazar's hand. Lazar responded limply, with a faint, confused smile on his face.

"My friend doesn't seem to feel too well. How about if I give you two a ride home?"

"I think I'll call my dad."

"Have it your way. I found a flask of vodka in his pocket. I threw it away for him. I'd hate for him to get into trouble. But you don't want your dad to know his condition, right?"

"Are you kidding me? Lazar doesn't drink."

"Well, you are beautiful and a powerhouse. Maybe he just thought it made sense not to tell you. I don't know." He shrugged. "Russians."

"Shut up, Jeph. Just shut up." Cali's mind was racing. Her dad. How well did she know Lazar? How well would she ever get to know him if her dad thought he got drunk at the prom?

"Just a friendly offer." Jeph got up, took his tux jacket off the back of the chair.

"Yes. Thanks." A fear crept in. "But take me home first, then Lazar. I'll give you his address."

"As you wish."

They lifted Lazar by opposite shoulders and maneuvered him out of the prom. Lazar's arm was heavy across Cali's shoulders. She did not smell alcohol on him.

Echo hopped back into Galynn's esuoh so she could see Cali as the downstate politician. Her face was red, and she was near tears. Cali must be experiencing these memories as Echo did.

Galynn asked her something about her legislative platform, and Cali pulled herself together as she talked about job training for students not bound for college.

Echo looked out at the clock behind the senator's desk. The half hour they had been granted was almost up, and Echo still had no idea where to look for Lazar's key. Opening doors might give a hint if she had hours or days to look, but really she had time for just one more question. It had to be the right one.

She went into Cali's esuoh again, whispered into the room, "What do you know about Lazar Kyrillovich?"

Cali rose in rage from her chair as a buzzing sound became perceptible.

Echo searched Cali's front room for the key. The buzzing item was a set of car keys about to vibrate themselves onto the floor.

When she touched the Oregon Shakespeare Festival keyring, she found herself in a room that dripped with disappointment and despair, from the barely serviceable furniture to the scratches and scars that marred the walls and the lintels of the doorway. On the other side of a shield of Plexiglas, scratched and scorched in places but still an impenetrable barrier, sat Lazar, wearing a shirt with horizontal black and white stripes. It had been only a couple of weeks since the prom, but he looked older and sadder, and an expression of confused submission hovered around his closed eyes.

Cali picked up the phone, and Lazar did the same. He didn't say anything, just sat there waiting, listening.

"Is it true?"

He gave a hopeless shrug. "I don't know. I don't remember."

"I never thought you—"

"I don't know who I am now. I fell asleep, and now I'm in a dream that doesn't end."

"Tell me you didn't do it."

"I don't know that. I don't even know myself. You need to go away now."

"I'll wait for you."

"No. You will do great things, and I will be here a long time, they say. I don't know."

"I'll send my father to help you."

"No one can help me."

"He'll try. I'll make him."

"Get out! Get out!" The shrieking voice came like a siren just outside the door. "I'm not falling for your ambush video. Get out!" Lazar sat there staring sadly at Cali as if he didn't hear anything. Echo felt her arm being pulled and then was in her own esuoh, as if the pulling had brought her there.

A voice came to her, not the shriek, but soft and hoarse and next to her ear. "We need to get out of here, or we'll both be talking to the police."

Echo was confused by the overlap of the worlds, but the jailhouse was fading, and the reality of the raven helping her find Lazar grew stronger. She got up from the chair, grabbed her bag just before she was forced to leave it behind, and walked behind the raven out of the office.

She had found a key, but it was not the one Jeph was looking for.

Chapter 19

The Rusty Blue Knight

When the bus driver called out the stop, Gray froze for a moment in his seat. He glanced back toward the girl, but she was gone. He said a silent goodbye to the rorrim and left the bus.

A cloud rolled across the sky, blocking the sun. It eased the strain on Gray's eyes and cooled the air. Was it an omen? Did weather *mean* something in Oge or was it just physical processes, as some of the Srelevart said? All around were streets, houses, trees, cars. Nothing spoke to him about where the Blue Knight lived. He started walking in a random direction, and a woman came his way, led by a tiny dog.

He asked her where to find the address.

"Back where you came from. It's the gravel street. That house would be on your left. I'm not sure of the numbers, but it's probably the one next to the intersection."

He went back. The house numbers were attached to a tall board fence and half hidden behind the branches of a tree with purple flowers. The gate, disguised to look like part of the fence, opened with a creak once he found the latch, and he slid inside and latched it behind him.

There was a sign on the lawn and another on the door. He didn't understand the words, but something in their shape and design said, *Go away.* Big straggly bushes embraced the house, and the weedy lawn was unkempt but not out of control. Gray put his sunglasses into his pocket and knocked, but nothing happened. The SUV in the driveway said nothing about who or what was in the house. He knocked again.

Now he heard movement inside, something falling. He knocked once more.

Cursing, more things falling, and the door swung open to an old man with watery blue eyes and a ragged growth of beard. "I never thought I'd see you again."

Gray stared at him, searching for the police detective at the scene of his mother's death. He had been a knight in armor, fighting evil and righting wrongs. "Are you the Blue Knight?"

"I was never who you thought I was, but—" He kicked a garbage bag aside so that he could open the door and waved vaguely toward a couple of kitchen chairs piled with books and papers. Then he headed out of the room, saying, "Take one of those chairs," as he went.

Gray went to the chair with the smaller pile, turned around looking for a place to put the unstable mountain of papers, and finally put it on the floor under the chair. He sat down.

The only light in the room came through half-closed blinds on a shaded window. All the other windows had curtains and shades drawn. Horizontal surfaces in the room held stacks of books and piles of paper like the one he had removed from the chair. The sofa next to the front window had a dirty blanket on it, and the low table in front of it held beer cans—tumbled together in a cascade that fell off the table and onto the floor—along with more paper and several yellow writing pads, all partially used. On the far wall, a bulletin board held a U.S. map with pushpins scattered across it and squares of paper arrayed around it.

The man came back carrying a beer. "You want one?"

Gray shook his head.

Travis sat on the sofa, swiped the empty cans into a garbage bag he pulled from under the table, and set the beer down. "So. You're awake."

"I wasn't sleeping—"

"I know. You always said you could see everything. What do you see now that you have your eyes open?"

"Less—and more. I just came into Oge—" *No.* He had to use Oge language. "Opened my eyes today."

"And I'm your first stop? I'm flattered."

What had Gray expected? He wanted to go into this man's esuoh, to learn more about him. He had seemed so big before, but Gray had been smaller, up until this very morning. Gray had found the Blue Knight in his esuoh with his head in his hands, showing nothing but his rusty armor.

All this was the man's armor. The fence, the bushes, the darkened windows, the clutter. Heat flowed through Gray from his feet to his face. He had invaded this man's inner space without permission. "May I come into your house?" He spoke more out of habit than rationally, but it felt right.

Travis set his beer down and looked at him with curiosity, then gave a laugh that turned into a cough. "Well, you're here now, right?"

Gray waited.

Travis rolled his eyes and shook his head. "Yes. You may come into my house. You may also have a beer."

Gray got up and walked around the room. When he came to the bulletin board on the far wall, Travis said to him, "Don't touch that."

He had found the center, the Oge version of the man's memory storage. He stood back and examined the board with its map and notes. It included a close-in photo of Cain's face, staring steadily at the camera, younger than now, but with the same icily imperious gaze. In the lower right-hand corner of the photo was a seven-point star with the words "Multnomah County Sheriff" in a circle inside it. "What is this?"

Travis got up heavily and walked over, bringing his beer. "It's a little research project of mine."

"You've got a picture of my father here."

"Oh, you found out about that, did you?"

"You knew, too? Why did everybody keep that secret from me?"

Travis held up both hands, palms toward him. "The social worker thought you would be better off not knowing."

How would it have changed his life to know that the man who killed his mother was his own father? Gray sighed. "Maybe. But I know now. Why is he here?"

Travis looked Gray up and down and set the beer down on a black desk with a black computer lurking in the shadows. "OK. The mystery of your mother's case for me wasn't who but how."

Gray tried to bring back the scene of his mother's death in his mind, using the adult words and concepts he hadn't known then. Cain wanted his mother's rorrim, but Gray had taken it under the bed and crossed over. She told Cain to leave. They struggled. She died. "How did she die?"

"That's my question. There was no obvious cause of death, and believe me, they looked. The autopsy gave no explanation."

A scrap of memory fluttered through Gray's mind, and he wished he could go into his esuoh to examine it. A circle of children and adults illumined by firelight. Campfire? Fireplace? He remembered the reddish light and the dancing flames. His mother held him, and the old lady with the firelight glinting off her gold tooth said, "He stole her soul!" in a scary voice. The rest of the kids said, "Ooooo!" and Gray's mother's arms tightened around him. The old woman winked at him and went on with the story.

Gray shook his head. There were other fantastic stories. A bear changed into a man, or a lost girl worked for a mysterious old woman for a hundred years that passed in the blink of an eye. Douglas and the other Srelevart had taught Gray to analyze the old stories in the context of Ytilaer, to find psychic processes and solutions to Oge problems.

Travis was watching him. "Did you remember something else?"

"No," Gray said. "Just an old story my mom's grandmother used to tell."

Travis shrugged and moved on to a group of papers. He flipped through them—they seemed to be small news items printed from the web. "Over the past few weeks, there's been a spate of deaths in Portland with no identifiable cause, even on autopsy. One or two or a handful every night."

Gray turned to stare at him. "Who are the victims?"

"Mostly homeless. They die in their sleep. Nobody cares enough to follow up." He picked up his beer and went over to sit on the sofa. "But tell me how you want me to help you."

Gray looked over the bulletin board one last time, wishing he could take a picture of it and store it in his esuoh. Then he followed Travis across the room and sat on the chair he had cleared before. "I have a friend, Echo, who's gone missing. I want you to help me find her."

"When did you last see her?"

"About noon. She was on her way to Salem to meet a state senator—"

"That *does* sound dangerous." An ironic smile touched Travis's mouth and then flitted away. "Did she tell you when she planned to be back?"

"This afternoon," Gray said, keenly aware of how insignificant it sounded.

"So she's not actually missing." Travis sat back on the sofa and crossed his ankle over his knee. "Did you two have a fight or anything?"

Gray felt his face flare red. *I was angry that she came into my esuoh without an invitation, but she didn't even notice it.* He remembered the little dance step she did telling him about her job. He sighed. "No. She was happy to be working."

Travis put his foot on the floor and leaned forward with his forearms on his knees. "So she was happy to be leaving. She went to Salem, which is not exactly Mogadishu. And she said she'd be back today."

"She *said* she would see me tomorrow morning, but that might be too late."

"Too late for what?"

"She's in danger." Gray felt his neck muscles tightening and his voice rising in pitch. He took a deep breath and willed himself to speak carefully. "Cain—" He forced himself to reiterate, "my father," as if it was a mark of shame he needed to embrace. "Cain and a guy named Jeph Blackthorne are working together on some kind of 'project,' and Echo has gone to work for them."

"A project," Travis said, his voice even, the question in the word more than the tone.

"They're looking for a man Jeph knew in high school. But why aren't they looking for it themselves?"

Travis nodded. "That's a question." Nevertheless, he shrugged. "But what's the danger?"

Gray struggled with the straitjacket of Oge explanations. "You remember when I was a kid, what I said Cain looked like?"

Travis nodded. "Unfortunately, yes. The judge and jury didn't exactly see him the same way."

Gray felt his face flush red. "I know. I know. But listen. He was *really* a monster—and still is. I just saw him yesterday and today. I saw the cowboy outfit with the red boots, but that's just a mask—he manipulates other people's perception of reality. Underneath, he's the same." *And underneath that, he's not flat black but shades of slate and charcoal.* Gray held his breath, wondering if this man, his designated savior, would even hear him out.

"OK," Travis said. "Bear with me on this. You're wandering into the deep weeds here, and I'm trying to follow. You say your friend is in danger because she's working for somebody your father knows, and your father looks like a monster to you."

"That monster is *who he is*!" Now Gray really was shouting. "And Jeph—even Jeph's partner—and even Cain—say Jeph's a bad guy."

Travis leaned back on the sofa and crossed his arms across his abdomen.

Gray took a deep breath, reminded himself of who he was talking to, and tried again in a more even tone. "I know it's hard to understand and harder to believe—but these people are clever and ruthless and use Ytilaer to deceive and manipulate people."

Travis wiped his face with his hands. "OK. Let's come at this from another direction. Did she go of her own free will? Not kidnapped or anything?"

"She didn't understand." Tears of frustration beat against Gray's eyelids. "And now she's in Ytilaer, and getting hit by a car or something is kind of the least bad thing that could happen to her."

"I have to ask this. Is your friend—Echo?—real? Like what we're doing right now?"

Gray shook his head and started for the door. "I knew this wouldn't work."

Travis rose and followed him to the door. "I'm not saying I won't help. I'm asking a question. And you don't have to answer, but if you choose not to answer, it's an answer."

"Yes!" Gray shouted. "Yes, she exists in both worlds. Just as you exist in both worlds, as a man in rusty armor."

Travis gave Gray a cold stare.

"I'm sorry. I shouldn't have said that. I understand why you can't help me. It's too hard for people in Oge to understand."

"Sit down. I didn't say I wouldn't help you."

Gray thought about it, weighed the options—his dignity or Echo. He had already made his choice. He sat down.

Travis went back to the sofa. "Now, how did Echo get involved with Cain and Jeph?"

"Cain thought I could help with their project, but Jeph got to me first and found me with Echo. I left the coffee shop, and Echo stayed behind. And if you could see her in the other world—she's as bright as the sun."

"And that means—?"

"She's like the three-year-old who sits down and plays Mozart by ear."

"A prodigy."

"Yeah. Quig and the others said that's why she should wait until she's an adult to find out about Ytilaer—the other way of looking at the world. Because she'll be powerful and needs maturity to use it right."

"So Jeph found Echo—"

"He offered her a job, crossed her over into Ytilaer, and sent her out into the world alone."

Travis looked thoughtful, then nodded. "Your story is utterly preposterous. But I may not have to believe it to help. What do you want from me?"

"I don't drive. Just take me to her, and help me talk to her."

Travis moved his head from side to side. "I'm not a licensed private investigator."

Gray shrugged. "I don't know what difference that makes. All I need is a ride to Salem."

Travis nodded at that. "What happens if we find her and she doesn't want to talk to you?"

Gray tried not to take in that possibility too deeply. "We come back and let her be. I'll pay what I owe you and try to get my job back."

"Let's see if you're serious. Five hundred dollars for a retainer, then two hundred a day plus expenses."

"Let's go to the bank and get started." Gray started walking for the door.

"OK, OK. I believe you mean it. But we'll go tomorrow. I don't want to make the trip and then have her show up at home today after we leave."

"But we may lose her. It may be too late."

"We won't lose her, but, as I said, I'm not going today. If you have to leave now, you'll need to find someone else." He ripped the corner off a newspaper and searched the debris on the coffee table until he came up with a pen. "Here's my number. Call me if you don't need me. Otherwise, bring the money, and I'll start tomorrow morning. Not too early."

The numbers on the slip of paper were large and a little shaky against a backdrop of unintelligible details. Like Oge in one picture. Gray put the paper into his pocket. He didn't bother to remind Travis he had the number already.

Travis walked him to the door.

CHAPTER 20

A Bend in the Road

ECHO STOOD IN THE COURTYARD OF THE GREAT CASTLE, while Galynn perched in one of the ancient oaks nearby.

Echo still held her staff with the river stone embedded in the top, still wore her rough wizarding robe, still saw the Capitol as a castle on a hill. She knew two things that were as real as true could be. She didn't get the key, and she didn't want to tell Jeph about it.

But there was no getting around it. She pulled her phone out of her bag and found a small, shiny box with no opening. She turned it this way and that. Gray always used voice commands—Echo had helped him set them up—but she had never set hers. She looked away from the phone, using muscle memory to find the button. She pressed it and said, "Call Jeph." All she got was a boop tone and nothing.

Wait. She had never called Jeph, so her phone didn't have his number. She reached deep into her bag, thinking of Jeph's key, and felt the business card. Pulling out the small handcuffs, she walked over to the raven under the oak tree. "I'm having trouble with my voice commands. Would you dial this number?"

The raven took the handcuffs in her wing and looked at it, then turned a tilted head toward Echo. She turned over the handcuffs and stared at the other side of the card—too long. What would make the card so interesting? Jeph's face, of course.

Could Galynn know him? The possibilities were sliding into place—asking whether Echo's life had been transformed, the way she looked at the card. If she was working for Jeph, wouldn't she know the mission? And if Jeph thought Echo needed help, wouldn't he tell her—or just send Galynn instead of her?

Echo held out her hand for the card. "I'll find someone else."

The bird gave a long *caw*. "Give me the phone." She used a wing feather to dial the number and handed the phone and the handcuffs back to Echo.

There was no time to ask about Galynn and Jeph, because the connection was complete and Echo was inside Meghan's esuoh. The room was full of Meghan saying, "Jeph Blackthorne, Success Transformation, Reputation Management. How may I help you?"

Echo answered that she was calling for Jeph, then opened a door and left Meghan's esuoh to wait outside in the courtyard.

"Echo!" Jeph's voice came from inside her esuoh. "We were just talking about you. What's the news?"

She went into her wagon and found him sitting on her bench with an arm flung along its back. His position invited her to sit beside him, but she was afraid of his disappointment. She made a chair and sat on it. "It's been quite an adventure."

There was a long silence, with Jeph sitting in perfect stillness and the smile frozen on his face.

She began to wonder if there was a glitch in the phone signal. "Are you there?"

Jeph's voice was as cold as his frozen face. "I'm waiting for the answer."

"How did you get into my esuoh?"

A frosty look crossed his face. "It's all electricity." He took his arm off the back of the bench and sat with his elbows on his knees, piercing her with his gaze.

She dove into what she had to tell. "I had a hard time keeping the conversation going while I searched for the key."

There was a deep, dissonant hum to the silence.

"I ran out of time and couldn't explore her upstairs."

The hum rose in intensity.

Echo got to the point. "There wasn't any key."

"There what?" Through her window she saw lightning strike the tree she was standing under. It left her staff a smoking ruin and broke its stone into several chunks of river rock. Her clothing changed to the ragged garb she had worn from the time of the game. "I depended on you. I taught you everything you needed to know."

"You didn't prepare me for how hard it would be, and I'm doing better than expected."

That snagged him. "Who expected?"

"Anyone." She didn't want him to know she had help. "Better than anyone could have expected."

"Fine. Just come back to Portland. I'll come up with Plan B."

"No. Listen. There was no key. I found one that took me to the last time she saw him, and there's no connection now. But I got a lead."

"What lead?"

"Am I still on the case?" She couldn't let this opportunity escape her now.

"Who is the lead?" His voice carried frustration that bordered on desperation.

"Is there enough on the card to cover a motel?"

"Marlo will cover it. Where are you going? Who are you going to see?"

"I'll tell you all about it when I get back with the key." Outside the window, her hand found the hangup button, and she was alone in her esuoh with reality creeping in like smoke.

Echo sighed as she tossed her phone and Jeph's card back into her bag. She sat on a stone bench outside the ruins of the crumbling castle, now a tourist attraction with people taking photos of their kids climbing over the stones. She wore her ragged clothes, and the remains of her burnt staff lay at her feet. She took a last look at it and tossed it aside, where it became a dead, lichen-covered branch from the oak tree overhead.

She looked up, and Galynn was standing there, looking at her intently through her closed raven's eye.

Echo started.

"Did you fall asleep?"

"No. I was just thinking about what to do next."

"What did your boss say?"

Echo stared at her, trying to see what the girl and the raven had in common. Friend or enemy? Helper or trickster? She *wanted* to trust her, to have someone to talk to about all this. She held herself back, went for the neutral reply. "It wasn't good. I didn't accomplish what I was supposed to."

"What was that?"

She sighed. "I'm not supposed to tell anyone."

The raven shook back her feathers. "So back to Portland?"

Echo thought, but she had already decided. "I can't lose this job on the first day." She stood up. "I need to catch a bus to the library. There is a library in this town, right?"

Galynn perched on the bench beside her. "Sure. Every Podunk town has a library. But you've got one in your pocket."

Echo sighed. "I can't use it."

Galynn cawed. "OK. I've got one in my pocket. What do you need to know?"

Echo hesitated. Say she got a ride to the library, somehow. Then she got information, however that would work. Then what? At every step, she was stymied by the way she perceived—and didn't perceive—the world. Gray got around in the dream world, but, now that she thought about it, he didn't go to strange towns to find things alone. She hated to admit he was right, but she needed help.

And here was help. Galynn seemed to know Jeph, whatever the implications of that might be. But she had already saved Echo's life, possibly more than once. So would she risk giving too much information to Galynn or find another random stranger who would probably be worse? It was either that or go home to the failure of a life she had before she started this morning. "Who is Cali Zielinski's father?"

"That's all?"

Echo shrugged. "It's a place to start."

Galynn thumbed the screen with her wing feather like a cartoon bird. "Zielinski is the eighth most common surname in Poland."

"Try Ashland."

"Still a lot. Robert, Vincent, John, Shirley."

"Let me think. Try attorney."

"OK. Here's a Newton Zielinski." She swiped the screen with her wing feathers. "He looks old enough to be her father."

"That must be him. I wonder if the train goes down there."

"Nope. My mom and I took the Coast Starlight down to San Francisco last spring break. It goes through Klamath Falls, not Ashland."

"How far is that?"

"Too far to walk." The bird ruffled her wings in an avian shrug. "I've got a better idea."

Echo waited, calculating the options.

"Take a car."

"That's a great idea. I don't have a driver's license."

"I do."

"And I suppose you have a car, too. That's why you took the train from Portland."

"It's at my mom's house. She bought it for me, so I don't have to bug her to take me places. She has her own car."

"She's going to let you drive a stranger to Ashland?" Echo felt that as more hope than objection.

"Sure." The raven cocked its head to one side. "If she doesn't know."

"Oh, great. She'll accuse me of kidnapping you. There must be another way."

"I'm just kidding. Of course I'll tell her who I'm with and where we're going. She lets me do everything."

"Really?" Hearing herself, Echo expected Galynn to reply, *Define real,* as Theo the Dragon Woman did. "If she says it's OK. If not, I'll find another way."

Echo and Galynn waited by the side of the road until another horse-drawn wagon came. It was old and rickety, and the horse was very slow. A few other people climbed on behind them, and the wagon meandered through the streets of the city, allowing passengers to come and go.

The down time and slower pace of the horse cart gave Echo a chance to notice that she hadn't eaten anything since sometime yesterday, unless you count dream food, which she didn't. She didn't see any way to rectify that problem, so she went outside on her porch to watch the eagles. Sitting there, it crossed her mind that she should be organizing her front room or looking upstairs at her memories, but she could do that after a few minutes.

When she went back inside, she discovered that someone was shaking her.

"Would you wake up? The driver is going to take us back to Salem if we don't get off."

Echo returned to her front room to discover that the horse-drawn cart had turned into a mass-transit dragon, with twenty or more seats strapped to its back. Echo and Galynn were the last passengers to depart.

They stepped down to a stone road up a steep hill, and Galynn led the way up and up and up.

At the top, they found a palace with a dozen or more dragons waiting patiently along the road, talking to each other in deep, rumbly voices in a language Echo didn't understand. They paid no attention to the two women as they walked by.

"This is good. Mom is having a party. I can get us some food, and she'll be distracted."

"I thought you were going to tell her."

Galynn went through a door into a side building. In the semi-darkness, Echo saw two dragons sleeping, one larger than the other. They each had four seats strapped on them.

"You wait in the car."

Echo felt the car door even as she experienced the climb to the back of the dragon. "Tell her."

"I'll tell her. Stop nagging."

Echo hopped into Galynn's esuoh and looked out her window. Galynn wound among the guests in a large backyard, where uniformed caterers served meat, salads, and desserts to people dressed in business casual, standing around in small groups with glasses of wine or beer in their hands. Then the distance became too great for Echo to maintain the connection. The image flickered, and Echo fell back into her own esuoh.

She went onto her porch again and focused on one eagle until she was riding with it, seeing the world it saw.

She felt something pecking at her hand.

She went back into her wagon and looked out the window. The raven was very close to her eyes, tilting its head this way and that.

"You sleep like the dead."

Echo straightened in her seat. The scene was different again. It was a car; her hands and eyes agreed. When she raised her hand above her head, she felt the cloth ceiling of a car but saw only the bright lights of a new-car showroom.

"I brought food and two overnight bags. Some clothes for me and some you can borrow."

"What did your mother say?"

"It's fine."

She started the engine, and light dawned behind them as she backed the car—which had become a yellow mid-sixties convertible with the top down—down the driveway and onto the road southbound.

Chapter 21

Jungle Excursion

Echo sat in Galynn's esuoh, looking out her window at the gray hood of the sensible sedan driving down Interstate 5 through the green fields of the southern Willamette Valley. With a shrug of pity for her driver and host, she went back into the reality she saw. The yellow convertible sped down a highway with a brown bluff on the left and blue ocean crashing against rocks on the right. In her esuoh she heard the radio playing the chorus of "Born to Be Wild" over and over. It was freedom, release from responsibility, and the beginning of a grand adventure. She leaned back in the seat and felt the wind riffle through her hair. "You're a good driver."

"Thanks, I guess," Galynn said. "It's I–5, not the Grand Prix."

"Better than a bus."

"You really know how to flatter a person."

Echo laughed. "What did your mom say, really?"

"She told the catering manager to make sure there was enough pasta salad, and then she told me, 'Uh-huh. Yeah. That will be fine.' And then she found a lady wandering around the house looking for a bathroom and took her to find it."

"I don't want you to get into trouble," Echo said. *Or myself either*, she didn't say.

"I left her a note, because she won't remember I was there."

Echo knew what it was like not to be noticed. She had lived in the shadow of her older sister, Diana, the bright spark of the family. As she remembered Diana, the sun went behind a cloud and the radio station changed to angry-sad music. Echo went into her esuoh to turn it off, and she returned to an old gray car—not old enough to be classic or new enough to be exciting, but gray inside and out—driving down a gray highway with gray-green grassland all around them.

When Galynn's phone exploded into manic guitar chords, she swerved, and the rumble strip sounded an accompanying drumbeat. She glanced at the phone, then tossed it aside. A text followed, which Galynn looked at, then threw the phone down again. A while later, Galynn took an exit.

"Are we there?" Echo asked.

"Rest area. I need to make a stop."

After parking the car, Galynn grabbed her phone and stepped out. "I'm going for a walk."

Echo wondered about the secrecy, so she went into Galynn's esuoh to listen.

An attractive woman, about Marlo's age, with black hair tied into a lump on top of her head and matching University of Oregon sweatshirt and sweatpants, appeared in Galynn's front room like a hologram. "Where the *hell* are you?" Her voice was high-pitched, angry, and panicked, like the ringtone of Galynn's phone.

"I told you I was going to Emma's. Don't you remember?"

"No, I don't." Galynn's mother put a hand on one hip. "There was so much going on. So the first person I called was Emma. She hasn't seen you since spring break."

The words, *Oh, shit,* ran through the room like a whisper on a breeze. "OK. I'm in a rest area south of Eugene."

"What the hell, Galynn? Have you taken leave of your senses?"

"I'm helping a friend get down to Ashland for a job. We'll be back tomorrow."

"Who is this friend? What kind of job?"

"I met her on the train. She's old. Like in her twenties. She's with Jeph—like you."

The woman's eyes got wide. "With Jeph how?"

Galynn laughed. "Not like that. She walks around with her eyes closed, but she's not blind. She works for him."

"Is Jeph there?"

"No. If he were, she wouldn't need my help, would she?"

Galynn walked over to a picnic table and perched on the bench. The connection glitched, and Echo needed to move a little closer. She tried to act casual, but the mother disappeared as Galynn looked pointedly at Echo. Catching the look, Echo pretended to look the other way.

"Galynn, are you there?" her mother's voice came back, insistently.

"We're on our way to Ashland, but we're totally fine. I'm still figuring all this out, but Jeph is paying for gas and everything. We're going to stay in a motel tonight and get back to Salem tomorrow afternoon. It's fun for me, work for her."

"Just leave her there at the rest area and come home."

"I can't do that. She needs my help. She's really pathetic."

"Galynn, this is dangerous. You're only seventeen—"

"Yeah, and I remember what Grandma said you did when you were seventeen."

"Leave me out of it. That's how I know it's dangerous."

"This is not like that. We're going to talk to some boring old fart. Cali Zielinski's father."

"I *ought* to call the police."

"You won't call the police."

"Are you testing me?"

"Not at all. I just know you're smarter than that. First, I'm not in any danger. Second, there's no point in pissing off Jeph, even if you don't hang around with him as much anymore. And third, you'll have a hard time explaining to the police how I was kidnapped by a blind woman, when the only one who has *stolen* a car is me. That will look good on my college applications."

"Galynn, if you don't turn around and come straight back—"

Echo whispered, "It's too late to drive back. Much safer tomorrow."

Galynn repeated. "It's too late to drive back. It will be much safer tomorrow."

"I'm going to sell that car."

"I'm just helping a friend in need."

"Where will you stay?"

"I don't know. My friend has a credit card to cover expenses. Someplace decent. I'll pick it out because she's kind of an idiot."

The woman sighed. "I'll get you a room at the Ashland Grande."

"Really? You're the best."

"I'd rather she slept in Lithia Park, but I want you safe. When you get there, go directly to the room and stay there all night. Order room service on my account, but don't leave the hotel. Then come directly home tomorrow."

"After we see the lawyer. Expect me around two or three. I'll be fine."

The woman disappeared.

Echo felt a touch on her arm and left Galynn's front room and went out into a dark jungle, where the trees dripped with snakes and she could see no path out.

"All taken care of," Galynn said. "You told me it was too late to go back, didn't you? My mom used to do that shit to me."

Echo shivered as all the snakes turned to look at her, tasting the air with their tongues. Galynn led her back to the car.

After the rest stop, the car was a jungle jeep with open sides. Gone was the wide-open highway with the ocean panoramas or even the gray grasslands. The road was hemmed in by the jungle like an animal being swallowed by a snake. As they drove, branches slapped at the windshield, and snakes fell from branches onto and sometimes into the Jeep. Rain poured in buckets, dripping through the canvas ceiling and blowing in at the windows.

Echo crept into Galynn's front room and looked out at the hills and vistas of the Rogue River Valley, turned to gold by the setting sun.

"Why do you keep doing that?"

"What?" Echo stepped back into the jungle darkness.

Galynn looked straight ahead as she drove. She didn't react to the rain; she didn't push the snakes off her shoulders. Although the path of the car wound like a snake through the jungle, her wing feathers stayed steady on the wheel, as appropriate for a freeway. "Going into my head, like some kind of stalker. You heard that whole conversation with my mom, didn't you?"

"Jeph said people in the ordinary world wouldn't know."

Now Galynn looked across at her. "That's how much you know about me. I've been in your fancy dream world before. And I *know* Jeph. But you know that, too, because you spied on my mom and me."

Busted. "I needed to know what was happening." Echo picked up a snake about the circumference of a pencil crawling in through the window and tossed it outside again. "When did you get into the dream world?"

"What do you see right now?"

"You wouldn't like it. Rain and jungle and snakes."

Echo felt Galynn's attention as she pushed the head of an enormous python out the window and watched its heavy body fall beside the car with a thump.

"You kind of deserve it."

"Probably. I was supposed to ask permission, but Jeph said normal people don't know you're there."

"That's where you went wrong, thinking I'm 'normal people.'"

Echo nodded. Was the rain lightening? "I'll ask from now on."

"We'll talk about that." She picked up her phone and held it in her wing for a moment, then set it down again. "And you won't listen in on my phone calls."

"It worked, didn't it?"

Galynn squawked. "You think you're the first one to think of 'It'll be safer to keep going'? Please. You're talking to an expert."

"So what's your connection with Jeph?" Echo felt the question with renewed urgency. "Will your mother tell him you're helping me?"

"She hasn't spoken to him in months. Since she caught him trying to introduce me to your world."

"Trying?"

"He was at our house. My mom went to get some drinks, and I asked him about it. He said he thought I had potential and let me cross over."

"What did you see?"

"Barbie house. Everything bright and plastic. It changed my life. Then my mom came back and lost her mind. Made me cross back and threw Jeph out of the house. But the last thing he said to me was that he'd see me again."

Echo was stunned. The rain had lifted, and the snakes stopped dropping from the trees, but the car still slithered through the jungle. "Did he contact you before we met?"

"No. Did he tell you to look for me?"

Echo shrugged and released a sigh. "He assumed I could do this on my own after a couple of hours of training."

"No shit. What made you think you could do it?"

"I have a friend who's been in this world since he was seven. He gets along fine."

Galynn flapped her wings and settled into driving again. "Are you getting along fine?"

"I'd have probably died in the parking lot before I ever got to Senator Zielinski's office if it hadn't been for you. I forgot to jump into someone's head to look." *And I'd have been looking all day for the senator's office. And I couldn't have kept her occupied while I searched for the key. Was Jeph setting me up for failure?*

The bird gave a *kak-kak-kak* that might have been laughter. "The snakes don't bother you?"

"They're just dream snakes. It's what it might mean that's disturbing." Echo waited a beat, looking around. "I don't see them right now."

"Maybe because you've stopped lying to me."

Echo thought about that. Maybe.

"I can be more helpful if I know what you're looking for," Galynn said.

"I signed a nondisclosure agreement."

"What aren't you supposed to disclose?"

That was the question, wasn't it? She went into her esuoh and looked through the short-term memories. She found Marlo's office, the one-page background check form, the pages and pages of the nondisclosure form. She had read it—at least she had run her eyes down the page—but here in her memories it was a blank page littered with the phrases "COMPANY SHALL" and "APPLICANT SHALL NOT," with doodled marginalia of Echo cleaning toilets or answering the phone or dressed in spy clothes with a gun on her hip. "What I got from his assistant was that I wasn't supposed to talk about the people I'm researching."

Galynn shifted her wings in a shrug. "Do what you have to do. If I were in your place, I would want a look around, too. So here's my deal. As long as you stay in your world, I'll help you on this project."

Echo let that sink in.

"*If* you tell me what you're looking for, *then* you can look out my eyes. Don't think you can do it without telling me, because I'll know, and I'll stop helping you. Equal footing or nothing. I'm pretty sure Jeph wouldn't be happy to find out you're leaving big stomping footprints all over the place. He might like to hire a replacement."

Echo sat silently for a while, as the trees closed in tighter and tighter, until one was growing inside the car. The rain and snakes were back, and one crawled down her neck. She ran into her esuoh and sat on her porch for a while.

When she came out, they were driving through a red desert like the landscape of Mars, but the sun was shining and the car was dry, and it seemed inevitable that she would take Galynn's deal.

But not yet.

Galynn marched up to the front desk of the Ashland Grande Hotel as Echo stood aside and gazed around the lobby. It looked like something abandoned and left to the elements for a hundred years. The furniture was broken; the windows let in the wet wind, and there was evidence everywhere that animals made their homes here. She wanted the comfort of knowing what it looked like in the physical world, but she refrained from entering Galynn's esuoh, because accepting Galynn's deal would be a bridge she couldn't uncross.

Galynn talked with the clerk, a tall, hump-backed man with a youthful face. He wore an old-fashioned suit that dripped rainwater, streaming from his black hair down his face to his clothing, which stuck to his thin, bent body.

Carrying a rusty key, Galynn grabbed one of the bags and led the way to the ancient, creaking elevator. Echo took up the other bag and followed, riding in silence up to a room in the same state of ruin as the lobby.

She sat on the filthy and broken bed and looked out at the tree next to the window, dead and lightning-splintered.

"How is it?" she asked Galynn.

"Expensive," Galynn said. "How's yours?"

"Decrepit."

Galynn smiled. "Do you want a look?"

Echo had crossed the line so far that the last mile probably wouldn't matter, but all the same. "Not now."

They ate from the room service menu—Echo ordered an appetizer of bread sticks and bottled water, which looked like wooden sticks but tasted fine. While they ate, Galynn watched out the window and described the festive street life of an Ashland summer night, people in their theatre-going attire exiting the various venues of the Oregon Shakespeare Festival and wandering down the street in search of a late dinner or a nightcap.

Echo sat in her own front room watching monkeys scream and fight in the lower canopy across the street of the city being reclaimed by the jungle.

Galynn complained about Echo's silence, but Echo ignored her. She was exhausted but not sleepy. She wandered through the upstairs hallways of her esuoh, experiencing the emotions that radiated from each door but choosing not to go inside.

At some point in the night, a doorknob throbbed with urgency. She went in and found herself in an abandoned city, at a sidewalk cafe where tiny metal tables sat rusting under a thick gray sky.

She sat at a table, waiting for someone, but she wasn't sure who. There was a pile of blackened ashes beside her that looked vaguely like the remains of rose stems.

She looked around and found a man sitting at the next table over, his back turned toward her. She didn't know when he had arrived, but there he was. He looked like Gray but different. She scooted her chair around and the sound of it startled the man, who turned back to her with eyebrows raised in surprise.

It was Gray. His eyes were closed—which disappointed her because she wanted to see them again. Nevertheless, he smiled at her, seeming glad and sad at the same time. He moved his chair to her table and sat down. But not across from her—instead, at a ninety-degree angle, so that they faced different directions.

"Is this my dream or yours?" she asked him.

"I'm not sure. I don't remember ever dreaming before."

"Oh, come on. I'm in your world now."

"I'm out of it."

She sat with that for a moment. "You're not in the dream world?"

"Ytilaer. I left it."

"After I left?"

"Because you left. Partly."

Now she looked at him. He continued to stare off into the distance, the muscles around his eyes working. She wanted to shake him, slap him, reach over and kiss him on the lips. Something that would wake him up. "Where's your rorrim?"

"Lost it."

Her breath caught at that. If it were hers, she would be devastated. But he never used it, anyway. "You're really stuck in the physical world? Cain said he had one that he wanted to give you."

"It belonged to my mother. He took it out of my hand the night he killed her."

"Oh, Gray."

"We're fine now." He gripped the table as if he were about to flip it over. "He's my *dad*." The way he spit out the words showed it was anything but fine.

"I'm sorry."

He let go the table, sat back in the chair. "He had to find me. Maybe it should have been sooner."

She sighed. "I thought we told each other everything. Back when we were friends."

"We're not friends?"

They had years of shared life, seeing each other every day. She shrugged. "I don't know what we are." She looked at him again, noticing the hard line of his jaw, the dark growth of beard. "What do you think?"

He turned toward her. "Everything is changing. We can't go back. I don't know what's forward."

"I know." She looked away toward the crumbling buildings, so gray that they seemed to merge into the sky. "All that time together. Doing homework. Meeting for coffee. Ignoring the mean kids. Telling Aunt Doris you weren't autistic. You never told me. Why didn't you tell me?" she asked the city, as if Gray were not there.

"What do you want to know?" he said.

She swept the dead roses off the table with her arm. "Damn it, Gray! I want to know why you didn't tell me!"

He disappeared like a magic trick.

She slammed the door and went to sit on her front porch.

CHAPTER 22

Finding Echo

G RAY FELT STRANGE OPENING THE DOOR TO THE UGLY MUG, seeing the small cafe the way people in Oge always dreamed it.

Gray and Echo had been meeting early in the morning here since they started drinking coffee. He was always first to arrive, because Echo was always late. The bearded owner—Gray was surprised at how much he looked like the friendly dwarf he saw in Ytilaer—manned the counter, just as he had almost every day. But today, as well as the big smile, Gray saw crinkles around his open brown eyes.

"Hey!" The coffee shop owner paused for a few seconds, his mouth open but not speaking. Then, finally, "What can I get for you?"

Gray felt the request for an explanation, and almost felt he owed one, given their long acquaintance. But he didn't know what he could say. *Yesterday I was blind but now I see*, might be believable, but it wasn't true, and the truth wouldn't be believable. He asked for the usual, then sat at the table for half an hour. When Echo didn't show, he tried calling her, but got no response.

A dream from the night before hovered at the edge of his memory, taunting him. Did she tell him where she was, where she was going? If she did, he didn't remember.

Feeling a sense of impending doom out of step with the sunny morning, he went to Aunt Doris's house.

Aunt Doris opened her front door and met Gray on her porch before he knocked. She wore a pink and purple track suit, and her hair stood up all over her head. "Where is she?"

He stepped back, almost tumbled backwards down her steps. He stood on the first step, looking up at her. She had always been formidable—like a mysterious Russian witch, capable of both kindness and great harm—and he had mostly avoided her. Now she looked down at him, her eyes narrowed, her forehead sewn with wrinkles, her mouth tight. He was tempted to run away, but he felt something like new power in his resolve. He took one step up so he was eye to eye with her.

Her eyes widened, but she leaned forward, fists on her hips, waiting for an answer.

"Didn't she come home last night?" Gray asked.

She deflated a little. "I thought she was with you."

Gray had to admit, at least to himself, that that would have been nice—and better than where she was—but he couldn't say that to Aunt Doris. "The last time I saw her was noon yesterday, and I'm worried about her."

"Oh, Lord. I've had a bad feeling about this ever since I saw his face on that business card. Nobody looks that good without being a creep."

He didn't need to ask who "nobody" was.

Aunt Doris went back into her house, and Gray followed her inside.

She led him into her kitchen. Some of the decor in her kitchen were the same as he had seen in Ytilaer. Flowers on the windowsill, a clock on the wall in the form of a long-tailed cat, whose eyes and tail wagged as it ticked. Unpainted wooden cabinets and floor and vibrant colors in the decorations. The Srelevart said that these congruities showed a person integrated in the inner and outer life. Maybe Ytilaer was not the only way to see.

"Sit down." She pointed to the kitchen table surrounded by windows and overlooking a backyard full of color. "I'll get you some coffee."

She brought two mugs and sat down across from him. "What do you know about where Echo went?"

"I was hoping she contacted you."

"What's going on—and why are your eyes open?"

He had known this question would come up, but he hadn't figured out how to deal with it. Or rather he had, but he wasn't comfortable with the decision. "I'll tell you, and you won't believe it, and I can't prove it."

"Try me."

"I've been seeing a different version of reality, Ytilaer, since I was seven. I didn't want to be in this version for reasons that evaporated yesterday. I came out and lost my ability to get back in."

She stared at him with her top lip curled slightly. "You expect me to believe that?"

"No. I expect you not to believe that. Echo crossed into Ytilaer and went to Salem yesterday on a job assignment for Jeph. If she's not back now, I've got an appointment with a retired police detective to go search for her." He got up to go. "Thanks for the coffee."

"Stop."

He turned to look back at her.

"You went to the police?"

"There's nothing they can do. Imagine trying to explain this situation to them. She's of legal age and hasn't been gone long by their standards."

"And this detective? Does he believe you?"

"No. But he believes I have the money to pay him to help me."

She nodded once, then got up from the table. "Let's go."

"Uh, the detective—"

"Where is he? The least I can do is drive you there." She led him out the back door and into the garage.

As GRAY GOT OUT OF THE CAR, he turned and looked back at the small, white-haired woman behind the wheel. "Really. We've got this, and we need someone to tell us if Echo gets back while we're gone." He watched her face, wondering what she would do after he closed the door. "And thanks."

"You find her." She leaned forward for full eye contact. "I'm holding you responsible."

"For what? Why?"

"Because if anything happens to her, I'm going to have to kill that Jeph person, and I'm too old for prison."

He tried to smile as he shut the door.

The window rolled down. "Be careful." She drove away.

When Travis opened the door, his eyes were red but focused. He was dressed in fresh jeans, white shirt with the collar open, and a black leather jacket. A black athletic bag sat by the door.

Gray handed him an envelope with five hundred-dollar bills.

"Cash? I'll write you a receipt." He went back into the house. "You could have brought a check, but this will probably come in handy for incidental expenses." He turned in his tracks. "Last name still Birdsong?"

Standing at the door, Gray answered absently, but the inner voices were shouting all the things that might have happened to Echo. Hit by a car on the way to her appointment. Lost in her own labyrinth and unaware of anything in the outside world. Corrupted into unscrupulous use of Ytilaer's powers. No. He couldn't believe that about Echo. He wouldn't. But she might not know any better. The possibility nagged.

Travis came back out holding out a piece of paper, which he handed to Gray. "OK. Where do I start?"

"Where do *you* start?"

"I know you're planning to come along to talk to the girl, but I'm the bloodhound here. Where do I start?"

"The last time I saw her, she was on her way to Salem to talk to Cali Zielinski. But that was nearly a full day ago, and she's not back. What if—?"

"Nope. We follow the trail. If we think we know the answer, we're less observant." He picked up the athletic bag and turned to lock the door, then headed for the vehicle at a brisk pace. He tossed the bag into the back of the faded beige SUV and unlocked the passenger door. He climbed into the driver's seat and started the engine as Gray stepped in.

Travis pulled out of the driveway into the gravel street and then into the mundane unknowns of Oge.

C H A P T E R 23

Secrets Revealed

IN THE MORNING, ECHO STOOD under warm rain coming through a hole in the roof with the falling water singing in sibilant whispers, *Am I the chosen one?*

A distant drumming brought her back to the jungle, and a familiar voice, Galynn's. "Get out of the shower. You're using all the hot water in the hotel."

Echo stepped out from under the hole in the roof and grabbed a bit of cloth hanging from a tree limb that had invaded the ancient building. The fact that it felt like a fluffy towel instead of a greasy rag reminded her where she was, and she found the handle for the shower and turned it off.

When she came out, Galynn was pecking at a wooden tray filled with roasted beetles and termites, cut pieces of snake and lizard, and a small, long-legged bird, with its feathers off and its white eyes turned accusingly toward Echo.

"I ordered breakfast. Help yourself." Galynn went into the room where the shower was.

A raven might have ordered insects for food, but Galynn wouldn't, and the hotel they were staying in wouldn't serve them if she had. While the rain was pouring in the other room, she ran her hand over the food. The long-legged bird felt soft, and when she pinched it, it squished like bread. The pile of beetles seemed flat and left her fingers greasy, and the termites were warm and formless. The lizard and snake pieces were cold and wet. She wiped her hands on her pants and walked away from the tray. She was hungry, but not that hungry.

There were two canvas backpacks on the bed, one open and spilling out its contents. Galynn had said she brought clothes for Echo. The unopened bag contained Barbie clothes—Echo's size, but pink and sparkly, with big bows and girly flounces—the sort of clothes Echo associated with her sister Diana. Echo shoved them back into the backpack and kept her own foolish outfit.

She sat at the window and looked down at the jungle city. In the upper canopy, screeching monkeys swung on vines from intertwined branches to ruined buildings. On the ancient street, men in sweat-stained jungle clothing drove roofless Jeeps and Land Rovers. The vehicles trundled over bumps and ruts among new trees growing where the road had been. On the sidewalk, a tiger whose coat seemed to glow in the morning light slunk along with the walk of a movie star.

Galynn came out, drying her hair with a rag like the one Echo had found. "Did you—" She walked over to the tray for a closer look. "Did you pinch the croissant?"

Echo turned back and stared at Galynn's finger pointing at the bird. "Is that a croissant?"

"Oh, for God's sake." She picked up the bird and threw it to Echo. "I'm not going to make you a sammich. I'm not your mom."

Echo caught it, and with the word attached, she could feel the light bread in her hand. "What else is there?"

"Seriously?"

"Yes."

"Bacon, melon, strawberries, blueberries. Did you stick your fingers in the eggs, too?"

Echo turned to the window again and took a bite of the croissant. "Thanks for ordering this."

"What did you think it was?"

"You don't want to know."

Echo heard rattling silverware like a bell behind her, then a smaller wooden tray appeared in her peripheral vision.

"Here. Don't look at it. Bacon, eggs, fruit. Coffee. Nothing you would be afraid to eat—or tell me about."

Echo extended her hand while looking the opposite direction and felt cold ceramic.

"There's a fork if people in the dream world use forks."

Echo found it, and with a little practice found she could eat while still focusing on the jungle outside. A mighty wind rose behind her, but she refused to turn, and it eventually resolved itself into the sound of a hair dryer.

When the wind stopped, Galynn hopped around the room, pulling clothes from one of the two canvas rucksacks. "I brought you some clothes. Stuff my mom likes."

"I'm good."

"You sure? Those look like you've slept in them."

Echo looked down at the ratty tunic and torn pants. Every rip and smudge told a story. Her clothes weren't glamorous, but they were as much a part of her as her own skin. "Worse than that," she told Galynn. "But this outfit is who I am."

"If you say so." Galynn tossed the bag by the door and started repacking hers. "So what's the plan?"

"Newton Zielinski." The name felt ominous. Her early perception of the dream world as a game was developing cracks with pain showing through them.

"I know that. What are you trying to find out?"

"I haven't gone back into your head yet." She was resisting the inevitable. She was on a train heading for a cliff, and it was too late to get off. In fact, she hungered for the flight; she had to see it through. But Galynn— "Something tells me it's a bad idea."

"Oh, come on. You wouldn't have gotten through your first interview without me. You wouldn't have gotten *here*. God knows where you would have ended up if you had tried it by yourself."

Echo shuddered. She was lost in the jungle *with* Galynn; where would she be without her?

The bird pointed her sharp beak at Echo. "I don't want to be the lovely assistant anymore."

Echo looked at her companion again. "Beautiful and terrifying. But not lovely."

"What the hell is that supposed to mean?"

"I'm sorry. I didn't mean to say that out loud. You look like a human-sized raven, not a magician's assistant."

"Huh." Galynn preened her feathers.

Echo pushed away the food and finished her coffee. "Do we have his address?"

"Yeah. But I'm not going to take you there unless you give me the rest of the story. Otherwise, we can go back to Salem, and I'll drop you off at the bus stop."

Echo froze. From inside her esuoh, a voice on the radio sang in a soothing tone with sweet, sweet strings: *Go back to Salem. Let it all go. There's something wrong here. Go back to your calm and boring life.*

And the answering voice, dark and raspy and hungry. *You'll never know what would have happened.*

"There's a man named Lazar Kyrillovich," Echo said, relieved to feel the tale spinning out of her like a spider's web and at the same time afraid Jeph would find out. But she went on with it anyway, because what else could she do? "And Jeph wants his key."

THE BUILDING WHERE GALYNN SAID NEWTON ZIELINSKI'S OFFICE was located looked to Echo like a grand hotel somewhere in the tropics of the British Colonial period. A white-washed stucco building, two stories high, shining in the wavering heat of a jungle clearing.

A breeze greeted Echo and Galynn as they crossed from the blazing outdoors into the shade of the interior. Oriental rugs softened the wooden floors. Huge fans swung lazily overhead, stirring up the air so that the sheer curtains fluttered in the breeze. It was still hot, inside as well as out, and sweat shone on the face of a woman standing at the desk in her white 1920s-style dress and pith helmet, holding a cigarette on a long black enameled cigarette holder. She spoke to a dark-faced man who, in his white suit, looked like a photographic negative.

Echo pointed to the two people. "We can ask there."

"What? Him? He works for the real estate company that owns this building. The sign says Zielinski's office is upstairs." Galynn led the way up two flights of stairs, then down a hallway, and stopped at a room with a tray of empty dishes on the floor beside it. She put her hand on the knob.

"Shouldn't we knock?" Echo asked her.

"Funny question coming from you." Galynn pushed open the door and led the way into the sitting room of a suite. A young woman in a long slim skirt and curly short black hair sat at a small desk, making a ruckus on an old-fashioned typewriter. Beyond her, an older man—maybe a few years younger than Aunt Doris—dressed in a pale blue seersucker suit was sitting on a striped sofa reading a newspaper with narrow columns and no photos, a tiny coffee cup on the end table beside him.

"May I help you?" the young woman asked.

"We'd like to see Newton Zielinski," Echo said. "We only need a few minutes of his time."

The young woman looked at them with a perfectly straight face and said, "I'm sorry. He's busy now. Would you like to make an appointment?"

Echo stared at her. "He's sitting right there drinking coffee and reading a newspaper. I'm sure he can spare a couple of minutes."

The young woman looked steadily at Echo. "He's in his office, and I know whether he's busy or not."

Echo was about to accuse her of gaslighting when Galynn stepped forward. She stretched her wings and struck an elegant pose that Echo couldn't help but admire. "Please tell him that his daughter told us to come and see him."

Both Echo and the young woman stared at Galynn. The young woman picked up the phone and in less than a minute, she escorted them to the sofa that she had pretended not to see.

Newton Zielinski, attorney at law, folded the newspaper and set it aside. He finished the coffee in the small cup. "How can I help you?"

"We've just been to see your daughter in Salem," Echo said. "We've come out from Pennsylvania looking for my cousin, Lazar Kyrillovich. My mother is his father's sister. My family has a tractor repair business, and we'd like to offer him a job, give him a new start."

He leaned back in his seat. "That's very generous. What prompted this kindness?"

Echo cursed herself. So many lies to invent, so little time to perfect them. She seemed to be always grabbing one on the fly, using whatever words floated in the air at the moment, and it left her unprepared to deal with their twisting, turning, slithering possibilities. This man's ostensibly innocent question felt like a trap. "Oh, you know," she said at last. "Family."

Echo didn't know where the trap was or what would spring it, so she ran into his esuoh to look for the key.

It was a pub in rich reds and dark wood, with a scuffed floor and the smell of pipe tobacco infusing the air. At the far end was a fireplace surrounded by bookshelves with a prominent painting of a man Echo didn't recognize. She threaded through the tables to the bookshelves and found a series of identical books with unmarked spines. She stopped and turned in place, looking for something *different*. Searching the upstairs in Cali's esuoh had turned out to be a waste of time. All she needed to find the key was to ask the right question.

The question didn't begin with *who, what, when, where, how,* or *why*. It was a mystery encapsulated in two words, whispered into the silence: "Lazar Kyrillovich."

Nothing happened.

A quick look out Newt's front window showed Galynn talking to him and Echo staring into space. *Well, that didn't work.* Echo opened her mouth to shout, but while the breath entered her being, she heard something, a soft buzzing, more a disturbance of the air than precisely a sound. She followed the vibration to a small statue of a woman with a mostly naked man lying dead across her lap. The woman looked down at the man with deep sadness, and even though the two of them seemed to be about the same age, her expression captured a mother's grief.

Echo reached out to the key, hesitating before touching it, because sorrow flowed out of it like a river pouring out of a cave. She tried to think of Jeph and her prospects for prosperity, but this statuette expressed where she had been bound from the first moment Jeph spoke to her in the cafe, only two days ago. She steeled herself to accept the totality of the adventure she had chosen and placed her hand on the statue. It became a door into a law office with a broad desk, seen from Newt Zielinski's viewpoint. A small, sad-looking woman sat across from him, kneading a handkerchief in her hands.

"We'll pay you." She held her spine straight and looked at him through tear-reddened eyes. "I don't know how. But my son is innocent."

Every criminal's mom declared her darling boy to be innocent, but this one—funny-looking and frumpy, with thick eyebrows and a long nose—he reluctantly believed. He was falling in love with her, but not *that* kind of love.

"My son is a good boy. He doesn't drink—his father has drinking problem—and he wouldn't drive someone else's car."

"Let's just say for the sake of argument that you're right." He was mustering the emotional distance it took to do a good job at this, but it wasn't easy.

She opened her mouth to speak.

"No. Really," he said. "I do believe you. But you have to look at it from the point of view of the judge and jury. Lazar was found passed out behind the wheel after the collision. His fingerprints were on the wheel. No one else was there. He had party drugs in his system. The techs say the car was going ninety in a twenty-five zone, and two children died besides the driver of the other car. Lazar has no driver's license, and even though it's his first DUII, he could get three consecutive ten-year sentences."

"He is innocent."

"And then there's the trial. He doesn't remember what happened to him, so he's not much help with his defense. Cali has offered to be a character witness—"

"No." She spoke as firmly as her son had when Newt made the proposal to him. "He was very sure. Cali should not testify."

Cali had insisted on being a character witness. Newt had been adamant that she shouldn't. And now he felt no satisfaction that these two suffering people, mother and son, stood on his side in the conflict between Cali's courage and his care for the well-being of his daughter. Buffeted between powerful motivations, he sat stiller than still, waiting.

"She must be free to follow her own path, with no scandal of defending a man accused of murder. That's what he said."

Newt took off his glasses and rubbed his face with one hand, then put his glasses back on. "So what you're telling me is that he wants a trial, with no rebuttal against the prosecution? You know he can get a court-appointed attorney to mangle this case almost as badly as he's insisting I do it."

"We will pay."

He rolled his eyes. "It's not about the money." He collected his thoughts. "That's one option. There are others."

She waited. She put her handkerchief away and folded her hands on her lap like a sleeping cat.

"Given his—condition—we could plead guilty except for insanity."

"He is not insane."

"I know. I've talked to him. His conversation is, well, colorful, but I believe he has his faculties. But he could serve his sentence in a psychiatric facility instead of prison. It might be safer for him, and the court might give him some leniency."

A shiver ran through her, and she shook her head. "His grandfather was a dissident who spent many years in Soviet mental hospital for 'sluggish schizophrenia.' When he came out, he was empty shell."

"You understand this is not the Soviet Union."

She shook her head, more emphatically than before.

Newton sighed. "Lazar refused as well." He folded his hands together on the desk. "Which leaves the last—and really the best—option. He pleads guilty, and we try to bargain down to a lesser charge. It still means prison time, but we may be able to reduce it."

"He's not guilty."

"It could be as little as fifteen years. He could get time off for good behavior, be out in his early thirties."

"To say he is guilty would be lie. I believe there is word for that."

"It's not suborning perjury to advocate for the best deal my client can get out of a bad situation."

"He's innocent."

It was infuriating. "If you believe he's innocent, it seems that you would want to get as close an approximation to justice as we can." *If you believe—* why did he say that? Of course she believed.

"He's seen the tapestry."

Lazar had used the same words, staring at Newt over the conference table—yes, staring at him, even with his eyes closed—and said "No" to the most sensible option. Just like that. When Newton asked for an explanation, Lazar had said, "I've seen the tapestry." It struck Newton suddenly how much the boy looked like his mother. The fine masculine features that Cali thought so handsome were, in this woman, at best, "handsome." Didn't matter. There was steel in that spine, despite the tears.

"What is this tapestry?" Newt asked the woman.

She shrugged. "I don't understand, but I believe him."

"Could you talk to him about it? He's of age, so he has the final say, but maybe you could . . . ." He didn't mention the fury that had taken over him. He had yelled at the boy, had barely prevented himself from slapping him, and the boy—young man—just looked at him sympathetically and said, "The pattern is established. My thread is only part of the picture."

She watched Newt carefully. "He said you tried very hard to persuade him."

"I'm ashamed that I yelled at him."

"He was grateful for your concern."

He sighed again—he seemed to do that a lot at times like this—and flipped through his notes. *No. There's nothing else.* He slapped the file closed with more force than he intended. "So you're onboard with this. A trial with no answer to the accusations."

She shrugged. "Please give us time. We will pay you."

"He will go to prison for a long time."

She stood, strong in her sadness. "Do whatever he tells you to do." She walked toward the door, turned back as she reached it. "Thank you."

As the door closed on the woman, Echo found it closed on her as well. She still held the statue of the woman with her dead son. The woman's face was older now; it was Lazar's mother. She went into her esuoh and drew a picture of it in her newest sketchbook, then looked outside.

The man was yelling at Galynn, with the veins standing out on his neck and forehead. Galynn squawked once and stood there with her beak pointed at him. On a shelf near the door was the statue Echo had found in his esuoh.

Echo came out of her esuoh to receive the full bellows of the man's rage. "I don't know what your game is, but that family has suffered enough from frauds like you. Get the hell out of my office."

Galynn hopped toward the door, and while the man's attention was diverted, Echo grabbed the statuette off the shelf. She could hold it in one hand, but it had the weight of something ten times that size.

Chapter 24

Navigating Oge

Gray rode with one hand on the door handle and one on the dashboard, white-knuckling as Travis sped through traffic. Not just the traffic but time itself seemed out of control.

"Tell me about this girl." Travis spoke without taking his eyes off the road.

"She's beautiful and full of light."

"That's like your black monster, isn't it?"

"No! How could you even think that?"

"Slow down, cowboy. I don't mean she *is* like your black monster. I mean, the way you see her is like the way you see him. Other people don't see her that way. If I were walking down the street, not in your—world or whatever—I couldn't say, 'Oh, there's a girl who's beautiful and full of light. That must be Gray's girlfriend.'"

He hated having her called his girlfriend. He had never had the opportunity—courage—to talk to her about that. She might laugh if she heard it. In fact, she absolutely would laugh. He focused on the issue at hand. "OK. That's true. Other people don't see her the same way I do."

"Thank you." Travis looked over his shoulder and changed lanes. "If she were with us right now, you and I would see her the same, right?"

"I think people in Oge filter differently, but true, more or less."

"And you told me you weren't sure I was the Blue Knight."

"I'm sorry. It's the way I always thought of you—"

"Not a problem." Still facing forward, Travis waved in Gray's general direction. "I was flattered—and you did call me the Blue Knight when you were seven. I've changed a lot since then, but you would be more likely to recognize me if we saw things the same way."

"OK." Something in the tone of his voice and the pacing of his words told Gray Travis was building up to something.

"If your girlfriend—"

"Echo," Gray corrected him.

"Echo—were in the next car over—"

Gray looked, because he had to, and saw a woman a little younger than Aunt Doris bouncing in the driver's seat singing music Gray couldn't hear.

"—Neither of us would know her."

Gray pointed over his shoulder. "That's not Echo, but I get your point."

"What if Echo is not beautiful? What if she has a face like a deflated football?"

The idea terrified Gray. Not so much that she might not be as beautiful as he saw her as that he might discover himself to be someone who only looks at the outside. "In seventh and eighth grades, especially right after she came to our school, some of the mean kids called her Broken Mirror."

"Now that's helpful. There was something about her that reminded them of a broken mirror."

"Well, yes. But they didn't see what she was really like—"

"It's OK. Let's just stipulate that you know her better than they ever did, and they don't deserve to kiss the ground she walks on." He looked over at Gray, whose face felt hot. "But can you see how that information will make it easier for *us* to find her? Easier than 'beautiful and full of light'?"

Gray took a deep, slow breath. "She has scars on her face, like a broken mirror, from a traffic accident when she was a kid. She mentioned it a few times, when we were first getting to know each other, but the subject seemed painful, so I didn't ask about it. I never saw the scars and didn't give them much thought."

Travis nodded. "We need information that people who know nothing about her would see without being in your other—"

"Ytilaer."

"Ytilaer. I'll get it if you keep correcting me."

The traffic around them picked up speed as they came to a place where two highways came together like a confluence of rivers, flowing through stands of tall, majestic trees.

Travis maneuvered through the stream with his eyes forward and his lips tightly closed. "Let's have a word for the kind of information I'm asking you for. *Facts*. True things everybody can see."

Among the Srelevart, *facts* more often referred to the ways Oge obscured reality, although Quig, of course, always took issue with that. Gray sat for a moment with this new definition. It put Quig in a new light and gave Gray a different framework to think about Echo. "Because she's in Ytilaer, she has her eyes closed to everyone outside it. She's taller than I am, and she laughs a lot. She's told me that her hair is shorter than mine and it's reddish-brown. She came to Oregon in seventh grade, after her parents and sister died in a traffic accident. She lives with her grandmother's sister—her only living relative—in Sellwood."

Travis nodded. "OK. That's helpful. What does she like?"

"She likes people, which makes it especially hard that they're so afraid of her. She's not mean in return, although she slapped a guy in seventh grade after he hit me in the back of the head."

Travis grinned. "I like her, but I hope we won't find her in jail for assault or battery." He waited a bit. "Anything else you can think of? How does she dress?"

"Clothes." Gray shrugged. "I never really noticed."

Travis smiled sadly and shook his head. "My wife said I never noticed her clothes, either."

TRAVIS PARKED THE CAR IN FRONT OF THE CAPITOL and turned off the engine. "This is it."

Gray stepped out of the vehicle. Over the sound of traffic and the pounding of construction equipment, the scent of newly mown grass flowed to him on a light breeze, carrying him back to a spring day in seventh grade. Gray and Echo had come with a busload of classmates on a field trip, riding in a vehicle that seemed to Gray like a truckload of chickens on their way to slaughter. Most of the kids in school ignored him, and Gray appreciated that, but there were always one or two who would do something clever like smacking him in the head and asking, "Who hit you?" This time, Echo turned around and slapped the kid back. "Some asshole nobody cares to know."

She turned around and sat down to a chorus of "Whoa" and "Zing" and "Got you," followed by the bully's voice on the verge of tears, discovering for the first time that this wasn't the road to popularity. Gray felt sorry for him—and humiliated for himself.

As the class walked up the steps to the white marble building, Gray told Echo it was like a castle on a hill. She said it was pretty pathetic for a castle, but there was a gold man on top of it. When he told her it was a wizard with a long staff, she laughed as if he had said something clever. But now the wizard with the long staff was a gilded pioneer holding an axe and some kind of cloth on his shoulder.

He followed Travis through the rotunda, the hoots and animal cries from that memory following him up the steps to the gift shop, where Travis asked the clerk where the senate offices were. She gave directions, and he strode off, Gray walking fast to keep up.

Down a narrow hallway, past a man in khakis and collared knit shirt talking with a man in a business suit, past open offices where assistants at desks talked on telephones. Travis stopped at one and asked where he could find Cali Zielinski. The woman stood up and stepped into the hallway to give directions. Down the hall, on the right. Travis strode off, and she smiled at Gray as he walked by.

Travis stopped before a dark wooden desk, where a young man in a navy suit sat typing on a computer.

After a few seconds, the man looked up. "Yes?"

"We want to talk to Cali Zielinski."

He looked at his screen, typing a few last keystrokes, then turned to them. "Do you have an appointment?"

"No. But we only need five minutes."

The man looked sympathetic. "She's booked today. Would you like to make an appointment for next week sometime?"

Gray felt his legs go weak.

Travis spoke up. "As I said, we only need a few minutes, and the matter is urgent."

"She's in a hearing now. Would you like to wait?"

Travis nodded, without looking for Gray's opinion. "Yes. We'll wait."

"Can you tell me what it's about?" the man asked.

"It's personal," Travis said. "About a young woman who interviewed her yesterday."

The assistant held them in a hard, steady gaze.

Gray felt the man's hostility and wanted to soften it. "Her name was Echo. She had her eyes closed. I'm worried that she might be in danger."

Travis chimed in. "She's unstable. Her family is worried."

When the assistant spoke again, his tone was cold, and his face still withheld its expression. "And you are?"

Travis answered before Gray could speak. "This is her brother, Gray, and I'm a friend of the family. My name is Travis Rankin. I'm a retired police detective. We really only need a couple of minutes."

"Please have a seat. She'll call as soon as the hearing is over." He sat down, pulled out his phone, and began texting.

As they sat side by side, Gray hissed at Travis. "Brother?"

"Keep it simple. If you start in on your dangerous other world, she'll kick us out before we begin."

Gray absorbed that. *Oge is just as hard to navigate as Ytilaer.* He looked out the window and wondered how Echo had gotten here without help. The assistant's posture as he spoke on the phone caught his attention. It wouldn't have mattered, except it did. He held the phone close to himself, and his back was toward them. When he glanced over his shoulder, Gray prodded Travis with his elbow.

"I see it." Travis whispered so softly that Gray could barely hear him.

Gray stared out the window at the branches waving against the taciturn blue sky.

Chapter 25
The Esuoh of the World

GALYNN LED THE WAY DOWN THE JUNGLE STREET. "What did you grab off the shelf?"

Echo felt things rolling and slithering underfoot, like moving vines or snakes under the detritus. She didn't look down. "A statue. Something I've seen before, but I can't place it."

"Let me see."

Echo held it out to her, keeping it firmly in her grasp.

"That?" Galynn reached for it. "Can I look at it?"

"It's a key. Maybe even *the* key. But I doubt it."

"Could you just open your hand, then?"

"Is there a place to sit? I don't want to drop it."

The bird turned her head upward and made an arc with her beak. She hopped to a nearby moss-covered monolith, toppled on its side, and sat.

Echo sat beside her and opened her hand.

"It's a doll," Galynn said, examining Echo's find.

"No." Echo looked away and wrapped her hand around it. It was smooth and circular with curved sides, flat on the bottom, round on top. "I feel the doll, but—" She opened her hand and looked at it cradled in her fingers. Now it felt like cold stone with folds of cloth carved into it. Rubbing the woman's face with her thumb, she felt the sadness and the chill of drying tears. "A woman holding her dead adult son."

"You mean the *Pieta*?"

"It's famous, right?"

"Kind of," Galynn said. "My father took me to see it in Rome last summer. There was a huge line."

"I guess that's why it looks familiar. But you don't see it?" Echo tried to resolve the conflicting senses of her touch and sight.

"I see a Russian nesting doll."

Echo shook her head. "There must be a connection to Lazar."

"Why?"

"Because it's here."

Galynn cocked her head to one side and came very close, her black beak nearly filling Echo's vision. "Isn't that backwards? Not that you found it because you were looking for it, but it's what you were looking for because you found it?"

Echo thought about that for a second. A chill ran through her like a cold wind blowing across her neck. "Maybe it found me."

Galynn shrugged with a ruffle of feathers and pulled out her phone. "You'll want to see this."

Echo went into Galynn's esuoh and looked out her window at what Galynn saw. Echo got only a glimpse at the periphery of Ashland in the physical world, where brightly dressed vacationers meandered down the sidewalks of a pretty Northwest city street. No vines or writhing snakes.

"Here, look at this." The phone went out of view as Galynn handed it to the scarred, damaged woman with closed eyes who sat beside her.

Echo had forgotten to wear the sunglasses. But that wasn't the matter at hand. "I'm in here. You look at it."

Galynn gave a high-pitched skronk. "Sorry."

The phone came back into view and there was a photo of the statue Echo had seen, but there was something different about it. "Could you zoom in?"

"You mean hold it closer? I'm not the phone." The statue zoomed into view, and Echo held the key close to the phone. It was a wooden doll with a slit around the middle. Painted on the doll was a queenly woman's face with enormous eyes and long nose, earrings and jeweled robe. Above and around her crown was a golden halo. In the doll's left hand, she held a painted cross. "OK. This doesn't work. Can you keep looking at the phone? I need to look at the key again."

Galynn gave a sighing caw.

Echo went into her esuoh and examined the key through her window. It was different from the statue on Galynn's phone, but where? The statue was incredibly detailed, down to the folds of the robe.

"Hello. I'm still here." Galynn sounded bored, tired, and out of patience.

"I'll be out in a minute."

She brought the key closer for a better look at the woman's face. That was it.

She ran back to Galynn's esuoh for a last look at the *Pieta* on her phone. "I found it. The face in the statue is young, but in the key she's old. Thick brows, a real nose. It's like someone else has been photoshopped onto the statue."

"So—"

The statue was the woman in Newton Zielinski's memory. "She's Lazar's mother," Echo said. "How can we find her?"

Galynn stood up and searched the horizon, looking like a raven doing her best impression of a meerkat. She sat on the bench next to Echo again. "I don't see her anywhere."

"Wait," Echo said. "You've got the library in your pocket. We got here. We can get to the next step."

Galynn held the phone with her finger-feathers and turned her beak toward Echo. "We had something to go on in Salem. What am I supposed to search for? Lazar's mom?"

"Kyrillovich," Echo said.

"Great." Galynn's tone was pessimistic, but her feathers were already scrolling. "How do you spell it?"

"I never saw it written," Echo said. Eventually, the search led to several ways the name *might* be spelled, but ended up going nowhere.

"She might not even have the same name as her son," Galynn said. "It's been known to happen."

"Maybe we can find something about the murder," Echo said, "or the trial."

Scrolling, scrolling. "Two local newspapers. One in Ashland—started in 2016, so not helpful. The other one in Medford, but nothing from the nineties online."

"Well—" This time it was Echo's turn to stand up and take in the scene. "I imagine Ashland has a library."

ECHO FOLLOWED GALYNN DOWN THE EMPTY THOROUGHFARE of the jungle-engulfed city until the raven veered up a steep incline into deeper jungle. Echo beat back vines that grasped her and branches that tried to smack her face.

The raven flew back. "Would you stop that? You look like a crazy person."

Echo stopped, breathless. "What are you talking about?"

"You're waving your arms like a windmill. You can ride in my head."

"I need to see this," Echo said.

"It's a library. You've never seen a library before?"

"Yes, but not like this. It must be a giant key; there's energy pulsing from it. It's at the top of this hill? I can't see for the jungle."

The raven clicked her beak a few times then gave a long harsh caw. "OK. Then trust me. There's no jungle."

"I can't help it if you don't see the jungle."

Galynn flapped her wings and hopped in a circle. "Listen to me. There are about twenty steps; we've done half of them. And there's no fucking jungle. You can come into my head when you want, but if you act weird, I'll go home without you."

Echo restrained herself from acting weird.

At the fifteenth of the twenty steps, a stone cliff came into view, barely visible through the trees and vines. By the eighteenth step, she could see the moss and other vegetation softening the strange formations of the cliff. At the twentieth, the cliff took the shape of a face with eyeholes high above where fires burned and an open mouth with missing lower teeth allowed entrance into a dark cavern.

Stepping over the threshold brought her into a different world. It wasn't a cave, and it was neither dark nor carved from stone. The chamber they entered was as big as the sky, and the Milky Way ran across it like the wake of Destiny. The floor consisted of books, magazines, photocopies, notes, pictures, flattened into paths winding through a dense forest of books. Galynn hopped nonchalantly among columns of books, whose tops extended like Dr. Seuss towers crazily out of sight. Everything hummed and spoke and sang—the stacks, the items, even the letters on the spines. They were a chorus in harmony and disharmony, telling a story bigger than Echo's ability to take it in.

She had arrived in the esuoh of the world. The windows were high overhead, visible only as patches of light far above, casting moving shadows across the stacks that climbed and climbed past them.

Other people were here, too. A woman in a path off to the side opened a book she had pulled from the stack where she stood. Light flowed out of it, and the woman stepped inside and disappeared. A short while later, she stepped out and replaced the book in the stack, the other books lifting themselves for her to slide it into place.

Galynn hopped along the path and around a bend up ahead.

Echo experienced the library with a buzzing intensity that scattered her thoughts and brought back her childhood sense of magical discovery. Echo reached out where she was and grabbed a book at random. It smelled of wet dirt and spring flowers. She opened it and stepped into a greenhouse. She walked through, looking at colorful annuals, ground covers, flowering shrubs, succulents and cactuses, ferns, orchids, and kitchen gardens. At the end of the greenhouse, a door labeled "Plan Your Garden" opened to the outdoors, and Echo walked out onto a wide area of reddish-beige dirt. She thought how nice it would be if it were covered with grass, and grass appeared—soft and lush. A green flower would go well with it, and five green flowers of different shapes and sizes appeared. She thought one into a corner of the yard. Nice, but not just right. She thought another into its place. Yes, that's the one. Now blue.

She was pulled out of that world like a toddler being lifted from a sandbox. Galynn shut the book and shoved it back. "Focus."

Echo followed like an obedient child, so full of this dream that she hardly knew what to "focus" on. She heard humming beside her and reached for it. She stepped into a world of sky, where she floated on an invisible raft that rose and fell on air currents as if on the ocean. Around her—above, below, three hundred sixty degrees times infinity—were aircraft, from historical flying machines to drones the size of an insect, jumbo jetliners, and futuristic spy planes. They all spewed streams of glowing numbers and formulas like chemtrails. Echo sat down on the raft to watch, comparing their flight to those of the eagles in front of her esuoh.

"What is that?"

Echo found herself falling and almost landed on the floor before she caught herself.

"Aviation theory? God, Echo. This is *your* mission, not mine. Let's keep going."

Mission? Echo tried to remember the mission, but another book opened, and she was in a garden even more amazing than the first. The black-barked trees were so gnarled that they looked as if they could speak, and nearby grew roses the size of basketballs. From the limb of a tree, a striped cat looked down at her, grinning.

The cat had such an intelligent expression that Echo thought it was worth a try to ask, "What's my mission?"

The cat blinked slowly at her and reopened its eyes. "That depends on what you're trying to accomplish."

"I always thought one day I would find myself and then I would know. But how can I find myself if I don't know who I am?"

"You don't find yourself. You build yourself brick by brick."

She was violently pulled out, and Galynn slammed the book into the stack. "Damn it, Echo. Your phone's ringing."

Echo reached into her bag for the vibrating object. She didn't want to talk in this sacred place, so she looked around for where to take a call. She found a phone booth constructed of names and phone numbers with yellow advertisements plastered on the windows. She sat on the bench and touched the glass at the bottom of her phone. "Hello?"

"Echo."

The voice was familiar, but she couldn't place it right now. Names help-fully popped out from the background of Yellow Pages, temporarily larger and bold and back-lighted. Not Terence Stephens, who was in her fourth-grade class in Pennsylvania. Not Thomas Magnum, Aunt Doris's favorite TV detective. Not Gray's brother, Quig.

"Echo, are you there? Answer me."

"Who's calling, please?"

"What the hell? It's Jeph."

"Oh, yes." One of the yellow ads lit up, encircled by a red neon tube. "Jephthah Blackthorne III, Success Transformation, Reputation Management," and she reeled off the phone number from the ad. "I'm in the library. It's overwhelming. I could stay here forever."

"What are you doing in the library? That's not what I sent you for."

She thought about it for a few seconds. "We're following a key."

"You got the key?"

"Different key. Key to the key. I think." Then more to herself than to Jeph, "That's my mission."

"You said 'we.'"

"Yes. I've got a raven helping me."

"In the library. Helping you."

"She's a very smart raven."

"I suppose you told her everything."

"I didn't have to tell her much. Like I said, she's a very smart raven. You might even know her. You and her mother—" She stopped herself from giggling.

"Damn," he muttered. Then to her. "This might work out. You say you're on the track of the key?"

"Yes. We've been to two places. The next one is the third. Third time's the charm." She laughed like a drunk person; she didn't know why. It was a like the effect of the dinosaur key Jeph had given her, but now the laugh-ter didn't feel pressed upon her, but as if it bubbled up from a spring deep within. A voice from inside, sounding like her mother, said, *Echo, you're being ridiculous.* She was being ridiculous, and the accusation itself struck her as ridiculous. She flexed her cheeks to keep from laughing.

"Come back to Portland as soon as you get it. Bring the raven with you."

"Sure, I'll bring the raven. You need to clear it with her mom, though. Can we get back to work now?"

"Yes. Exactly. Get back to work. And get out of the library."

Echo threw the phone back into her bag and left the phone booth.

The raven was standing there peering at her with closed eyes. "He said I could come back to Portland with you?"

"You heard that?"

"Just because you're looking at a phone book doesn't mean no one can hear you."

Echo felt deflated. "I was in a phone booth."

"Actually, you were standing next to the shelf of Yellow Pages."

Echo sighed. "OK. Let's get back to work."

Galynn led the way through the library, and Echo followed dutifully, ignoring the song of Sirens coming from the ocean adventure on her left and the smell of Cajun fare coming from the kitchen on her right.

They walked to a huge wooden desk piled with ancient books and manuscripts, where an orangutan wearing an ID lanyard that read, "Sir Terry," sat eating a banana. "Ook?"

Galynn walked up to the desk. "We want to find out about a murder trial that happened in Ashland about twenty years ago."

"We have microfilm upstairs." The orangutan led up a winding and rickety staircase to the place where memories were stored, followed by a raven and a fool.

THE RAVEN AND THE ORANGUTAN HUDDLED OVER A MAGICAL DEVICE that was supposed to present memories as reflections in a bowl of water. Leaving them to the effort, Echo stared out the window at an ocean as big as the world.

The raven squawked. "Echo, would you come here? When was the trial?"

Echo stayed at the window, looking back over her shoulder. "He's been in prison twenty years, so about that. I don't know exactly when he got out."

Outside the window, giants rose out of the land like time-lapse trees, then fought and died, their bodies becoming land that pushed away the ocean and grew into mountains. Dinosaurs meandered the hills, then dissolved into the earth. A silver flood flowed into the valleys, lapping at the edges of the mountains, and then withdrew, leaving behind buildings, streets, roads. Again and again the waves broke against the mountains, and each time there were more buildings, more houses, more streets, more people walking along those streets.

Behind her, Galynn thanked the librarian and said she had it now. Then Galynn spoke in Echo's ear. "Let's get this thing done. I should get paid for this if I'm going to do all the work."

Echo left the panorama and followed Galynn to the Histor-O-Meter.

"Come on into my head," Galynn said. "Let's look at this together."

Echo went into Galynn's esuoh and looked out at the clean, comfortable, not at all whimsical library. Galynn slid a roll of microfilm into the reader and scrolled through the pages too fast to read.

Echo reached into her bag and pulled out the key. The wooden nesting doll that Galynn saw was cute, but it didn't speak to Echo. She left Galynn's esuoh and went out into the world. A fog of sadness rolled out of the statue. It was room temperature but cooling fast. When the statue was too cold to touch, Echo said, "Stop."

"No. It's—" Galynn kept scrolling.

The statue returned to room temperature, and the sadness left the room.

"You need to go back. You missed it."

"OK. Then you do it."

Echo took the handle and turned it back, focusing on the statue.

"You're not even looking at the machine." The raven sounded exasperated. "How can you know—"

But she could. The statue iced over, and Echo slowed down. Fog so filled the room that she couldn't see the machine, and she stopped. Echo was floating in a pool of ice water. She went behind Galynn's eyes to find the photo. Nothing spoke to her there, so she went out into the world to look at it.

The woman in the statue sat alone in a courtroom with space between her seat and the chairs around her. No one seemed to notice that she was weeping with a dead man spread across her lap. The man at the defense table—teenager, really—turned to look at the woman, startling Echo with his gaze. Both the dead man and the man on trial had their eyes closed; the one in Echo's lap was cold as stone, and the other had had something happen to him that no one understood. They were the same.

The man on trial was Lazar. He was lithe and dark-haired, very handsome, close to Gray's age, and when he turned briefly to look at his mom, his face expressed monumental sadness and fear. The judge slammed the gavel, and all the people stood to leave. The woman also got up, becoming a middle-aged woman with mousy blonde hair and unfashionable clothes, running to the defendant before they could take him away.

A sheriff's deputy came with shackles in hand, but the defense attorney waved him away. "His mother" was all she heard of the words he spoke.

The deputy nodded and stepped back. The mother ran up and hugged her son. He kept saying, "It's the way it needs to be."

She laid her head against his chest. "I know you didn't do it."

He held her at arm's length, looking at her through closed eyes, then turned and held out his arms to the deputy, who stepped forward with the shackles again.

Newton Zielinski grasped the woman's shoulders in a side hug, and she sobbed, watching her son being led away.

Out of the corner of her eye, Echo caught a familiar figure leaving the courtroom with the others. Jeph, the same age as Lazar, with a thoughtful expression. Taking it all in, considering the implications. The crowd pushed Jeph outside the door.

Echo turned to Galynn. "It's his mom."

"Well, duh. But who is she?"

"Can you print out her face from the image?"

"What image? All we have is a grainy picture of a courtroom with the backs of a lot of people's heads."

"OK. Let's find a better clue."

"I didn't plan to stay in the library all day."

"Let's go backwards."

Echo held the statue and watched the days and weeks slide by. She felt the ice again, not as cold as before, but noticeable. "Slow down."

Galynn slowed down, scrolling, scrolling.

"There she is."

It was the face of the key, beaten down by time but lit by a glimmer of hope.

Galynn summarized the article for Echo. "She's asking if anyone saw an accident during the night of May twenty-ninth to thirtieth. Her name is Irina Simon."

"Lazar's name is Kyrillovich, not Simon," Echo said. "That's probably why we couldn't find her online."

"Are you sure she's the right one?" Galynn asked.

Echo didn't even need to pause to think about it. "No doubt."

"Here's a phone number, but I would bet my car that it's the lawyer's."

Echo left Galynn's esuoh and held her phone out to her. "Dial it."

"Are you kidding? He just threw us out of his office."

"Maybe he won't remember my voice," Echo said.

The raven sighed and dialed the number. Echo went into her esuoh for the conversation.

The assistant answered. Echo could see the attorney's office, the rackety typewriter, a chipped coffee mug of stained white ceramic on the desk beside her. "Newton Zielinski's office."

"Good morning." Galynn nudged Echo. "Excuse me, good afternoon. I was just browsing old issues of the *Ashland Tidings*, and I ran across an article asking for information about a traffic crash. I have something to share."

"When was that?" the woman asked.

"Date!" Echo whispered to Galynn. Galynn whispered the answer, and Echo repeated it.

"That was more than twenty years ago," the woman said.

"I know. But I do have new information."

The line clicked, and then Newton Zielinski picked up again. He was sitting at a table in his pub, and a file was open in front of him. "Yes?" There were years of weariness in his voice.

She jumped into the seat across from him. "I have new information for Irina Simon about what happened to her son."

"I don't know what your game is, young lady, but that woman has suffered enough."

"I know why his eyes were closed." She got up and searched quickly, running her hand along his bookshelves. Maybe there was another key? Any kind of hint. "His mother might be interested."

She felt a vibration, soft as a cat's purr. She asked him, "What did you give his mother?"

An image came into view, like a home movie playing in the air. Christmas. A boy in a red jacket and a Seahawks watch cap carrying a box—Newt had packed it with fruit, meat, treats from the Russian market, and an envelope containing hundred-dollar bills hidden in the tea box, all the while humming "Mary, Did You Know?" without even noticing. Sitting in his car parked up the street like a stalker or a detective on surveillance, he watched the boy set the box on her porch and run away. Good boy. Just as instructed. Newt waited until Irina opened the door and found the box before he drove away. The secrecy would keep her from giving it back. He felt like Scrooge redeemed.

Irina lived in a compact ranch-style home on a street with no sidewalks, the house numbers screwed into the wall beside the front door. Even though Echo had never been there, the street name was as familiar as her own address.

"You could have told me when you were here," Zielinski said.

"OK. If you don't want to know—" She hung up the phone and turned to Galynn. "I've got the address. Write this down."

Galynn mapped it into her GPS, and they left the library.

Chapter 26

The Hunt Continues

It seemed like a lifetime of waiting before a slim, blonde woman in a power suit entered the corridor, her gaze focused on Gray and Travis like an angry hawk. Senator Cali Zielinski. She strode down the corridor and paused in front of them. "Are you here to explain why the girl with her eyes closed came by yesterday?"

Gray looked at Travis. *Explain?* Travis gazed steadily at the woman without speaking.

Her assistant spoke from behind her, glancing down at his desk. "Travis Rankin and Gray Birdsong."

She turned to look at him, then back at Travis.

Travis held out his hand, but she led the way toward her office door. He whispered to Gray, "Let me do the talking."

"Come in," she said, looking over her shoulder to her assistant. "Five minutes." It wasn't a question.

Her office had three walls of bookshelves of a rich, reddish wood and a desk, large but not grand, with simple wood-and-fabric chairs in front of it. A leather sofa off to the side faced the tree-shaded windows.

"Please sit."

They sat.

She stood by her desk, looking down on them. "What's this all about?"

"I'm a retired police detective, a friend of the family. This is the young lady's brother."

Gray squirmed. His mission was too important for lying. It was also too precarious for truth-telling. He felt Cain standing over him, smiling and saying, *Good job, son.*

She crossed her arms over her abdomen. "Nice story. I don't believe it, but go on."

"She's in danger," Gray said. "She doesn't see—" But a narrow-eyed look from Travis stopped him mid-sentence.

"She managed well." The woman looked over their heads, around the room, craning her neck to look out the window. Then she focused on them, studying their faces with narrowed eyes. "Her friend did most of the talking."

Gray and Travis looked at each other, Travis's expression showing the same question he felt.

Travis spoke: "Friend?"

The senator looked impatient. "I'm asking the questions."

Gray tried the direct approach. "We just want to know where Echo went from here."

She looked at him with narrowed eyes, her arms tight across her torso, her hands closed into fists. "How could I know that?"

"Did she ask anything that might give you a hint? Did any memories come to you suddenly out of nowhere?"

Now she dropped her arms and stood up straight, raised her head and spoke in a low voice as hard as steel. "I don't know what kind of game you people are playing, but you will not harass me or my friends for entertainment."

Travis sat back, eyes open wide. "Entertainment?"

Her eyes narrowed and blinked rapidly. "Get your cameras ready. This is my statement. Lazar Kyrillovich was a teenaged boy who made a mistake. Yes, I liked him, and I'm not ashamed of it. I was a teenager, too. The last time I saw him was in the Jackson County Jail while he was waiting for trial. I don't know what happened to him, but for that girl to come here with her eyes closed the same way his were was a cruel prank. He's paid his debt; he's a free man now. And he deserves to be left alone. If you think this would be good entertainment on YouTube, go ahead and post it. I can't stop you, and I'm not going to deny him." She pressed a button on her phone. "I've asked these officers to escort you out. I don't want to see any of your crew again."

Two men wearing Capitol Security badges entered the room, their guns holstered but their faces grim and set. Travis led the way out, and Gray got one last look at Senator Cali Zielinski, on the verge of tears.

Outside the senator's office, the security guards checked Gray's and Travis's IDs, then escorted the duo to the door of the Capitol and watched from the steps as they walked toward the SUV. Gray waited until they were out of earshot to speak. "That went well." He hoped Travis didn't notice the sarcasm. The bright lights and shiny surfaces were irritating him, the agreed-upon realities, *facts*, that revealed exactly nothing.

Travis glanced back at him but kept walking.

Travis got into the car, pulled a small laptop out of his bag and fired it up. Gray climbed into the passenger seat and waited, his head in his hands and his elbows on the dashboard. He tried to think about what Cali Zielinski had said, but all he could hear were voices mocking him. *She's gone, and you don't know where. You should have come yesterday. You should have known this wouldn't work.* He kept expecting the engine to start for the trip back to Portland. When it didn't, he lifted his head to watch Travis, chewing on the inside of his cheek as he tapped and read, tapped and read on his laptop.

After a bit, he looked up at Gray. "Nice work." He typed some more. "Did Echo do that?"

"What?" *What* did *Echo do to reduce a state senator to helpless rage?*

"Make her think of her old boyfriend who just got out of prison?"

That pulled Gray out of his fog of self-recrimination. Of course there had to be a connection between whatever Echo did and what Cali had experienced—unless Cali had been pining with love for her high-school boyfriend, which was unlikely. "If she went through the senator's memories and found something, that would have made Cali experience the memory as if it had just suddenly come to the surface." Gray was alarmed at the idea of Echo doing that. Imagine going to a friend's house and digging through the boxes of keepsakes in the back of their closet. He suppressed a shiver of revulsion. "Yeah, probably."

Travis checked his notebook. "Lazar Kyrillovich." He wrote in it. "Cheer up. This isn't a dead end." He pulled his phone out of his pocket and scrolled. He spoke without looking up. "Next stop, Ashland?"

"Ashland?"

"You don't need magic if you've got logic. The senator's district is southern Jackson County—Ashland. If the guy Echo is looking for went to high school with her, it's probably Ashland High School. Second, the senator's father is a defense attorney—in Ashland."

"Wait? How did you get that?"

"Didn't you see the picture of him on her shelf?"

"I just saw one of a girl and an older man."

"That was the senator as a high-school student with her father, in Rome, with the Colosseum in the background. The man's a lawyer. Her father. And what do you know but there's a defense attorney named Zielinski in Ashland?" He smiled a triumphant smile. "Data, patterns, truth, just like in your magic world."

"How do you know he's a lawyer?"

Travis shrugged. "He looks like one. Plus Google. How many attorneys named Zielinski do you think there are?"

Gray stared at him.

"Exactly. Not rare, but not like Miller, Moore, or Taylor."

Gray wanted to go into his esuoh and look at the picture again. He tried to remember, but all he got was a girl and a middle-aged man—older than Quig, younger than Douglas—in front of a building. Nothing about the scene said "lawyer" to him. But what could he have learned in Ytilaer without invading Cali's esuoh? "Ashland."

CHAPTER 27

Grabbing the Brass Ring

As Echo and Galynn left the library, the jungle grew more cartoonish. The monkeys became funny instead of menacing. The birds in the trees performed doo-wop hits, and the people walking down the street had big noses, long legs, and huge feet.

While Galynn drove, Echo went into her esuoh and celebrated her triumph. She did a little happy dance in the small space, swirling her magic chair into Aunt Doris's empty kitchen and back again. She had met challenges, made discoveries, found a friend and helper, and now she was reaching the pinnacle of her quest. Sure, there might still be obstacles, but she had proved her ability to jump over them.

She imagined the pleased surprise on Jeph's face when she delivered the key. "I wasn't sure for a while there if you would pull it off," he would say. He would receive the final key, whatever it was, and hand her a check, with enough zeroes to pay for an apartment for six months. Then he would call in Marlo to show Echo her new desk. Would he give her a mirror for her own use? Maybe not right away, but she had already proved she could survive in this world, so she could wait.

And Gray— *Shit.* She had told him she would see him at Ugly Mug this morning. No, wait. Yesterday morning? But he would get over it, especially when she told him she could stay on in Sellwood and wouldn't have to move.

And Aunt Doris. If she didn't have to provide a place for Echo, she could move into senior housing and not have to buy a house in the boonies away from all her friends.

The key of the sad mother, sitting safely on the table in Echo's esuoh, radiated waves of sorrow, but Echo resolutely clung to the promise of success and the sunny skies she insisted were ahead.

Outside her window, the jungle had melted into savannah. The other cars were open Jeeps with goofy faces. A hippopotamus in a tutu danced next to a pond, and a zebra blew a whistle at a soccer game featuring spiral-horned kudus versus blaze-faced blesbok, whose goalie had just impaled the ball on its gently curving horn.

The mother's sadness nagged at Echo wordlessly, like a cat scratching at a door, but Echo chalked it up to the fact that she had never had much experience with things coming together the way they were right now.

"We're here." Galynn's voice filtered into Echo's esuoh, and Echo went out to complete the last step of her journey.

The raven led the way to Irina's house, a thatch-roofed hut with a house cat on the porch. The orange cat had the head and mane of a lion, and it sat next to the door, washing itself with one leg sticking up.

The door opened, and an old woman in a tattered shawl appeared in the doorway. Her face was very wrinkled, and it took Echo a time to recognize the woman in the statue.

Galynn spoke first. "Irina Simon? Do you mind if we talk to you for a few minutes?"

The woman didn't answer. She looked at Galynn blankly as if she were a door-knocking evangelist, then at Echo. Her eyes widened, and she opened the door. "I have been expecting you." She spoke in a pronounced but understandable foreign accent. "My son told me you would come. Come in, please."

She was expecting them? Lazar had told her? How did he know?

Irina stepped aside for Galynn and Echo to enter, and they walked into a small, shabby room with two doors leading off it—which made it larger on the inside than on the outside, but not necessarily by very much.

"Please sit down." She indicated a wooden bench like a church pew against an outer wall with a low, rough-hewn wooden table before it. Galynn sat, but before Echo could sit beside her, the woman stopped her. "No, this chair for you." She pointed to a wooden chair on the other side of the table with a basket of knitting next to it. The chair faced a quarter-turn away from a stone fireplace with a weak little blaze struggling to stay alight. It was chilly in the room, even though it was a warm spring day.

Why this chair? Obviously it was the one the woman herself used when she was alone, but should Echo thank her or be wary of her plans?

"You would like tea?" she asked, and both Echo and Galynn said yes. For Echo, it was a chance to catch her breath and understand this place. The raven sat expressionless on the bench, watching the woman go through the door next to the fireplace and close it behind her.

Echo glanced over her shoulder, then leaned forward and asked in a stage whisper, "May I come into your house?"

"Why so polite all of a sudden? Not much to see."

Galynn turned her gaze around the room so that Echo could take in the thrift-store furniture, the threadbare Oriental rug, the religious pictures on various walls, the battered coffee table in front of the sofa. There was no fireplace, but there was a basket of knitting beside the faded and scratched rocking chair where Echo had been invited to sit. The room was spotlessly clean. There was no television.

Echo was still in Galynn's esuoh when Irina came back into the room carrying a tray with a teapot and three matching cups with a small bowl of sugar and pitcher of cream. They were made of translucent china with red roses painted on them. The tea set was the most beautiful thing in the room. The tea was fragrant like flowers.

Irina filled a cup and turned to offer it to Echo. "Cream or sugar?"

But Echo was still in Galynn's esuoh, and she miscalculated the placement of the cup. Instead of taking it, she knocked it to the floor. Both the cup and saucer broke into many pieces.

"I'm so sorry." This woman didn't have much, but Echo had broken it. "Let me—" But what could she do? Give her money? Fix the cup? Echo went back into her own esuoh and saw something almost alive in its brightness lying broken on the floor.

"It's all right." Irina set down the tray and quickly picked up the pieces. "Let me get another." She carried the broken cup and saucer back into the kitchen.

The raven squawked. "Way to go."

"It was an accident." A stray shard lay on the floor, still glowing. Echo picked it up and cradled it in her hand.

Irina came back with another cup and saucer of the same set. She filled the cup, then handed it to Echo carefully, holding the saucer firmly until Echo got a grip.

She sat down next to Galynn and took a sip of her own tea. "You're searching for my son?"

Galynn took up the interview. "Where is he?"

"He is in Depoe Bay, working with my husband." She set the cup and saucer down and smoothed the lap of her dress. "My son was only eighteen when he went to prison. Now he is thirty-eight and a convicted murderer. My husband started Krill Whale Watching Tours to give Lazar a future. I say 'my husband,' but we are divorced. But he loves his son, as I do."

She got up and walked over to a shelf that seemed to hang from the stone wall. She took down an ancient book that looked much used and went back to sit beside Galynn, but spoke to Echo. "I will show photographs to your friend. Lazar said you need to explore my house." She opened the book on her lap. "He is our only son, all we have left, but Lazar said it is in God's hands. So do what you must."

Echo entered Irina's esuoh with a sense of trepidation, carrying the weeping-woman key in her hand. Why did she feel such reticence? She had been specifically invited. Lazar was in the dream world. Had he traveled through his mother's inner space this way?

Irina's esuoh was like her physical house, as Echo had seen it in the dream world: threadbare rug, hard wooden chairs, a cold and empty fireplace.

On one wall was a painting on a wooden board that looked, from a distance, to be three feet square, but it swelled to more than life size as Echo walked closer. It glowed with an inner illumination, like a flatscreen TV. The painting contained many people and told a story Echo didn't know. All eyes watched—some in hostile agitation, some in gobsmacked wonder, some in adoration—the drama at the center of the image. Two men with halos met near the mouth of a cave. One in red and blue clothing with writing on his halo held up a hand in a strange gesture. The other, with a halo of plain gold, stood in the mouth of a cave, wrapped like a mummy, with only his face exposed. The one in red and blue seemed sad. The mummy looked at him as if he were a good friend late for an appointment, but everything was fine now that he was here.

Two men scurried to remove the mummy's wrappings, and two women kneeled before the man in red and blue. Words in an unknown language written across the top of the board spoke a message Echo couldn't understand.

A straight-backed chair faced the painting. The chair called to Echo with a promise of understanding, so she sat and gazed at the scene. The figures in the painting seemed both moving and still. The image communicated triumphant joy that forded but didn't bridge a deep river of sorrow. When she felt cold, like what flowed off the woman's key, rising to her ankles, she got up from the chair and strode away from the painting.

Outside Irina's window, Galynn tried to appear interested in photos of Lazar as a small boy with dark, curly hair riding on the shoulders of a huge man with an even bigger smile, his wife coming up to his shoulders beside him, wearing a mid-calf skirt, a scarf around her hair, and a friendly but shy smile.

"That picture was taken in Moscow when Lazar was two. We had just gotten permission to come to America. We thought our lives were just beginning."

We thought. The sadness of those words landed like the crack of a whip. What really happened to Lazar? His mother thought he was innocent. Well, she would. Newt Zielinski thought he was innocent. OK, he was the attorney. But the question Echo had tried to avoid for so long demanded to be asked. What was Jeph's part in all of this? Why would he pour his beneficence on this man, a stranger to him, and why through Echo? Why didn't he do it himself?

The key she had brought from Newton Zielinski's office was ice cold, and it vibrated as if it were shivering. But Lazar was out of prison. He would work with his father, and maybe there would be happiness in the rest of his life.

The voice of safety and security spoke again from the depths of her esuoh. *It's not too late to go back to your old life, pretend you never started this journey.* But it was too late. If she went back, she would spend the rest of her boring life wondering what would have happened. *You will sacrifice everything for this.* Everything was a small price to pay to find out.

Echo took the statue to a rickety ladder going up into a dark loft. But the statue's vibrations wavered as she looked upward, and the cold became lukewarm, like a fish dying in the sunlight.

She turned and went through the corner of the hut that served as a kitchen, small and cramped, just a couple of shelves on the wall, a tiny table, and one chair. She turned to the basement door, banded with iron and locked with a huge rusted padlock. When she pressed the key against it, the padlock dropped open. She stood at the top of the stairs and looked down into the darkness.

"Echo!"

She jumped back, startled.

"Echo!" It was Galynn, calling her in a whisper.

She went back to Irina's front room. Outside Irina's window, her hands emptied the teapot and with a sigh picked up the shards of the broken cup from the counter and threw them into the trash under the sink. She put the cream into the refrigerator.

Echo opened a door from Irina's esuoh into Galynn's. "She could hear you in the kitchen," she made her physical voice say. It sounded tinny and awkward coming through Galynn's ears, but Galynn didn't seem to notice.

"Look." Galynn held up a flyer for Krill Whale Watching in Depoe Bay. It included a photo of Nikolai and Lazar Kyrillovich, proprietors, standing in front of a huge inflatable boat, both smiling. The younger man had a horizontal scar, like a knife wound, under his right eye. "We know where he is. We can leave now."

"Jeph doesn't need a *physical* location. He needs a key."

"Why?"

Why indeed? "I don't know. Let me just find it. Look at the photos. I'll be back as soon as I can."

"I don't know what to say."

"Just keep telling her he's cute."

"I already did that."

"Then ask about his interests. Did he like sports, play an instrument? Was he good at school? You're better at conversation than I am."

"It's harder with old people. I'm used to my mom's friends—and my dad's. Press the button and they keep talking until you make your excuses and leave. But she's really listening. I'm a little afraid of her."

"She's harmless."

"That's why she's so scary."

Echo rolled her eyes. "I'll be back as fast as I can." She went back into Irina's esuoh.

Chapter 28

The Real Irina

THE BASEMENT DOOR STOOD OPEN, and the yawning gap breathed like a cave. Echo waited for a mummy to walk out of it, but no one did. On an impulse, before stepping into the darkness, she went back to the kitchen table and picked up the key again, maybe as a weapon, maybe for luck. Maybe in case she later found something labeled "Drink Me" and would need a key to help her reach it.

The stairs and walls were damp, slippery stone, and the key was cold and wet in her hand. The steps dipped in the center, as if they had been used by centuries of pilgrims. Echo felt along the wall for a light switch and, no surprise, didn't find one.

At the first step, fear caught her from behind and tried to pull her backwards from the stairs. Voices shouted at her from her own esuoh. *This is dangerous. You'll never come out. You'll die down there.* Echo tried to reason with them. She was sitting in a chair in the shabby but comfortable living room of a nice lady in Ashland, Oregon. Nothing was going to happen. *No! Death is waiting!*

Echo shivered but kept walking, anticipating Jeph's esteem, Gray's friendship, her new and prosperous life that depended on succeeding at this assignment. As she walked downward, the stones vibrated—not chaotically like an earthquake nor rhythmically like a machine, but continuously rumbling in a slow and sinuous rhythm under her feet.

At the first turning of the stair was a door like one in a cheap apartment. Inside, a man shouted in a foreign language. She touched the doorknob, and it opened. She hardly had time to register that there were two people in the room before she slid into the consciousness of the woman, Irina. The man was her husband, he of the massive build and big smile. Now he was angry, not at Irina, but at everything, and Irina was there. Echo felt Irina's fear, her love, her overarching sadness, as big as his but with no outlet. The man poured himself half a tumbler of a clear liquid from a tall bottle, drank it in one swallow, and smashed the glass against the wall. He shouted, and Echo heard him in a foreign language and also understood his words.

"It's bullshit. My son wouldn't do that."

"No. He would not," Irina said.

"Justice. We were promised justice." He walked over and shouted in her face. "Where is justice?"

A wave of fear washed over Irina, and then calmness took hold. "Injustice is everywhere. Our Lord—"

"Damn 'our Lord.'" He stared at her with his fist closing and opening, then walked back to the kitchen table. "Damn him to hell, just as he has damned our son to hell." He put his head in his hands and sobbed.

Fear came over Irina. She felt alone, unknown, unprotected, in an empty, cold, and unfeeling universe. The feeling was so powerful that it ejected Echo from the room.

She stood in the hallway, leaning against the door, until her heart stopped pounding, then began the descent again.

At the second turning of the stair was a heavy metal door with a wire-enforced window. Echo went through and found herself sitting at a battered metal table with a sheet of scratched Plexiglas between her and Lazar, who had his eyes closed. It was the same place she had sat in Cali Zielinski's memory, but now it looked as if the film crew had put a blue filter on the camera.

Irina held a clunky phone receiver against her ear. The boy on the other end of the line, so close and yet a million miles away, kept saying, "They tell me I killed some people. I don't remember anything. I don't know. I don't know. I don't know."

Echo felt tears running down Irina's face. She wiped them away again and again, but still they fell. A huge weight pressed down on her, like all the sorrow of the world. If he was found guilty, Irina would be in prison with him. Despair enfolded her, and Echo found herself outside the door.

At the third turning of the stair was a wooden double door. Echo stepped through and found herself in the first row of a room full of angry and curious people. Her head was buzzing. At the side, a bearded man with red suspenders read from a piece of paper. The words got tangled on the way; Irina couldn't quite understand them. But one slipped through: "Guilty." Someone cried out, and the judge hammered, and Irina realized she was the one who had made the noise. She heard something behind her and looked back. The boy Jeph, who Lazar had thought was a friend, met her eye and gave her a flash of a smile—a smirk of victory—and returned his attention to the judge. Hot rage flowed through Irina. If she had been close enough, she could have choked him and scratched his eyes out. And then Echo was back on the stairs again.

The stairway ended at last, opening onto cold, dry sand reflecting the light of the unnaturally huge white moon. The smell of ocean filtered in from beyond sand dunes, and off in the distance, bright colorful lights glimmered like the carnival pier of her dream.

The key pulled her toward the sound that continued to vibrate the sand under the starless sky. Miniature avalanches rolled off tiny dunes under her feet. She followed a depression in the dry sand that led away from the ocean, toward a tiny dark structure too far away to identify.

As she walked, the statue she carried captured the vibration, which resolved into music, faint and distant, deep bass like giants shaking the foundations of the earth with their singing. The vibration shook Echo's bones—well, not her bones, since they were stacked in a chair at Irina's house, but it felt like it. It felt like an electrical charge, without the burning. She pushed forward toward the structure and the sound.

After hours of walking, she came to a waist-high retaining wall made of rough, flat stones. Sand had gathered against it but had not overcome it. She climbed to a gravel-paved pathway and sat on the wall with the statue in her lap, resting and looking toward the ocean. Even after all this time, the moon was at the same place in the sky. Was the moon stationary here, or had time stopped? An answer came from deep within her that the questions were irrelevant. She struggled to her feet and followed the path.

The structure turned out to be a small building on an island in the middle of a reflecting pool. The moon threw Echo's shadow like a monster on the glistening surface of the water. The singing was clearly audible now. Not just the earth-shaking basses, but soaring sopranos and midrange parts marching like pilgrims on a journey. As she followed the path around the pond, with the grassy lakeshore to her left and the retaining wall holding back sand and forest to her right, the moon crept onto the surface of the lake until from the other side it was like a luminescent painting on the vibrating water.

Silhouetted by the moonlight, the building became a domed gazebo made of metal wrought into vines and topped by a cross with two extra bars, the top one half the length of the middle and the third near the bottom of the vertical, slanted at a forty-five-degree angle. Light shone through the emptiness of the gazebo.

Echo couldn't say what she expected, but this was not it. Nice scenery, but there was nothing here.

She turned in a circle where she stood. The lake and gazebo sat in an expanse of sand embraced by a forest. How long had she been walking? Was Galynn even at Irina's house still? Had Echo's intuition led her to the wrong place? It would have been more logical to go toward the light. And now what? Go back?

She had come this far. There was a bench in the gazebo that reminded her of her front porch. She would sit for a time. Maybe a plan would come.

There was no bridge over the lake, but she could see white stair steps under the water, and it seemed unlikely that the water would be deep. Walking down the stairs, she found the lake so cold that she almost went back, but curiosity was stronger than her desire for comfort. Three steps took her to waist deep, and the next was such a drop that her head went under. She panicked for an instant, trying to swim, but then it was as if arms lifted her up—although she felt no arms—and her foot found the next step, and her head emerged from the water. After that, the upward steps brought her quickly to the island side.

As soon as she set foot on land, the scene changed. The full moon illuminated everything like a spotlight. The gazebo had become a tiny domed building, its walls covered with white, blooming roses. All around on the little island was a garden of lilies with a path running through it. And Echo herself was clean and dry.

She walked to the door and pushed, then pulled. Nothing happened. Then she held the key up to the door, and it opened to receive her. She looked in at the velvet darkness and stepped inside.

As she closed the door behind her, she became aware of a faint flickering light like a candle, but bluish, bouncing off the ceiling over the top of a head-high wall at the far end of the building. Tiny glimmers of escaping light marked the edges of double doors leading through the wall. The invisible singers seemed to line the outer wall of the building.

Despite the radiance, when Echo walked forward, she collided with something warm and cloth-covered. A person. "I'm sorry."

"Don't be." A woman spoke with Irina's voice, but no accent. "I've been waiting for you."

"For me?"

"Well, no." The woman turned again toward the front of the building. "Not *for* you, but I knew you were coming. You have questions."

Echo shrugged. "I always do. And now more than usual. Do you know the answers?"

The woman stood still, her head tilted as if taking a cue from the music. "We have time before the procession begins. Let's go sit in the garden." She led out the door to the path through the lily beds and around the building to a wooden bench overlooking the lake where the big moon shone down on them with smiling perplexity.

The woman sat on the bench and turned her face to the moonlight as if it warmed her like the sun. She patted the bench beside her. "Sit. Ask."

Echo stared at her. She had Irina's face, but free of all its worry and sadness. "Are you Irina?"

She sat silent for a second, like a bodyguard conferring with the command center. "That's not the question you've come for, but it's worth answering. I am Irina's inmost self. You may call me her soul, although there are many names, and the definitions don't capture the meaning. We are three: The outer Irina is the body, which receives the gift of physical experience and the ability to change the world. The Irina you met, who is showing baby pictures of Lazar to your friend, is the middle Irina, her 'mind' or 'personality' or 'self.' Again, the words shift like footprints in dry sand."

Echo stared out at the image of the moon on the vibrating water. "And I?"

"You bring your personality to meet Irina's soul. Lazar said there is a tool, a mirror, that allows you to walk in other people's territories. It is very *interesting*, no?" She said "interesting" like it was a bad thing.

"Yes."

"Also very dangerous."

Echo shrugged. "It's not real."

"My dear one. It is more real than anything you can imagine. You think dangers that don't touch the body are not dangers. But consider what happens when the body loses contact with the mind or soul."

Echo remembered her grandmother, near the end of her struggle with Alzheimer's, sitting in a chair staring into space. Echo had been about ten, and her father had explained with tears in his eyes that his mother's mind had gotten lost. She shivered at the thought.

"Tell me your real question."

There was a question, not the one she had been sent to ask, pounding on a door somewhere, demanding to be let out and answered. Irina couldn't know the answer, but Echo asked it anyway. "Why does Jeph want me to find Lazar's key?"

She expected Irina to shrug, to say something passive, but fire flashed through her eyes. It died down, leaving Irina with a stiffer spine and an expression of firm expectation. "You ask this question even though you already know the answer, because it demands a choice you would rather not make." She turned and looked Echo full in the eye for a few seconds that seemed to stretch into hours, then she turned to the moon again.

Echo's understanding of reality shook. "It was all lies and betrayal," she said, speaking to herself, as if her lungs were empty of air. "He drugged Lazar, and every step along the way, they protected Jeph by protecting Cali. She saved herself but abandoned Lazar to his fate." A cloud drifted across the moon, putting Echo into darkness. "And Jeph left Lazar to take responsibility for the deaths." Her stomach churned.

Irina spoke at last. "It is not enough that Lazar must spend twenty years in prison. Jeph has plans for him. Something worse than death, but Lazar would not tell me more."

Echo saw her mission in a new way. She wasn't the private eye; she was the hit man. She wasn't the rescuer; she was the betrayer. Echo stared out past the moonlit lake to the castles she had built in the air: Jeph's esteem, her great job, her apartment in Sellwood. They smashed like Christmas ornaments hit with a baseball bat. After this whole fiasco, would Gray even want to be her friend anymore?

Utterly deflated and incapable of expressing the humiliation and despair she felt, she stood and brushed off her clothes. "Well, then." Her finger caught in a rip on her coat and tore it some more. "Thank you for that. I'll go back to Portland, and maybe Gray can help me get out of here."

"Please sit." Irina spoke quietly but with authority that brooked no dissent. "I have a message for you from Lazar." She sat silent, staring toward the moon for a moment, her lips moving slightly, whether speaking or simply trembling Echo couldn't tell. Echo waited. "The key is inside the chapel. It is a tiny cross on a chain, lying on the floor in a shaft of light."

"But—"

"Take it to Jeph as planned. Then go home."

A tsunami arose in Echo's chest, threatening to escape through her eyes. "You can't mean it. You just said—"

"My mother's heart says, 'Leave the key and run away.' But Lazar asks you to take the key to Jeph. And I trust Lazar more than myself."

Echo thought about that. Had there ever been anyone she trusted more than herself? She imagined it as something both comforting and terrifying. But she had come so far, aiding Jeph in his purpose. Maybe she could make this right.

"I'll take the key."

"Yes." Irina stared across the lake, her fingers counting something and her lips moving soundlessly.

Echo waited another minute, but Irina never looked at her. She went back into the chapel and found a small object glimmering on the floor. She hadn't seen it before. It was a silver three-bar cross like the one on top of the chapel, about half the length of her pinky, on a light-weight silver chain. It was so small that she was afraid of losing it, so she hung it around her neck and turned to leave the building. But before she reached the door, she went back to put Irina's key in its place, thinking it would be safer to leave it there.

When she closed the door behind her, the scene changed. Gone were the gardens, the chapel, even the lake. The moon shone down on a vast expanse of dry sand that shifted and squeaked under Echo's feet. It was only a few minutes' walk to the stairs up to Irina's kitchen.

In Irina's esuoh, the wooden picture had changed. Instead of a man dressed like a mummy coming out of the cave, a lone woman struggled to carry the mummy back into the cave. Gone were the jubilant and angry crowds. Even the teacher in red and blue was gone. From a hole in the sky, painted light blue with rays streaking outward like a magic portal, a hand extended, thumb and third finger folded together, the other fingers standing, the same gesture the teacher held in the other painting.

Through Irina's window, Echo saw both Galynn and herself apparently snoozing. Irina had set the photo album aside and sat staring at a picture of the teacher on the wall, fingering a woolen beaded bracelet in her lap.

CHAPTER 29

Return

ECHO CAME OUT OF IRINA'S ESUOH into the small, dismal room. Galynn sat with her head lolled to one side, her beak open, snoring slightly. Irina still held the bracelet in her hand, counting the beads. She didn't seem to be sleeping, although her eyes were closed, because she was in Oge.

Echo stretched and walked over and touched Galynn's wing. "I think we've kept Irina long enough."

Irina turned to face them. "Did you get what you wanted?"

"Yes." Echo wished she hadn't.

"That's good. My son said it was important. When you see him, will you give him his mother's love?"

When you see him? But there was only one answer to that question. "Yes, I will."

Galynn sat up at that. "Sorry. I didn't mean to fall asleep."

Irina smiled. "I understand, Galynn. Traveling is hard, and you have long drive this afternoon."

Galynn stood up. "Thanks for the tea. Nicholas and Alexandra, right?" Irina nodded. "I'll tell my mother about it. I think she'll like it."

Irina stood and slid the bracelet onto her wrist. She walked them to the door.

Galynn went out first, and Echo paused at the door, looking down at Irina, who was, like her esuoh, bigger on the inside than out. Echo felt the burden of what she had been asked to do. Did Irina—*this* Irina—know? She turned and went out the door.

A cold, greasy rain was falling from a gray sky.

Galynn watched the door close behind them and then almost danced with delight. "You got it? Where do we go next?"

Echo didn't answer. Galynn's car had become a cart, the two-wheeled, open manure wagon she had seen in movies about the French Revolution. Galynn climbed up to the driver's seat. Echo hesitated a beat before realizing *she* wasn't going to the guillotine but helping drive someone else. In the back of the cart, a dark-haired man in rags lay face down, unmoving, on a pile of filthy hay. Echo turned toward the front. It was too terrible to look.

Galynn started the engine.

Echo heard the engine, but saw a tired horse turn back balefully at the crack of the whip.

"Well?" Galynn said.

"Well, what?" Echo heard the irritability that had crept into her voice.

"You don't get to back out on me now. You promised to tell me the plan."

The plan. "I don't have a plan. I need to think." *I'm a fool who walks with my head in the clouds and my feet on the edge of a cliff, and Galynn is a fool to trust me.*

"But did you get it?"

"Get what?" *I was wrong about Jeph. There's darkness at the end of this journey.*

"The key! The key! Did. You. Get. The. Key?" She drove for a while, and the rain turned to thick fog. "Where do we go next?"

The key. Echo touched it without looking at it. It was the size and elongated shape of a tiny Atlantic auger seashell she had found on a beach trip with her family, long lost now.

"That's it? Let me see."

Echo pulled the yarn off her neck and handed it to Galynn.

She studied it, her raven's head turning curiously from side to side. "It's a chip from the cup you broke."

Echo held out her hand to get it back.

"Don't put it on your neck." Galynn put the item in her hand and Echo felt it with her fingertips—the sharp edges, the yarn wrapped around it.

"Why not?"

"The string could break. You don't want to lose it."

That was true. *She said take it to Jeph and go home.*

"Put it in your bag somewhere safe."

Echo thought about it. *She said when you see him* . . . . She found the inner pocket of her bag and zipped the key inside.

"Where to next?"

"We're finished with Ashland."

"OK. Portland, here we come."

Echo went into her esuoh and onto her porch, where she absorbed the silence of the swirling fog.

THE FOG OUTSIDE ECHO'S ESUOH HID THE CHASM beyond the porch rail. It was like a movie screen poised to reveal monsters and heroes, but they never emerged from formlessness. The fog came closer, and even the porch rail disappeared. If the fog overtook her, would she forget everything? She would be OK with that.

She felt more than heard someone calling her. "Wake up."

She rose and went back into her esuoh, fingers of fog following her through the door and swirling in the room like otherworldly home-buyers checking out the real estate. Echo left her esuoh.

The raven squawked at her. "I'm starved."

Echo felt a gnawing in the pit of her stomach but no room to put anything there. She dug into her bag and found the debit card Jeph had given her. She handed it over. "Get yourself something. I'm not hungry."

"Let's pull over at this truck stop."

"Fine." Without thinking about it, she turned to the back of the tumbril. "Do you want anything?"

The dark-haired man, unmoving in the straw, didn't answer.

"Who are you talking to?" the raven squawked, looking forward still.

What if I told her? Would it make any difference? So far, she and Galynn had been going in the same direction—Jeph's direction. What would happen if Echo revealed the change? "Sorry. I was dreaming."

"I wish I were. Driving is boring, and you're just sleeping through it."

Not sleeping. Maybe never again. "I'll wait out here."

"You sure?" Not getting an answer, Galynn shrugged and left the wagon.

Once Galynn had entered the long log structure, Echo turned to get a better look at the man in the cart. His hair was short with threads of gray in it. His bare arm was bruised, wiry, and well-muscled, but not young or old.

"Hey!"

He didn't move. Was he dead? She was about to crawl back to check when her phone rang.

She reached into her bag and the glass box leaped into her hand. Jeph or a spammer? Gray or Aunt Doris? She stared at its featureless black surface debating the risks and rewards of the various conversations. At this moment, she would choose the straightforward avarice of a phone scam.

But before she could decide whether to answer, she felt Jeph's presence in her esuoh. The phone had stopped ringing, and she felt the quiet hum of a connection. She had to talk to him, ready or not.

She found him at her table of memories, casually flipping through the unfiled sketchbooks. Images flitted through her mind: Galynn, Irina's soul, her sister Diana. *Need a distraction.* "Want some ice cream?" she asked him. At once, all her sketchbooks filed themselves as if at the command of a Sorceror's Apprentice, leaving one random image—even Echo herself didn't know when it came from—of a tall, stout, red-haired woman in a pink sundress, walking down a busy summer street and rapturously licking a marionberry ice cream cone.

He turned to look at her, his expression a mix of irritation and wonder. "Echo." He seemed a little off—nothing she could point to exactly, but rumpled, lumpy, grumpy. "Haven't heard from you for a while."

What had he seen in her memories? She wanted to run over and shove him away from the table, but she opted for a more measured response. "What are you doing here?"

He glanced once again at her sketchbooks, now on their shelf shoulder to shoulder like little soccer players defending against a penalty kick, and gave her his full attention. "I need some good news."

Echo felt her face flush at the memory of the last time she talked to Jeph. Floating through the joyful whimsy of the library, she was confident that her mission was almost finished, and she was looking forward to the rewards. All that success now lay at her feet like bright bits of broken glass. Instinctively, she didn't want to tell him the truth, but she hadn't had time to come up with a lie, particularly one that would stand against Jeph's scrutiny.

He eyed her steadily and reached out, hovering his hand over her bookshelf. All the little combatant sketchbooks stood down—Echo wasn't even sure what she had done to militarize them—and became simply black saddle-stitched books whose only connection to each other was in their content. Without even looking at them, he took a sketchbook from the shelf, flipping through its pages. "So you went to see Lazar's mom. How is she?"

Irina's image of Jeph in the courtroom flashed through Echo's memory as she walked over and took the sketchbook from his hand, then slid it onto her shelf. "She's fine."

He opened a door and pulled her by her wrist into his esuoh. It was still spacious, but the expensive furnishings seemed like cheap knockoffs, shiny on the surface but structurally unsound. She reached for a door back into her own esuoh, but it didn't appear at her hand. She tried again and again. Fear crept in from the edges of her consciousness.

Jeph pulled the small handcuffs out of his pocket and dangled them before her. "You're twenty-four hours late, and I've still got your key."

Her first impulse was to try to wrest it from him, but she mastered herself, created a chair and sat down, casually. She didn't want him to know she had changed sides. "I thought it was your key."

"It connects us. But what you need to know is that it opens your basement door." His face wore the same triumphant-malicious smile Irina had seen in the courtroom.

"Where the creepy-crawlies are?"

The smile grew a shade broader, and then he glitched, like a video with an uncertain internet signal. "Just give me Lazar's key."

How hard was he working to maintain this connection across hundreds of miles? She babbled, using time against him. "Well, first we went to Newton Zielinski's office. Cali's father; he was Lazar's defense attorney." *Keep talking. Keep talking.* "It was hard to get into his esuoh, and once I was there, it took a while to find the next key."

He took a step toward her. "Give me the key."

"I did find a key in his office," she said, stepping back, "but it wasn't Lazar's key. It was his mother's."

Jeph froze, his hand reaching out for her, then flashed several times, both he and his esuoh disappearing, leaving Echo in the tumbril. Then she was in his esuoh again. "Hand it over," he said, desperation creeping into his voice. "I need it." His suit looked like it was too big for him, and his teeth seemed sharper.

Give him the key, Irina had said. Go back to Portland. "OK. OK." She reached into her big magic bag of everything, where she had found the key every time she searched. Her arm went deep into its inner reaches and grasped a familiar object. Her fingers recognized thick paper, a small rectangle. "Here it is."

He held his hand out.

She looked at the key, the handcuffs she had found in her dream, and she invested it with everything she now knew about Jeph—the cowardice, the malice, the pathetic manipulation, the extraordinary efforts to appear what he was not. He shrunk in her perception to a funny-horror cartoon creature with an overlarge coat covering big round shoulders connected to his bald head by a skinny, curving neck. "You're a joke," she said to him.

So much for not revealing that she had switched sides.

Jeph's esuoh disappeared, and she was again in the wagon with the prisoner behind her. She pushed her thumb around the glass near the bottom of the phone and finally slid over the hangup button. She ripped the card into tiny pieces and flung both the phone and the bits of paper across the parking lot. She heard an impact like something hitting a garbage container, then glass breaking.

If she had ever been unsure, Echo knew now that she wasn't going back to Portland. She would go to Depoe Bay and warn Lazar that Jeph was coming.

Galynn flew up to the driver's seat and tossed something into Echo's lap. It was a sandwich in a plastic container. Echo still couldn't stomach the idea of food. She stashed it in her bag for later.

"Did you just throw your phone out the window?"

"I hate robocalls."

Galynn gave her a look that was piercing even with her bird's eyes closed. "You want to go pick it up? It might be fixable."

Echo sighed, adrenalin still coursing through her system. "Let's just go back to Salem."

"You mean Portland, right?

CHAPTER 30

The End of the Journey

ECHO, SITTING ON THE FRONT PORCH OF HER ESUOH, felt or heard something and fought her way out of the purple fog that embraced her like a blanket.

She went out into the world and looked around. She was still in the cart with Galynn, driving through a dark and starless night. "Where are we?"

"Five miles from Salem."

"Drop me at the train station." Aunt Doris had taken a bus with a group of friends down to Mystic Mountain Casino, halfway to the coast, and they had caught it at the Salem train station.

"There's no train—"

Echo cut her off. "It'll be fine."

"You can come into my head and look around outside. It's ten o'clock. There'll be no one there until morning."

Echo felt her vulnerability as a tightness in her chest and a roaring of blood in her ears. "I'll be fine."

The raven drove for a minute or two, facing straight ahead. "You're dumping me."

"That's not—"

"Bullshit! You wouldn't have gotten this far without me, and now you think you can just tell me to go back home to my mom while you get all the credit?"

"There's no credit. I'm a fool, and Jeph is not what I thought he was. He's dangerous. I don't know his plans for Lazar, but they're not good." The man in the tumbril groaned in the darkness and shifted position. "I'll return the key to Lazar so he can protect himself from Jeph's scheme—whatever it is."

"You're not just dumping me. You're dumping Jeph, too."

That caught Echo up short. *Dumping Jeph.* She had aged a hundred years in her journey to meet Irina's soul, and in that time her perception of Galynn had gone from being a street-smart savvy traveler to a seventeen-year-old high school girl who was vulnerable to a predator. Echo cringed at the knowledge that she herself might have developed a crush on Jeph if she weren't protected by the armor of her ugly face.

But Galynn wasn't finished— "The one who gave you a job and a chance and let you into that world where some people would like to be but can't. Just because you met some pious sock who's so boring she put us both to sleep."

Echo didn't know how to answer and felt too weak to speak. "Just let me off at the train station."

Galynn didn't say any more, but the cart slowed, and Echo could tell by its movements that it was getting off the highway.

"Thanks."

"Don't thank me. We were supposed to be partners."

Partners. Echo went into her esuoh and pulled down the ladder to her upstairs. She knew how Galynn felt, and she might be able to use that knowledge to make it easier for Galynn to deal with the situation.

She searched for the right door, trying to remember how she fooled Chris the IT guy in Jeph's office. She had chosen one of his favorite things and ruined it for him. She didn't want to do that again. She would make her own key this time.

She opened door after door, finding them dark, empty, or boring—the buzzing of a fly against a summer window or staring out at the rain while her sister carried on an animated conversation in the next room, the voice and tone fascinating, the words undecipherable. Eventually, the search seemed so futile that she gave up.

At that moment, she found the door, buzzing like a hornet's nest in sunshine. She went inside and was twelve again on a summer night in her parents' backyard. It was her sister's nineteenth birthday party, end-of-school party, going-off-to-college party. Echo had been told to stay in her room and let Diana say goodbye to her friends in peace. But nobody understood that Echo walked in Diana's sunlight. Even though she lacked her sister's intelligence, beauty, and grace, she admired—and wanted—Diana's friends: musicians, drama geeks, and the smart rejects who would come back to their twentieth reunion in a Lamborghini, showing off pictures of their recent vacation in the Seychelles.

Compared to them, Echo's sixth-grade classmates seemed silly, dull, awkward, and provincial. Echo felt the coming loss as deeply as any of the ones *invited* to the party, and being excluded seemed like an insult as well as an injury. So she attended in secret.

Her father had built his daughters a treehouse in their family's backyard. But by the time it was built, Echo was coming into the right age to use it, and Diana was too old. Thus it became Echo's treehouse, with cushions, books, and drawings—a refuge where she could be herself. It had windows and a couple of knotholes in the floor where she could see everything that happened in the yard. So she was there that evening when the yard was lit up with white Christmas lights, and the air was full of laughter and music and clever banter and reminiscences. Echo sat above and watched, feeling as if she were almost part of it.

At some point in the evening, her sister looked up and noticed that Echo was spying on her party. She went in to their father and demanded that he do something. He came and climbed up the ladder and told Echo to come inside. It was bad enough climbing down the ladder like a chastened puppy and going into the house. But a few minutes later, Diana came into her room and excoriated her for invading the party. Told Echo it was time to get a life of her own. Then she went back to the party, and seconds later laughter filtered up through Echo's window like fingers pointing at her.

She went to sleep with her heart transformed into a lead weight of humiliation.

Standing now in the memory of her room back then, and having lived through the whole thing again in just a few seconds, she saw it all both as her twelve-year-old self and the one who was now the same age Diana had been. She could imagine Diana's feelings of being trapped by a little sister, not having any privacy, always being admired and copied so that even her very self seemed threatened. The feelings wound and twisted together like a ball of snakes. Echo couldn't get her metaphorical arms around them, but with concentration, she did get her dream arms around them, patting at the bulging surface until she compressed them into a key in the shape of a Mayan-calendar paperweight.

The paperweight was heavy, like the end of the world, and giving it to Galynn felt like kicking a puppy to make it go away from danger. But it would end the argument, and Galynn would be safe. It would have been better, maybe, to find a sunnier moment, like the end of summer camp when she was eight, when she was glad to have been there and glad to be going home. But the way she felt now, she wasn't sure she could find that door. Anyway, Diana's last party was the one that buzzed, so it must be the right one.

Right?

Echo sighed and went into Galynn's esuoh. Outside her windows was a clear night, well after sunset but illumined to near daylight by streetlights and car lights and lighted signs.

She picked up a photo album that lay open on a desk. There was Echo nearly getting run over in the parking lot of the train station. Echo in the hotel refusing to eat until Galynn explained what was on the tray. Echo in the library looking out the window while Galynn found her way through the microfiche. As she had placed the spider in Chris's memory in Jeph's office, she now laid the paperweight on the open album. The pictures changed, but she didn't stay to look at them. The decision was behind her; now she was living out the consequences. She went back into her own esuoh.

She wished she could show appreciation instead of this.

She went back out into the tumbril.

THE END OF THE JOURNEY passed in a cavelike blackness. Their vehicle had become a car in a haunted-house ride like What You Did, but in this ride there were no red-eyed monsters leaping out of corners or lighted displays of ghoulery. Just darkness—flat, hard, and empty.

As the car slowed for its last turn, Echo went into to Galynn's esuoh to see the parking lot from her eyes. Streetlights lit the empty parking lot. The car came to a stop facing the building with two or three cars moving along the street in front of the building to their right and train tracks running behind the building in a realm of darkness on their left. Even that darkness was not as deep as the one Echo saw in the world.

"Get out." Galynn's voice was hard and cold.

Seeing through Galynn's eyes, Echo found the door handle.

"I said get out. We're not partners; you don't get to be in my head."

Echo opened the door.

"You did something to me." She looked confused and angry.

Echo looked back at her in surprise. "You noticed?"

"You took something away. I remember it like a dream. Everything was fine. We were doing this thing together. But now I know you never wanted me along. You're tired of me. Well, fine. Get out."

"That's not it. I was just—"

"Get out." The raven stared straight ahead, its beak trembling.

Echo stepped out and looked back. "Go to your mom's house. I'll find you after this is all over and tell you everything."

"Go to hell." She sped away from the parking lot, leaving Echo alone in darkness.

The Next Journey

Yes, this journey ends here, but a new journey begins in the second and last book of this series, *The Fool Arises Dreaming*, as Echo attempts to repair the chaos she's caused.